Empty Cradle

Penrose & Pyke Mysteries, Book 8

Rose Pascoe

Published by Flax Bay Books, 2025

Copyright

EMPTY CRADLE

ISBN: 978-1067024345 (Softcover POD)

978-1067024338 (Epub)

Publisher: Flax Bay Books, New Zealand

Cover design: Rose Pascoe
Cover images from Shutterstock and Adobe Stock Images

Contents

An Unwanted Case

Grace Penrose Pyke cast aside her anatomy textbook, narrowly missing the border collie snoozing beside her. Blaze looked up at her with a hopeful perk to her head. Inactivity did not come naturally to either of them.

"Shall we visit the detectives in their lair, Blaze?"

Grace's husband, Charlie, was working in the house next door, which belonged to his business partner, Alistair Stewart. It was also the office of their private detective agency. She stopped by the kitchen for a plate of freshly baked scones as an excuse to interrupt the men at their work. They probably needed a little cheering up, because Alistair was chest-deep in a challenging fraud case, and Charlie was helping him wade through the deluge of documents.

It was partly her fault. A year ago, Charlie had promised her he would stay away from dangerous investigations, because they had decided to start a family. It hadn't worked out so far for either of them. Forcing Charlie to work behind a desk was akin to putting a tiger in a cage and poking it, while Grace's failure to conceive a child had only added to the tension.

As she and Blaze passed an open window on route to the Stewarts' door, Grace overheard what sounded like an argument between Charlie and Alistair. The two men were as close as father and son, and she'd never heard them so much as raise their voices before, except in jest. Common decency told her to walk away, but her insatiable curiosity drove her on. Grace gestured for Blaze to stay outside and keep quiet while she crept into the house. Fortunately, the office door was ajar.

"Please, Alistair," Charlie said. "You know I wouldn't ask if it wasn't important to me. Can't we swap cases? You could take the kidnapping, while I handle your fraud case."

Grace had never heard her husband plead with his business partner like this. Why would he want to swap a kidnapping case, which was exactly the kind of excitement and intrigue Charlie thrived on, for a dull fraud investigation? Unless ... She had thought Charlie had brushed off his own experience of being kidnapped a year ago, but perhaps she was wrong.

When Alistair replied, his usual soft Scottish burr had a hard edge. "You know that makes no sense, Charlie. I can't let my client down by stopping in the middle of a complex investigation. Besides, you are better suited to the new case than me, because you might need the skills of your tracking dog."

"Can't we refuse to take on the kidnapping? I don't want to risk Grace's fragile state of health by taking this case."

Fragile? Grace felt like storming into the office and giving her husband a piece of her mind. Did Charlie think she had been so badly affected by his disappearance last year that she couldn't cope with him investigating another person's kidnapping? She held back because Charlie sounded uncharacteristically agitated, when he was famous for staying calm in a crisis. Grace crept a little closer to the door, intrigued by what this new case involved.

"Charlie, need I remind you what is at stake? Isn't that more important than Grace's feelings?"

"Nothing is more important than Grace, Alistair. How would you feel if it was your wife?" A sharp intake of breath followed Charlie's harsh retort. "Alistair, I'm so sorry. Forgive me for being so tactless after all you've been through. When we have time, I'd appreciate your wise counsel."

"I understand how you feel, Charlie, but I doubt there is much I can do to help. I don't wish to sound heartless, but the sad fact is that you and Grace will have to learn to live with the fickleness of fate, just as my first wife and I had to."

A frown creased Grace's forehead as she realised the men were talking about their struggle to conceive, since Alistair's one regret was that his first wife's longstanding illness had left her unable to have children. What could their personal problems possibly have to do with her husband refusing a kidnapping case?

A rustling of papers, the soft tread of feet towards the hat stand. Grace had seconds to move if she didn't want to be caught eavesdropping.

"Take the case, Charlie," Alistair said, "or you'll lie awake every night for the rest of your life wondering if you could have saved that baby boy. I've got to go. I'm already late for a meeting."

Grace's heart lurched. A baby had been kidnapped. No wonder Charlie was reluctant to take the case. She and Charlie had tried to make light of their own childless state, but each month that passed added more strain to their relationship.

Before Grace could duck into another room to avoid being seen, Alistair dashed out the door and cannoned into her, sending the plate of scones flying. She stood her ground and took the offensive. "Charlie will take the kidnapping case, Alistair." She tried to say the words calmly, but each syllable cut through gritted teeth. "I will assist, if my husband doesn't think me so fragile that I will blow away in the breeze."

Alistair opened his mouth to apologise, but Grace cut him off. "Don't look at me like that, Alistair. I'm perfectly fine and you're late for a meeting. Go."

Despite being a respected and feared former detective inspector with over thirty years' experience of taking down hardened criminals, Alistair Stewart let out a squeak and scuttled around her. He fled out the door, grabbing a scone off the floor as he went. Charlie watched him go with the look of a man who longed to follow. At any other time, Grace might have been amused at seeing these two tough former policemen cowering from her, but she was not in the mood.

She crossed her arms and attempted to fill the doorway with her narrow frame. "I. Am. Not. Fragile."

Charlie shrank backwards as if she had slapped him, but he recovered quickly. "Perhaps fragile was a poor word choice, my love. But you did collapse at work two months ago."

"The police surgeon was grossly exaggerating to call it a collapse. I may have dozed off for a moment, but that was perfectly understandable given how busy I was with final exams."

"Dozed off? *Dozed off?* Grace, need I remind you that you were found lying unconscious on the mortuary floor? Face down. Out cold." Charlie held up his hand to fend off her response. "Final exams, working for the police surgeon, helping at the Lavender House medical clinic, and working for our private investigation business, as well as running a household, fighting for the right to vote, and all the other things you do. Was it any wonder your body collapsed in protest?"

Charlie paused to allow her to admit it. When she didn't, his muscled arms crossed over his broad chest as he made full use of his height advantage. "I meant it when I insisted you take two months off."

They had had a fearful row over it – their first serious fight. Charlie had gone so far as to suggest she take an entire year off her medical studies, after pointing out they were now financially able to cope on his income after receiving a huge reward for their honeymoon investigation. To his credit, he had realised his error of judgement at once, but Grace had been furious by that point. After calming down, two days later, they had compromised by agreeing to a two-month break over summer between her final exams and the start of the new term at medical school. Grace had also vowed never to lose her temper again, because she couldn't bear to see the pain she had caused him. On the other hand, their reconciliation had been wonderfully memorable.

Realising she couldn't out-intimidate him, Grace uncrossed her arms and shot her next arrow at his soft heart. "I had a delightful two weeks off over Christmas and New Year, my sweet. We had a splendid time on the Otago Peninsula, didn't we? Those moonlit

8

dips in the sea really were most invigorating. I am as refreshed, calm, and healthy as I will ever be."

Charlie's nostrils flared at the mention of moonlit bathing in the sea, which had been very invigorating indeed, given the secluded nature of the cove in which the holiday cottage nestled. Grace didn't mention that she had also taken great pride in mastering the art of bicycle riding, because Charlie had only succeeded in wobbling and crashing, before he declared he was a horse man and no ridiculous metal contraption would change that. Grace had wobbled and crashed too, but she had persevered through gravel-grazed knees because she knew she would need a form of transport when she qualified as a doctor at the end of the year. By the end of the week, she could ride the bicycle for miles at a frankly alarming speed, with the wind whipping her long hair into a black banner behind her. The freedom had been nothing short of exhilarating.

Her charm offensive failed. Charlie flexed his biceps and puffed out his broad chest. "Two full months away from work, Grace. I mean it."

Grace wished her husband wasn't six feet tall because she wanted to glare at him eye to eye. Eye to muscular shoulder put her at a distinct disadvantage physically, but she had her own strengths. She stroked soft fingers down his freshly shaven cheek. "Charlie, dearest heart, if I take any more time off, my brain will rot and dribble out my nose."

Charlie's feet shuffled ever so slightly, a sure sign he was about to say something she wouldn't want to hear. "It's just that you seem to have been so irritable the last few days. No, I didn't mean irritable. Just … distracted. Don't look at me like that, Grace. It makes me nervous."

"I have not been irritable!" Grace knew that yelling the words destroyed her argument, but she couldn't stop herself. Her long-suffering husband had that slapped-in-the-face look about him again. She took a deep, calming breath. "All right. I have been irritable. More than irritable. I've been miserable. I'm sorry,

Charlie, but I need to get back to work or I'll go insane. The truth is, I had such hopes after our delightful break away over Christmas, but it was all for nothing. Another month has passed and I am still not pregnant."

Charlie scooped her into his arms and crushed her to his body. "I'm sorry, my love. I should have realised."

Darn the man. Now she was going to cry.

"There's no hurry to start a family." Charlie wiped a tear from her cheek. "We can only hope that we'll be blessed with a child when the time is right. In the meantime, I would rather we enjoyed our time together without the pressure of this case. A baby has been kidnapped and held to ransom. It will certainly be harrowing and extremely stressful."

"Is it only me you are worried about, Charlie?" Grace whispered. "After what you went through a year ago, I would understand if it's too hard for you to cope with a kidnapping case."

Charlie stepped away and examined her face with the intensity he used for examining a crime scene. "Those few hours I was being held against my will were just as hard on you, Grace."

"All the more reason for us to work together on this case, since we both understand what the victim and family are going through. Together, we have a better chance of getting that precious wee baby back to his parents."

From the narrowing of his almond eyes, Grace thought he was about to put his foot down, but Charlie let out another long huff of breath and reached for his hat and coat. "The truth is, I can't turn this case down and I can't do it without you. I'll tell you about it on the way. Bring your medical bag. We'll take Blaze too."

Their border collie was waiting by the open front door, licking cream and strawberry jam off her nose and looking eager for action. Grace picked up the empty scone plate and went next door to collect her hat and medical bag.

They walked down High Street and stopped in the city only long enough to recruit Johnny Todd and his team of messenger boys as

10

helpers, before connecting to a tram towards the north end of Dunedin. A familiar route to Grace, as she was a student at the Otago Medical School. The trams were packed with passengers, so Charlie remained silent until they alighted at Dundas Street. He helped her down the step and kept holding her arm as they walked. Blaze trotted along beside Charlie's knee, now a well-trained detective dog after a year in their company.

"The baby was kidnapped overnight," Charlie said when they were clear of the crowd. "His father sent an urgent message to Alistair this morning to plead for our help, because the ransom demand told him not to contact the police."

As they approached the Dundas Street bridge over the Water of Leith, a young child tottered towards them, followed by a mother with bags under her eyes, who was pushing a baby carriage. The toddler ignored them in favour of Blaze, who allowed herself to be patted by clumsy hands. The mother murmured an apology as she pulled the child away, heading towards the nearby Dunedin Botanic Garden, Grace suspected, to wear the child out in pursuit of a peaceful afternoon.

Grace watched them hurry away. Perhaps Charlie was right. The kidnapping of an infant differed from the crimes they usually dealt with. Even murder investigations, horrendous as they were, involved a victim who could no longer be helped, except by arresting the killer. A kidnapping would bring tremendous pressure on them to find the baby before it was too late.

"How much time have we got before the ransom is due?" she asked.

"Four days. Friday at noon. It will be nearly impossible to find the kidnapper in such a short time unless we get a strong lead straight away. I'm hoping Blaze will be able to follow the trail. Grace, I want you to know that you can step away from the investigation at any time."

"Not with a baby's life at risk." Grace wondered how she would cope, but she also saw they had no choice. They couldn't let the parents down, because they had no other option if they couldn't call the police.

However, before she threw all her energy and skills at this case, she wanted to clear the air with her husband. She picked up a twig and dropped it over the rail of the bridge, a game she had often played with her brothers as a child. The twig spun around and around in a gentle eddy before becoming trapped in a fallen branch. Charlie came up beside her and dropped his twig, which caught the current and bobbed away towards the sea.

Typical, Grace thought, as she framed her conciliatory words carefully. "There are so many things I have struggled to achieve in my life, but I never for a moment thought that having a child would be one of them. I'm sorry if I have been impossible to live with lately, Charlie."

Her husband wrapped an arm around her shoulders. "You have nothing to apologise for, Grace. We've only been married for a year, and didn't we always say it would be better for you to finish your medical degree before having a child? Maybe fate is working in our favour."

"That's the point, Charlie. A year should be enough. But I am fine with it, honestly." Grace pushed herself off the bridge rail. "Come on, let's find ourselves a kidnapper."

Grace didn't want to trust to fate, but science had provided no answers. She had read everything she could find on the subject, which was lamentably little considering that female fertility was the very foundation of the human race. Most of what she read were clinical summaries of anatomy and function involving a husband and wife. One would think babies never sprang forth from an unmarried union.

Medical textbooks instructed doctors to advise "unnecessarily anxious" prospective mothers not to be alarmed until at least a year of "regular marital activity" had passed. That dreaded one-year mark was up in exactly eight days, twelve hours, and fifty-two minutes. Not that she was counting. Needless to say, her current childless state was not due to lack of "marital activity". One only had to look at her gorgeous and delightfully vigorous husband to know that. After the one-year mark, recommended options varied depending on the whims of the author, ranging from the pointless to the painful to the downright ridiculous. Worse still was their callous use of words like inadequate, barren, and sterile. Small wonder Grace had vowed never again to read another medical text on the subject.

They had passed the road around the back of the Dunedin Botanic Garden before Charlie spoke again. "I know this will sound patronising, but worrying about it won't help, Grace."

"How can I forget about it, when every second person I meet asks when they might expect 'the pitter patter of tiny feet' or assumes I am denying your conjugal rights for the sake of my career? As if the contents of my womb were any of their business. How would they like it if I asked them about their marital activities within five minutes of meeting?"

Charlie flicked a cautious glance at her before giving her a rueful smile. "I'd like to see you try."

"Maybe I will. I know we need to focus on the kidnapping, Charlie, but I felt I owed you an explanation for my irritability. Seriously, my love, I will try to be a better person and think only of our many blessings. At least with the ransom due on Friday, the investigation will be over before our wedding anniversary next week."

"I can't believe it's been nearly a year since we got married," Charlie said, changing the subject with annoyingly hearty cheerfulness. "So much has happened. A memorable honeymoon, Lavender House risen from the ashes, the business thriving. Not to forget one of the proudest moments of my life – walking you to the polling booth for the first ever vote open to all the women and men of New Zealand."

Grace smiled at the memory. Marching to the polling booth surrounded by fellow suffragists, singing and joyful. The year

1893 would go down in New Zealand's history as the start of a glorious new future of equality for women. The world took notice that day and hopefully changed for the better. "We have much to celebrate, my love. Whether or not we have children in the future, we will always have each other. That should be a cause for celebration, surely."

"My sentiments exactly." Charlie planted a lingering kiss on the sensitive skin behind her ear. They walked in comfortable silence before turning into one of the side streets leading up to the parkland that joined the Botanic Gardens to the Northern Cemetery.

Charlie glanced at the address in his hand and stopped at the last house on the street. "We're here. The client's name is Edward Barclay. The missing baby is his son, Oliver Barclay. We need to be sympathetic to their plight, but also careful about making promises. The odds of finding the child are not in our favour."

Grace examined the single-storey wooden dwelling in front of her. Fresh white paint, geraniums on the porch, pretty garden. The average person would never imagine it to be the scene of a heinous crime. But then the average person was so frequently wrong on such matters. However, in this case, Grace was surprised by the modest dwelling, because she had assumed the family must be wealthy. Unless Mr Edward Barclay or his wife had a very large trust fund under their pillows, they did not seem a likely target of a ransom demand.

Paternal Anger

Charlie took a moment to check the area around the Barclays' house for lurking criminals before approaching the front door. If the kidnapping had been organised by a criminal gang, they might have men watching for a police presence. Unlikely, but Charlie didn't want to take any risks when the ransom note had specifically said "no police", because private investigators would not be welcome either. Nervous kidnappers made rash decisions, and the stakes could not be higher with a vulnerable infant at risk.

The problem, from an investigation standpoint, was that here was no precedent on which to base this investigation. He couldn't recall a single kidnapping of a young child for ransom in this country. The rare cases involving young children were more often abductions by warring family members or infants taken by a mentally unstable person desperate for a child of their own.

Blaze scouted the area at his command, as she had been trained to do, and returned to his side without raising the alert. Charlie straightened his tie and knocked on the door, preparing to meet the parents at the worst moment of their lives.

The door crashed open before his knuckles finished the last knock. A gentleman aged in his late thirties or early forties lurched forward, almost landing in Charlie's arms. Mr Edward Barclay, father of the kidnapped child, judging from the wild glint in his eyes.

Barclay's face crumpled when he saw a young couple barely in their mid-twenties with a dog. He pulled back to block the doorway. "We're not receiving visitors and I don't give to charities."

Charlie replied in a tone designed to be both soothing and authoritative. "You must be Mr Barclay. I am Charlie Penrose

15

Pyke, private investigator and founding partner of the Southern Investigations Agency. May I introduce –"

Barclay cut him off with a bluntness that would have been impolite under ordinary circumstances. "You're too young to be a detective."

"I have been a detective for many years, Mr Barclay." Four years, to be precise, counting his time as a detective constable training under the most experienced officer in the police force, Alistair Stewart. No need to mention he had no experience whatsoever with kidnapping. Charlie held out a calling card, forcing Barclay to uncross his arms to take it. "May we come in, Mr Barclay? I'd prefer not to be seen on your doorstep."

Barclay grasped the card with one hand, running the other hand through dark red hair, which stood as upright as a rooster's comb. Charlie assessed their client as he waited for the man to step aside and let them in. Everything about him indicated a confident and well-to-do city gentleman, from his erect posture and the precisely trimmed moustache forming an arch over a resolute jaw, down to the immaculate black suit and polished shoes. The lack of a tie or cravat and the state of his hair suggested Barclay had been told his son was missing as he was dressing for his workday. Given the ransom demand, Charlie had assumed Mr Barclay would be a prominent business owner, but the modest house placed Barclay a little further down the scale, perhaps as an attorney or senior manager.

He might as well have been speaking a foreign language for all the response he got. Their client appeared paralysed by the situation, which was not unexpected, given the man was suffering an unfathomable shock. In Charlie's experience, men used to being in charge were often the most thrown out of kilter by being the victim of crime. It said a great deal for the man that he was not catatonic or panicking.

"We should go inside," Charlie repeated. "I don't want to alert the kidnapper to our presence if he is watching the house for signs of the police."

Barclay's mouth sagged open, then he all but yanked Charlie into the hall. When Charlie stepped past him, he realised Barclay only came up to his chin, which made him not much taller than Grace. He had seemed taller, more imposing, on the step. Barclay hesitated in the doorway, as if uncertain whether to close the door on Grace and the dog, who were waiting patiently on the porch with identically neutral expressions.

Charlie motioned for Blaze to sit and Grace to enter. "May I introduce our medical expert, Mrs Grace Penrose Pyke, and our specialist tracking dog, Blaze."

Barclay's attention passed straight over Grace as if she wasn't there, landing on Blaze with a spark of hope. "A tracking dog. Excellent. You'll want to get started immediately. I already know the blackguard who took my son. All I need from you is to find him and clap him in irons."

"We need to talk briefly first, Mr Barclay." If Barclay really did know the identity of the kidnapper, this just might be the shortest investigation on record – and thank goodness for that. But Charlie wasn't about to make the mistake of jumping to conclusions, especially with a child's life on the line. He gestured for Barclay to go ahead of him down the hall.

"Talk? I don't want to talk, I want action."

"I'll need to get details of the suspected kidnapper and a description of your child, as well as examining the nursery for evidence. We have to understand exactly what happened and why you believe this person took your son before we can proceed to a search and arrest. It shouldn't take long."

"Yes, yes, I see. Whatever you need." Barclay leaned forward to clasp Charlie's arm, his voice a whisper. "Nothing is more important to me than my precious son and heir. My wife is in the sitting room, but she won't be of any use, I'm afraid. Daisy has a delicate constitution, and Oliver's disappearance has shaken her to the core. If your wife is a nurse, perhaps she ought to give Daisy a sedative."

Charlie refrained from commenting until he had met the child's mother. Giving the shock Mrs Barclay had suffered, her husband could well be right, even if he had expressed it rather tactlessly. Grace met his eye but kept her expression blank, which must have taken an impressive amount of forbearance on her part.

Barclay took them into the first room on the right. "Daisy, my love, the private detective is here. He has a tracking dog."

And a wife, Charlie wanted to say but didn't, because social niceties were the last thing he expected of his client right now. Still, he wondered how Barclay could overlook Grace. Despite her slight build, her powerful presence lit any room she entered, in his mind at least.

Mrs Daisy Barclay was slumped in an armchair and appeared more in need of a restorative than a sedative. She tried to stand when they entered the room, but the poor woman looked as if her spine had turned to gelatine. Mr Barclay was at her side in an instant, urging her to sit down and taking her hand to comfort her. In better circumstances, Mr and Mrs Barclay would have made a handsome couple. Daisy was a perfect name for her. Flawless white skin, flaxen curls, and a sweet face that seemed designed to smile and laugh. But not today. Today, Daisy Barclay's eyes were puffy from crying, and the smile she attempted was all too fleeting.

"Mrs Barclay, may we express our sincere sympathy for the dreadful situation you and your husband find yourselves in? I am Charlie Penrose Pyke, a partner in the Southern Investigations Agency, and this is the agency's medical expert, Mrs Grace Penrose Pyke."

Despite her distressed state, Daisy was quick to pull herself together in the face of hope. "Thank you for coming so quickly, Mr Penrose Pyke. I asked Edward to contact you because we are desperate for help but cannot turn to the police." Daisy's gaze switched from Charlie to Grace, and the faint smile reappeared briefly. "Your skills won't be needed, Mrs Penrose Pyke. I'm not in need of medical care, whatever my husband may have told you."

"I didn't tell them you needed a nurse, Daisy," Barclay said gently. "But a strong sedative may be in order to spare your nerves this dreadful ordeal."

Charlie intervened, because it was clear Daisy didn't want or need a sedative, which was just as well, because he wanted both parents to be wide awake and united in their focus on their missing child. Besides, Charlie was in no mood to let Grace's skills be underestimated, even by a client in distress. "For the record, my wife is not a nurse. She is here as a partner in the detective agency and an essential member of the investigation team. Grace is in her final year of medical school and has such an excellent reputation for criminal forensics that she has a paid position working as an assistant to the police surgeon."

Both the Barclays' eyes widened at this news – the husband's in disbelief and the wife's with a spark of interest.

Grace glided forward, as serene as a swan, although her feelings were easy to read in the firm set of her lips. "Perhaps I could take Mrs Barclay to another room, whilst you gentlemen discuss the practicalities."

She assisted Daisy Barclay to rise, and they left the room without further ado, to Charlie's relief, knowing Grace would expertly soothe the devastated mother, while also drawing critical information from her. Edward Barclay followed them to the door, as if he was unsure whether he wanted his wife out of his sight, but Grace had closed the door before he could intervene.

"Perhaps it's for the best." Barclay said the words with a sad shake of his head. "Daisy blames herself, of course. I told her the time for recriminations will be when Oliver is safe at home again and the scoundrel is behind bars. Not that I blame her myself, naturally."

Charlie was left with the impression that Barclay really did believe his wife was partly to blame but that he was trying his best to be understanding. He couldn't allow that attitude to pass unchallenged. "You are right not to blame your wife, Mr Barclay. Nobody but the kidnapper is to blame. Why don't you take a seat and tell me whom you suspect." Charlie pointed to an armchair, which had its back to the door and clearly belonged to the man of the house, because the side table next to it held a pipe and tobacco pouch, as well as spectacles and a leather-bound Bible. Charlie sat in the facing chair.

Barclay hesitated, then sat. He picked up his pipe and jabbed the stem in Charlie's direction to emphasise his words. "The kidnapper's name is Nathan Locke. A jumped-up popinjay who thinks he is cleverer than his betters. He was my junior clerk at the Bank of New Zealand in Wellington, before I transferred to my current position as a senior bank clerk in Dunedin. I had Locke dismissed over a small sum of money that went missing two years ago."

"Two years ago? I have to say, it doesn't sound like a strong motive on the face of it, Mr Barclay."

"Locke denied stealing the money and made a dreadful fuss about losing his position. We had already exchanged harsh words over his inappropriate conduct towards my wife at the bank's Christmas social event."

Charlie raised an eyebrow.

"Nothing improper, you understand," Barclay hastened to add, "but Locke was overly familiar with my wife. Daisy is a pretty woman who is too sweet and innocent to know how to handle unwanted attention, so I had to step in. Locke felt the reprimand was undeserved and held a grudge against me. I believe he stole the money to make me, as his superior, look bad."

"But kidnapping a child …"

"Kidnapping for *ransom*, Mr Penrose Pyke. Locke was dismissed without references, naturally. He wrote me a letter

20

several weeks after his dismissal, which made the depth of his bitterness against me abundantly clear. I kept it." Barclay fished in his pocket and handed over the letter. "I dismissed it at the time as no more than a ridiculous threat from a desperate man."

The letter, which was no more than a brief note, no doubt written under the influence of alcohol and anger once Nathan Locke realised how difficult it would be to find a new position without a reference. Charlie read it aloud: *My life has been destroyed by your lies. I want compensation or I will tell the senior manager what really happened. Don't ignore me or you will regret it.*

"I take your point, Mr Barclay. The tone is definitely threatening and the compensation demand is telling. Did Mr Locke follow up his threat at the time?"

"No. I confronted him as soon as I received the note and told him to stop bothering me with his petty grievances or I would make sure he never worked again. I've no idea what sewer he disappeared down, but I made sure I circulated his identity to other banks so they wouldn't employ him either. Damned impertinence from a junior clerk, and a thief at that."

Charlie said nothing, hoping to draw Barclay into further disclosures. From the way Mr Barclay's moustache quivered and his face reddened, there was more to tell.

"The theft damaged my reputation as Locke's superior officer. I, who ought to have been lauded for discovering the theft, instead received the punishment of a transfer to Dunedin. They wanted to hush up the incident because the managing director was about to retire. Outrageous to penalise me for his crime."

"You did the right thing keeping the letter, Mr Barclay. At least it is a firm lead for me to follow, although I can't help but think two years is a long time to wait for revenge, especially when the incident occurred hundreds of miles away in Wellington."

"Criminals are not driven by logic, one assumes. I transferred to Dunedin and heard no more from Locke. Perhaps he didn't know where we were. Indeed, I would not have given him a second thought if my wife's companion hadn't mentioned seeing a man of his description talking to my wife in the Dunedin Botanic Garden three weeks ago. Perhaps seeing Daisy triggered his old resentment."

"Ah, I see. A recent sighting does sound suspicious. Are you sure it was Nathan Locke?"

"Daisy claimed the man was simply a stranger who had mistakenly believed she looked familiar, but Prudence's description matched Nathan Locke. When I pressed Daisy about the man, she admitted it was him, but she said she hadn't wanted to upset me by mentioning his name. Daisy assured me she hadn't seen him either before or since, but then there was the odd incident of the white rose on the sundial."

Charlie paused with his pencil poised over his notebook. "A white rose?"

"I woke early yesterday morning and noticed a single white rose sitting on the sundial outside the nursery window. It might have been nothing more than those cheeky devils who have nothing better to do than steal other people's flowers, but I thought I ought to mention it because Oliver was taken the following night."

"I'll make a note of it. One never knows what may prove relevant." Charlie flipped over to a new page. "I'll need a description of Nathan Locke."

Barclay's mouth turned lemon sour. "Prudence described him as 'tall and handsome, with curly blond hair and the profile of a Greek god'. Ridiculous. Women are rather prone to excess in these matters, and I would hardly describe him as more than a tall, blond man with unmemorable features, although he does have a fairly prominent nose. I suppose one might call him handsome in the shallow, showy way some young men seem to cultivate these days."

"I'll certainly look into it with urgency." A potential suspect was far better than the alternative – a kidnapping motivated purely by the ransom money, which could have been committed by anyone with sufficient greed and appalling morals. Once the child was gone, there would be precious few clues to track down. "Do you have any information on his current whereabouts, Mr Barclay?"

Barclay slammed his pipe down on the side table. "If I knew his current location, I would not have agreed to call you in. I would tackle the blackguard myself."

In Charlie's view, it was just as well Mrs Barclay had insisted on calling in a private detective. Edward Barclay might be a successful banker, but he would likely be no match for a younger, taller, resentful kidnapper with everything to lose. If indeed Nathan Locke was the kidnapper. Holding a baby to ransom seemed an extreme response to an old grudge, even if Locke's dismissal had been a major financial setback and a blow to his future prospects.

"I'd like to look at the nursery first," Charlie said, "and then we will attempt to track the kidnapper's movements with our dog. If we're unsuccessful, we'll need to use other means to locate Nathan Locke as soon as possible, which means I need you and your wife to make a list of anything you know about him that could assist us. Friends and colleagues from Locke's time in Wellington, and any hints about his current work or living arrangements that Mrs Barclay might have noted during their brief encounter three weeks ago. However, our best option would be to ask for assistance from the police."

Barclay was on his feet in an instant, his face a burning ember. "You can't tell the police. The ransom note said not to. Oliver might be harmed if we don't follow the kidnapper's instructions."

Charlie rose too. "Nevertheless, it would be best if the police are informed, because they have resources we cannot match for locating suspects. I have an excellent relationship with the local detective inspector, whom I can contact discreetly through a trusted friend away from the police station. I would insist that the police do not come here to your home. And, if it's not Locke, Detective Inspector Wallace will know of similar cases and potential suspects. He can also ensure the local beat constables keep an eye out for suspicious activity. You will appreciate that with such limited time, it would be best to have as much assistance as possible."

"No police," Mr Barclay snapped. "I would rather pay the ransom than risk my son's life. If that is too difficult for you, I'll engage someone else or search every damn house in Dunedin myself. Nathan Locke cannot be that hard to find if he has an eight-month-old child with him."

Maternal Anguish

Grace kept a firm grip on Daisy Barclay's arm as she guided her out of the sitting room and down the hall, opening doors until she found the kitchen. She had hoped to find a motherly housekeeper preparing a welcoming pot of tea and breakfast for Mrs Barclay, who had most likely not eaten.

"Do you have anyone who helps around the house, Mrs Barclay?" Grace asked. "A strong cup of tea would do you the world of good."

"Edward let our housekeeper go several weeks ago." This simple statement seemed to drag Daisy Barclay's sagging shoulders even lower, and her words held a touch of acidity. She heaved the kettle onto the lit stove as if it was weighted with lead, before gathering the tea caddy, cups, and spoons in a slow, mechanical response to a visitor's request for refreshment.

"I'll be back in a minute." Grace slipped out of the kitchen and ran on light feet down the hall to the sitting room. She eased the door open a crack in time to catch Edward Barclay's suspicions about Nathan Locke, staying only long enough to hear Mr Barclay state his reasons for suspecting him.

When Grace returned to the kitchen, she found Mrs Barclay sitting at the kitchen table, staring at the pale blue baby bootie she held in her palm. Her eyes shone with tears but they went unshed. The poor woman appeared to be shocked into immobility.

Grace rescued the whistling kettle to make tea, adding a dose of sugar to one cup and placing it by Daisy's hand. "You should eat something, Mrs Barclay, to keep your strength up. I don't mean to sound unsympathetic, but we have a difficult week ahead of us. Perhaps some toast?"

"I don't eat bread, Mrs Penrose Pyke." Daisy Barclay mumbled the words through the bootie she was now holding to her face.

"Later then. And do please call me Grace. We'll need to work together to get Oliver back as soon as possible."

"Ollie." Daisy tucked the bootie into her bodice. "Edward insists on calling him Oliver, but he is only a baby and Ollie suits him better. Edward didn't want me to contact your agency, but I have heard you and your husband perform miracles."

Grace put her hand on top of Daisy's trembling fingers. Daisy was holding her emotions together with impressive strength, but the depth of her fear showed in the vice-like grip with which she latched onto Grace's hand.

"We will do everything in our power to get Ollie back to you, Daisy. It might help if you had a woman friend or relative to come and stay with you for support."

"I have Prudence, who lives with us," Daisy said with a distinct lack of enthusiasm. "My only sister passed away last year after a long illness. I should have been at her side, but Edward wouldn't let me visit her sickbed or travel to her funeral because I was only months away from giving birth."

Grace's heart went out to her. "Are you still in contact with your sister's family?"

"I wrote to my brother-in-law, James Montgomery, for a while."

Grace thought Daisy was about to give a reason for falling out of touch with her brother-in-law, but she bent her head and kept her silence. Edward probably didn't like his wife writing to a man, even the husband of a beloved sister. "Is there a friend who could support you?"

"Nobody I could ask to come here. Don't worry about me, Grace. I am stronger than I look, and all I care about is getting Ollie back."

"I don't doubt it. Your husband believes a man called Nathan Locke is the kidnapper."

Daisy's grip tightened another notch. "Edward is wrong. Please, please, don't be distracted by his accusation. You'll only be wasting precious time because Mr Locke would never do such a dreadful thing."

"I believe you, Daisy, but I need to know why, because your husband seems certain he is to blame. I understand Mr Locke threatened Mr Barclay after he was dismissed from his position at the bank in Wellington."

"Please just believe me, Grace." Daisy's fingers slipped free as she transferred them to the cup and sipped tea, her eyes closed and her face blank. "You have to understand that Edward is a good husband, but he is prone to jealousy. It was such a trivial incident. Mr Locke bumped into me at the bank's Christmas party and spilled my drink. It was only elderflower cordial, so the stain barely showed, but Mr Locke was most apologetic. He fetched me a napkin and a fresh drink and stayed to chat with me for a minute or two. Edward doesn't like me talking to other men, but what could I do when the poor man was trying to make up for his clumsiness by being kind?"

"I understand," Grace said. She couldn't imagine being married to a man who was so jealous he wouldn't allow his wife to exchange a few words with a colleague at a social occasion. Dear Charlie didn't bat an eyelid over Grace conducting medical examinations of other men, although, of course, he was exceptional.

Daisy was looking at her with wide hazel eyes, which seemed to radiate injured innocence. "That brief conversation was all the connection I had with Mr Locke until I saw him again in Dunedin."

"In fact, I understand Mr Locke was dismissed over a rather more serious matter," Grace said. "A theft from the bank."

"I didn't know about the theft or his dismissal until our meeting in the Botanic Garden three weeks ago." Daisy glanced towards

27

the door and lowered her voice. "The encounter was entirely by chance, I swear, whatever Edward believes. I hadn't seen the man for over two years and I haven't seen him since. Indeed, Mr Locke appeared quite alarmed by my presence. I explained we had moved to Dunedin and naturally I asked after him out of politeness. It was only then I found out that Edward had him fired over a theft, which Mr Locke denied committing."

"Did he give you any indication of where he was currently living or working?"

"None at all, and I didn't ask. I was too upset by Edward's role in his dismissal."

"You believed Mr Locke?" Grace could see that she did, but wanted Daisy to confirm it.

"I don't know. He seemed an honest sort of man, but naturally I trusted my husband's judgement. Perhaps it was a misunderstanding. Mr Locke insisted he no longer harboured any ill will towards Edward and we parted on good terms. Unfortunately, we were seen talking in the gardens and Edward found out. He was angry, thinking Locke must have deliberately tracked us down, even though I swore we met by chance. Now you can see why I believe Locke to be innocent of taking Ollie."

Grace wasn't so sure. Even if it was a chance meeting, as Daisy said, it might have triggered old resentments. And then there was the matter of Edward Barclay's furious reaction to the meeting, which hinted that he feared a closer relationship than Daisy was admitting. "Mr Locke must be quite distinctive if the person who saw you could describe him accurately enough for your husband to recognise him after two years."

"He does rather stand out, because he is taller than most people and classically handsome, with pale blond hair."

"Daisy, may I ask who reported the chance encounter to your husband?"

"Prudence Winslow, who lives with us. Edward refers to her as my companion."

The pursing of Daisy's lips indicated Prudence was far from Daisy's ideal choice of companion. Grace let the silence hang until Daisy filled it.

"We met her through the local church soon after we arrived in Dunedin two years ago. Her mother passed away recently and Edward was kind enough to help her manage the sale of her family home, as she had nobody else to turn to. Edward has a senior position with a bank, you see, and thus the necessary financial skills and understanding of real estate."

"How thoughtful of him," Grace said. "How did Miss Winslow come to move in with you? Is she a particular friend of yours?"

"No, but Prudence needed a place to stay until she decided on her plans for the future, so Edward suggested she stay here and act as my companion. He felt it would be appropriate for me to have a woman of a similar age in the house while he was at work. Before Prudence moved in, which was about six weeks ago, I only had the company of the housekeeper, who came in for a few hours a day."

Grace read between the lines and assumed Edward did not approve of the housekeeper. Another potential suspect, if they had time to interview all the people who might have had a grudge against Edward Barclay, however minor. To a working woman, losing the few shillings a week she might earn as a daily housekeeper could mean the difference between hunger and comfort.

Daisy must have realised she hadn't provided a glowing reference for her companion because she added, "Prudence adores Ollie. She has been wonderful about seeing to him in the mornings so I can get some sleep. For the first few months, Ollie woke frequently. He has been much better since I started giving him a little solid food, although he has been fretful the last few nights. I sleep in the nursery so he doesn't disturb the rest of the household."

"It must be hard. I have friends with babies who say they would give almost anything to have a full night's sleep." The topic of sleep provided Grace with a convenient transition to the events of

29

the previous night. Specifically, why Daisy hadn't been disturbed by the intruder when she was sleeping in the nursery with Ollie. There was no easy way to say it, except to avoid making it sound like an accusation. "When did you discover Ollie was missing, Daisy?"

"This morning, when Prudence screamed." Daisy withdrew her hands into a tight ball in the centre of her chest. When she looked up again, tears were streaming down her cheeks. "I'm certain I didn't take any of my sleeping tonic last night. I'd swear to it ... only ... only I didn't hear a thing. Ollie was taken by God only knows who, and I slept through it. What sort of mother doesn't wake when her child is snatched in the night right under her nose? No wonder Edward blames me."

Grace was around the end of the table in an instant, taking Daisy in her arms and holding her until her sobs died away. It was all Grace could do to hold back her own tears. Charlie had been right when he said this case would take a toll on everyone involved, including themselves. But he had been wrong to try to stop her from joining the investigation, because Daisy Barclay needed her almost as much as little Ollie did.

Several minutes passed before Daisy's tears dried, leaving her limp against Grace's shoulder. Grace kept hold of her, but leaned back so she could look her in the eye. "Daisy, listen to me. It is *not* your fault. The kidnapper is the only person to blame for the appalling situation you find yourself in. I'm going to ask you to rest now, while my husband and I use our tracking dog to search for your precious baby Ollie. When we come back, I'll want you to tell me who you think could have done this if Nathan Locke didn't. It might be someone you know who needs money, or someone with a resentment against the family, or simply a person who wants a baby but can't have one of their own."

Daisy's frown suggested that she already had one or more suspects in mind, but she wasn't sure enough to share her views right now. "A little quiet time to get my thoughts in order would be appreciated. Are you going to give me a sedative?"

Grace smiled. "Now why would I want to do that when you have important work to do, making a list of potential suspects? However, I might tell your husband I have, for the sake of peace in the household."

Daisy smiled back, transforming her face. "I'm glad you're here, Grace."

Jealousy was not a trait Grace admired in a man, but she could see why Edward Barclay worried other men would find his wife attractive. She had that elusive quality of making a person feel better just by being in her presence, even now, in the worst possible circumstances. What Grace couldn't accept was Edward Barclay's anger at Daisy after her chance meeting with the attractive and younger Nathan Locke in the Botanic Garden. Unless Mr Barclay had a genuine reason to believe the meeting was not by chance.

Jealousy was not the only trait Grace disliked about their new client. His high-handed approach to inviting another woman into the house as Daisy's unwanted companion, his willingness to blame his wife for not preventing the kidnapping, his dismissal of her usefulness to the investigation – all this and more told Grace that Edward Barclay was a traditional husband who ruled by divine masculine right. Unfortunately, this only put him in the vast majority of ordinary men who took for granted their status as head of the household and protector of their family.

Grace didn't want to leave Daisy, but she seemed to have pulled herself together now and was busy putting together a tray with the makings of a light meal, as if she had taken to heart Grace's words about keeping up her strength and wanted to give the impression of a woman in control. Grace had always been the same. She hated people seeing her at her worst and strove to meet a crisis with action.

She was about to leave the kitchen when Daisy handed her a chipped enamel bowl filled with water. "For your dog," Daisy said. "It's a hot day."

The simple act of putting a dog before herself made Grace warm to Daisy even more. She took the bowl outside, finding Blaze at rest under a shady tree.

"We're relying on you, Blaze," Grace whispered as she put the bowl down. Oh, to be a dog and not have to worry about doing and saying the right thing in the complex world of humans. Grace worried that she had left their client with the impression that they would find Ollie. But then, this was hardly the time to tell Daisy that kidnappings often ended badly. Even Grace could not bring herself to admit that truth yet.

Mrs Barclay was probably in her late twenties, which was older than average for a first baby, while her husband might be as much as a decade older. Grace had been left in no doubt that little Ollie was adored by both parents with the fervent attachment that suggested a longed-for baby. Perhaps the kidnapper knew them well enough to realise the Barclays would do whatever it took to pay the ransom to get back their beloved son. She only hoped it would be enough.

Empty Cradle

Charlie followed Edward Barclay down the hall towards the nursery. The house was of a simple design: a central hallway leading from the front door with rooms off on either side. Barclay pointed out the location of his study, opposite the sitting room and adjoining the master bedroom, before striding off down the hallway, pointing alternately left and right. "Guest room, occupied by the only other occupant of the house, my wife's companion. Facilities, kitchen."

That left only one other room, the last on the right, facing north towards the area of bush and open land adjoining the Botanic Garden. Mr Barclay hesitated outside the room with his hand hovering over the doorknob as if it was too hot to touch, confirming Charlie's assumption that the remaining room was the nursery.

"Can you tell me about your wife's companion?" Charlie inquired, to give his client time to steady his nerves.

"Miss Prudence Winslow. She has been an invaluable support to my wife over the past few weeks, especially with Oliver. This morning, she left as soon as she discovered Oliver missing in order to search the neighbourhood for any sign of him. I would have done it myself if I hadn't had to wait for your arrival. I keep expecting her to walk through the door holding Oliver and laughing at his antics."

"I understand how hard this must be for you," Charlie said. "I'll need to speak to Miss Winslow as soon as possible. Do you have servants, living in or out?"

"None living in. A local lad helps in the garden when needed and his mother takes in the laundry and helps with spring cleaning.

Other than that, Prudence and Daisy manage the cooking and cleaning."

Charlie nodded, although he thought it a little unusual that a senior banker wouldn't employ more help. "I want to reassure you we will do everything possible to find your son, Mr Barclay. Is there someone you and your wife could call upon to support you during this difficult time? A relative or close friend, perhaps?"

"I don't need to be patted on the back and fussed over." Barclay's face reddened above the quivering ends of his moustache. "All I want is to have my son back."

"Of course." Charlie ignored the angry retort and stepped past Barclay to open the door into the nursery. He imagined how he would feel if his own child had been taken and was amazed Barclay could function at all.

The nursery was furnished with an exuberance of fresh blue wallpaper, and enough toys and baby paraphernalia to stock a small shop. A stranger entering would be left in no doubt the room belonged to a cherished first son. A cradle draped with fine white muslin stood in one corner. Beyond the cradle, the window stood open, looking out onto a small lawn and garden, with trees beyond. Soft blue curtains billowed in the breeze.

Edward Barclay stood in the doorway with his hands clasped, staring at the empty cradle as if the power of his faith could fill it.

Charlie took their client's arm and led him to the sole armchair. "I'll need a description of your son, Mr Barclay, including his age."

Barclay's eyes never left the cradle, but a wistful smile touched his lips. "Oliver is eight months old. A fine strapping lad. Blue-grey eyes like mine. Blond hair, like Daisy, but they do say a baby's hair can darken over time. Very well behaved and intelligent, unless he is hungry or tired."

"Eight months is such a lovely age," Charlie said. "Has Oliver started to crawl yet?"

"A little. Oliver said 'dada' for the first time last week."

"Oh, how lovely." Time was short, so Charlie eased into the critical questions. "I take it the kidnapper entered via the window during the night."

"Yes. I checked on Oliver when I retired at around eleven o'clock last night. I heard nothing until Prudence screamed when she went to get Oliver at about eight o'clock this morning. Prudence thought it odd that he and Daisy were sleeping so late, but she hadn't wanted to disturb them earlier. Normally, Oliver is awake by six o'clock, but he'd had a few restless nights, so we weren't too surprised he'd slept in."

"And Mrs Barclay?"

Barclay pointed to the open door to an adjoining room. "My wife was asleep in the small side room attached to the nursery. She'd been up with Oliver the previous nights and must have been exhausted. The sleeping arrangement was necessary, because I have an important position in the bank I work for and cannot afford to lose sleep when Oliver wakes during the night."

Charlie poked his head in and saw a simple day bed with a low set of drawers beside it. Despite the narrowness of the bed, it took up most of the room. Perhaps it had been used as quarters for a nanny in the past, or as a storage room. The room was only accessible through the nursery and had no window. From where Mrs Barclay had been sleeping to the child's cradle was only a few yards. Either the intruder had been extremely quiet or Mrs Barclay had been very deeply asleep after a series of disturbed nights.

A bottle of sleeping tonic sat on top of the drawers amongst a clutter of candlesticks, books, hairbrushes, a drained cup, and a full glass of water, suggesting that Mrs Barclay routinely slept next to the nursery. Charlie picked up the tonic bottle, noting that it was almost full, despite being issued by the pharmacy three weeks ago. If Mrs Barclay had used the sleeping tonic, she hadn't taken more than a few sips to help her drop off, presumably so she could wake if the child needed her. Charlie knew from talking to his best friend, Declan Kelly, that new mothers and fathers could become

35

so deprived of sleep that they learned to sleep through any amount of noise apart from the cries of their baby.

Charlie moved back to the main nursery area to inspect the window, which was intact and fully open. A deep gouge cut across the windowsill where a crowbar had been forced under the bottom of the window, leaving the flimsy window latch torn from its mounting. A tuft of soft blue wool had caught on the broken latch, presumably from the infant boy's nightclothes as he was taken out of the window. Charlie stared at the blue fluff and wished once again he could be anywhere but here.

The obvious question was why Mrs Barclay had not woken at the noise of the window being forced open. Was this what Mr Barclay meant when he said Daisy blamed herself? Charlie turned back to their client. "Did any of you hear the intruder breaking in, or any other unusual noise, Mr Barclay?"

"No. I did wonder if my wife had taken too much of her sleeping tonic by mistake, because it's hard to fathom how she didn't wake up. I heard nothing, but I am a sound sleeper and the master bedroom is on the far side of the house. Prudence didn't hear anything either, and she is sure she would have heard Oliver crying out if he had."

Charlie wasn't too surprised, knowing that some babies could sleep through anything once they were in a deep sleep. Besides, the kidnapper would have covered Oliver's mouth if he tried to cry out.

A sharp mark down the side of the window frame caught his eye. It continued around all sides of the window, leaving a cut through the paint and a thin line of putty on each side where the window had been sealed shut and painted over. The intruder had had to slice through the seal with a sharp knife, meaning the kidnapper had brought a knife with him, either knowing the window was sealed or expecting trouble. Hopefully the former, as it would have made sense for the kidnapper to make himself familiar with the house before risking a kidnapping.

Why seal the only window shut, sacrificing fresh air? Why not simply install a stronger lock on the inside if they were concerned about security, especially as the risk of fire was far higher than the likelihood of an intruder. Dunedin was a fairly safe city, and this part of town was by no means a rough area.

Barclay noticed his interest. "My wife asked me to seal the window to ensure it couldn't be opened. She has a nervous disposition, being relatively new to Dunedin and with a precious child to protect. If I had known what would happen, I'd have added bars."

Charlie left a pause to encourage further information, but Barclay said no more. "Do you have a photograph of Oliver?" He hadn't seen a single photograph in the house so far. Not even a wedding portrait.

"We have no photographs," Mr Barclay said. "The Bible tells us vanity is a sin."

Was it vanity to wish to capture an image of one's precious first child? Charlie knew he would take photographs every day, so as not to miss a moment of the baby's life. If he ever had a child. "Would friends or family have a photograph?"

"We have no family in Dunedin and few friends, aside from the church community, because we only moved here two years ago. I have my work colleagues and the gentlemen acquaintances from my club, but Daisy does not care to go out except to take fresh air. She was close to her sister when we lived in Wellington, but her sister died last year. Her parents are dead too."

A lonely life for a new mother, Charlie thought. Perhaps that was why she had a live-in companion. "We'll need to get more details from you and your wife as soon as we come back from attempting to track the kidnapper."

"I'll answer any questions you have," Barclay said, "but I don't want you distressing my wife any more than absolutely necessary. Daisy was in an excessively delicate state of mind even before this outrage. My wife was unable to conceive for several years, you see. I tried not to hold the fact that she had failed in her duty as a wife against her, but naturally Daisy felt it deeply. Unfortunately, the weakness of spirits she suffered after years of barrenness persisted even after Oliver's birth."

Failed in her duty as a wife? Charlie counted to ten silently to prevent himself from giving Barclay a piece of his mind. It was just as well Grace and Mrs Barclay were not here to hear this. However, it did seem odd that Daisy did not feel more joyful after the long-awaited child was born.

A sixth sense made him turn to the doorway, where Grace was standing, looking at Barclay with a glare that would melt every flake of snow on the Southern Alps.

"I've sent Mrs Barclay to rest, as you suggested, Mr Barclay," Grace said with the clinical briskness of a doctor dealing with a disagreeable patient. "She is not to be disturbed until we return."

Barclay shook his head at Charlie. "You see what I mean? This is why I asked Prudence Winslow to assist Daisy. Prudence is a marvel with Oliver and very tolerant of my wife's frailties."

"Your wife has had a dreadful shock, Mr Barclay," Charlie said. "She will need your utmost support and sympathy."

"Of course." Barclay said the words as if he sincerely meant them. Indeed, his tone gave the impression that he felt he was already doing his utmost for his wife. Perhaps he supposed a stiff upper lip and a firm hand were what she needed most, aside from a strong sedative.

"Where did you find the ransom note?" Charlie asked, trying to keep his tone businesslike and his focus on the daunting task ahead.

"Prudence found it in the cradle when she went to see to Oliver. I took it away before Daisy could see it, not wishing to upset her any more than necessary, but otherwise I touched nothing."

"Excellent. Please show me where it was and continue to leave everything untouched, although it would be as well to shut the window and fix the latch if you are concerned about security."

They went over to the cradle, where Mr Barclay pointed to the spot where once the baby's head must have lain. The blanket had been neatly turned down to remove Oliver. This small sign the kidnapper had treated the infant with care gave him a ray of hope. The worst case in any kidnapping was the victim being killed outright, and the body disposed of, to enable the kidnapper to collect the ransom without the risk and bother of caring for the victim. Not that Charlie would mention that harsh reality to the parents.

Barclay extracted the ransom note from his pocket and opened it up carefully, revealing a curl of pale blond hair. Nausea swelling in Charlie's stomach at the thought of a helpless infant waking in a stranger's arms without his mother to comfort him. Visions of his own fall into the hands of kidnappers flooded his brain with unwanted memories, but Charlie forced himself to consider the evidence methodically. The hair had been snipped, not yanked out by the roots. Another sign of care. Good.

He looked up to find Grace by his side, which was just as well, since his own hand was shaking. She gathered the hair into an envelope with forceps, before picking up the ransom note with the same care.

The ransom note read: *Money for baby. £200 by noon Friday. No police if you want to see the baby again.*

Charlie could see why Edward Barclay had removed the note to spare his wife the sight of the cruel words and the lock of hair. Several thoughts tumbled through his mind. The oddity of the note was foremost, followed by the short timeframe, it being late on Monday morning already. Unless Barclay kept that much money in a bank account or in cash hidden in a safe in the house, it would be a stretch to meet the ransom demand in the time available. That was a question to be asked later, and one Barclay had no doubt already considered. Two hundred pounds was a large amount, but probably not an insurmountable sum for a family like the Barclays. If Nathan Locke had failed to find work without references in the intervening two years, it was the level of compensation he might well demand for lost salary, without risking an excessive demand that the Barclays could not afford.

Evidently, Barclay's thoughts were running along the same lines. "Locke's given me only four days to get the ransom together. Four days! No prudent man would keep such a sum on hand. How am I supposed to release such an amount from my investments in a short time? And why should I pay for what is mine? I'll see the scoundrel behind bars for the rest of his miserable life, if it's the last thing I do."

"The handwriting does not match the letter Nathan Locke sent you," Charlie said.

Locke had written the threatening letter in the neat, precise hand of a bank clerk, even though he must have penned the threat in anger. He had even added the day and date as one would on normal correspondence, out of habit presumably, although he had refrained from adding the usual "yours sincerely". In contrast, the ransom note was chaotic, both in sentence structure and penmanship. The wording of the first sentence, "Money for baby", seemed particularly clumsy, especially when the kidnapper went to the trouble of constructing a longer final sentence. An educated person trying to disguise their status, perhaps? The writer would have been better to add in a few spelling mistakes in that case.

"He'd have been a fool not to disguise his handwriting," Barclay pointed out.

"Agreed. But it is difficult to disguise characteristic letters and features even when trying to write in a different hand." Charlie held out the two notes side by side. "The capital M of money in the ransom note is spiky and leans backwards, whereas Locke's letter is neatly penned with a rounded, forward-leaning capital M. Similarly, the word Friday appears in each note, but the capital F is far more ornate in the ransom demand than in the date on the letter. If anything, one would expect the ransom demand to be in simple block or printed letters if the kidnapper was trying to disguise their handwriting. And look at the very odd lower-case Y at the end of money, which is poorly aligned and misshapen, whereas Locke's Y is precise and neatly looped at the bottom."

"It's Locke," Barclay said. "He's trying to cover his tracks by writing like a madman. The man may be a scoundrel, but he's not stupid."

Grace used the forceps to transfer the ransom note into an envelope for further analysis. After she put the evidence into her medical bag, she twirled her index finger in a circle discreetly, indicating she wanted to examine the scene of the crime. Over the past year, they had developed a series of hand signals to communicate without speaking, after a misunderstanding during Charlie's kidnapping.

"Time to put our tracking dog to work before the trail goes cold," Charlie said. "With your permission, I'll bring the dog into the nursery to get the scent. It would be helpful if I could take Oliver's favourite toy or blanket."

While Mr Barclay rummaged in a basket of toys, Charlie sidled up to his wife. "Did Mrs Barclay give you any indication of Nathan Locke's location?"

"She doesn't know," Grace whispered. "According to her, they had nothing more than a single chance meeting in the Dunedin Botanic Garden. She is adamant that Locke is not the kidnapper." Grace's eyes flicked towards Barclay, who had pulled a toy out of the basket and was now retrieving a soft blue blanket from the linen shelf. "Barclay is excessively jealous and controlling."

Barclay came over and held out the blanket and a lop-sided monkey, which was heavily chewed and made with more love than skill. "Daisy made a set of animals for Oliver. I was trying to find his favourite one, the giraffe, but I couldn't see it in his toy basket." Barclay clutched the toy to his cheek – an oddly touching gesture from such a strait-laced gentleman – before handing the monkey and blanket over.

Charlie wanted to give Grace time to work her magic unobserved, so he took Edward Barclay back to the sitting room to

41

explain the next steps of the investigation and hand him their standard contract to read while they were out with Blaze. Grace was extracting a vial from her medical bag as they left, giving him a spark of hope that she was following a line of inquiry.

Once in the sitting room, Charlie moved to the window facing out onto the street and scanned the surrounding area. "Do you see that lad in the bush diagonally across the street, Mr Barclay?"

Barclay swept his gaze across the street. "No."

Excellent. Johnny Todd's messenger lads had been well trained in many skills they wouldn't want the police to know about. Watching unobserved was the least of them. Charlie opened the window and waved. A small hand emerged from the bush and waved back.

"Our surveillance team is already watching the house. They are messenger boys under the command of a young man called Johnny Todd. They may look like a bunch of street urchins, but they are loyal, discreet, and clever. If anyone else is watching the house, or approaches the house with a further ransom demand, they will spot him and follow him back to his hiding place."

Edward Barclay nodded vigorously. "I have to say I am impressed with your efficiency, Mr Penrose Pyke."

"I want to keep movements around the house to a minimum to avoid the kidnappers becoming suspicious. We'll use the lads to communicate. We need a password, so you know who you can trust." Charlie held up the monkey. "Does this toy have a name?"

"Mama Monkey."

"Good. Anyone I send to the house will give you the password 'Mama Monkey'. Otherwise, don't let them in. If you're sending a message to me, leave a broom on the porch and a lad will come. Ask him for the same password. I need to hear immediately if there are any developments, including further information on the location and time of the ransom drop. Is that clear?"

"Yes. What can I do?"

"Try to be patient. Have someone at home at all times, if possible, in case there is a message from me or the kidnapper. And, of course, you must get the ransom together as soon as possible."

Barclay glared at him. "You can't mean for me to pay the devil?"

"Mr Barclay, I hate to be blunt, but that might be our best option. Unless we can identify the location of the kidnapper quickly ... well, Dunedin is a big city."

Barclay blanched, but he held his nerve. "Whatever it takes, I want my son back and Nathan Locke behind bars. Do you understand?"

"Of course. We will put all our resources into it. Can I just reiterate that we would be better off with the police involved? We have an excellent rapport with a highly skilled detective inspector and his sergeant. They will be discreet."

"I suppose I must take your advice. But no uniformed coppers clumping around in their oversized boots waving truncheons."

"Agreed. I'll be back in a minute."

Charlie went out onto the porch. The messenger boy was on his way out the gate with a sample from Grace to take back to their laboratory, so Charlie called for him to wait while he scribbled a note for Johnny, instructing him to send a telegram to Wellington. Finding Nathan Locke was their top priority and the Wellington branch of the Bank of New Zealand was the only point of contact Charlie had to find a forwarding address. The Barclay family connections in Wellington were worth looking into as well.

With a low whistle, Charlie called Blaze, and they returned to the nursery. Fortunately, neither of the Barclays were there, because he didn't wish to cause them the distress of seeing Blaze take the scent. Grace wasn't there either. He knelt down to let the dog sniff the toy and blanket, as she had been trained to do. She whined and strained at the leash, eager to get on with the job she was born to do. The border collie had been with them for a year, having proven herself more adept at tracking than sheep herding.

Charlie was eager for action too. He tucked the blanket into his satchel and the monkey in his pocket, before glancing at his watch. Nearly eleven o'clock already. They had just four days to search an entire city, unless Blaze could track the kidnapper now.

He stopped briefly in the sitting room on his way out. "We may be gone for a while, Mr Barclay, but we will be back with more questions. Eat and rest if you can, but don't leave the house. I'd be grateful if you could make a list of anyone else who might hold a grudge or want money from you. Nathan Locke may be our man, but I would hate to waste days chasing him only to find we have ignored other possibilities, however slight."

"I understand. Anything else?"

"While we are gone, look around and see what else has been taken from the nursery, such as baby clothes and bedding."

"I wouldn't know," Barclay said. "I'll ask my wife."

"Take particular note of essentials such as baby bottles. Does your wife still feed him?"

Barclay gaped at him as if he was a moron. "Of course she feeds him!"

Charlie wanted to roll his eyes, but he could see from the man's confusion that he was going to have to spell it out to Barclay. "Milk, I mean. I need to know whether Oliver takes his milk from a bottle or whether your wife supplies it."

"I haven't seen any bottles." Barclay stammered the words as if it was an embarrassment to mention breast-feeding in company.

"Forgive my intrusive questions, but it is important to know if the kidnapper took what he would need to care for Oliver. If not, he will need to buy supplies. We can alert shops selling baby items to be on the lookout."

"Oh, well, yes, of course. Forgive my doubts, Mr Penrose Pyke. I can see now that you are a professional, despite your youth. Naturally, we will do whatever we can to help."

44

Charlie tossed up whether to ask a question that had been prickling his skin ever since he had entered the nursery, but he decided to hold back until he understood more about the relationship between Barclay and his wife.

As he left the sitting room, he glanced back down the corridor to check he hadn't been seeing things. But there it was, the key still in the outside of the nursery door, raising the disturbing question of why a nursery would ever need to be locked from the outside, or, indeed, locked at all. If Mrs Barclay was so nervous of intruders that she had asked for the window to be sealed, why wouldn't she have locked the door from the inside?

On the Trail

Grace was on her knees on a gravel path, examining footprints in the dirt of the flower garden, when Blaze ran around the side of the house with Charlie in tow.

She pointed to the criss-cross of prints with toes facing the nursery window, and the single pair of deeper footprints on top of them, pointing outward. "One man with average sized boots, unevenly worn on the inside edge of the ball of the foot. Old boots, judging from the lack of tread. The intruder spent some time cutting through the seal around the window, before taking the baby, and exiting in a single jump. No other trace evidence that I can see, other than slivers of paint and putty where he has sliced through the seal."

Charlie handed Blaze's leash to Grace so he could sketch the boot marks. His silence warned her not to ask further questions until they were away from the house. Then he snapped his notebook shut and unclipped the leash. Blaze shot forward at her sudden release but steadied herself and put her nose to the ground, heading towards the area of bush beyond the end of the road.

Their border collie had become an indispensable part of their lives in the year she had lived with them, but her tracking prowess had never been more vital than it was today. Without Blaze's extraordinary sense of smell, Grace knew it would be a hopeless task to track the kidnapper. The summer sun had dried out the soil to a shell too hard to capture footprints, except in the moist soil of the flower bed.

The ground sloped upwards beyond the house. Grace concentrated on following Blaze as the collie raced ahead, certain of her direction for the most part, although now and then Blaze slowed as she lost the scent. The trail went towards the Dunedin

Botanic Garden, which could be a problem, as Blaze would struggle to follow the scent there with all the people who would have passed through on a fine morning. Grace glanced across at Charlie, whose rigid jaw warned her he feared their search would be fruitless. It took little imagination to realise that a person ruthless enough to kidnap an infant would not hesitate to kill the child once the ransom had been paid, rather than risk being caught at the hand-over. But they also knew that giving in to fear wouldn't help find little Ollie.

Blaze stopped at the edge of the cemetery road. Charlie's eyes flicked to his wife as the dog paused and cast around for the scent. "How was Mrs Barclay, Grace? Her husband seems to think she is too delicate to cope with questioning. You heard the remark about her low spirits even after Oliver's birth."

Grace let out a grunt that had nothing to do with exertion. "Mrs Daisy Barclay is deeply shocked and devastated by Ollie's disappearance, but not, in my opinion, caught in the grip of melancholia or hysteria. She is certainly willing and able to answer questions when given the opportunity. Daisy calls him Ollie, by the way, while her husband insists on Oliver. It's not the only matter they disagree on."

"Perhaps Daisy is exhausted by the sleepless nights and the hours of work babies require, rather than in low spirits. After many years of trying to conceive, she must be overjoyed to have Ollie."

"Actually, Charlie, it is far from uncommon for women to suffer depressed spirits after giving birth, no matter how longed for and cherished the baby is. Such women need love and support, instead of constantly being told to pull themselves together and think about how fortunate they are. However, I didn't detect any sign of it in Daisy."

"Every wife deserves to feel loved, every day of her life."

Charlie's statement, spoken as a simple truth, melted Grace's heart. She flung her arms around him and kissed him soundly on the lips, causing blushes and titters from a pair of elderly ladies, who were ambling up the road towards the northern cemetery, carrying flowers.

The more wrinkled of the two ladies surprised Grace by letting out a whoop of delight. "Make every moment count, my dears, for life may be short and love is precious. With two beloved husbands six feet under marble, I know what I'm talking about."

Blaze had picked up the scent and was off again before Grace could think of an appropriate reply. Instead, she waved farewell as she hoisted her skirts and took off after the collie toward the Botanic Garden, which lay between them and the northern end of the city.

Once they reached the brow of the hill, Grace caught her breath. "It's odd that Daisy didn't wake up when the kidnapper broke in, although it's probably a blessing as she might have been injured or kidnapped too if she had confronted the intruder. Daisy thinks her husband blames her for taking too much sleeping tonic, even though she denies taking any."

"Edward Barclay does blame her for sleeping through the kidnapping," Charlie said, as they joined a path around the hillside, leading down into the lower gardens. "However, her bottle of sleeping tonic was almost full, despite being prescribed three weeks ago, which suggests she was telling the truth about not having taken any last night."

On such a glorious day, it wasn't long before they met couples and groups of women walking towards them up the path. Grace slipped her arm through her husband's and lowered her voice. "Which is why I took a sample from the dregs of the cocoa she drank before going to bed. I don't like the way this investigation is going, Charlie. If Daisy was deliberately drugged last night, then either the kidnapping was an extraordinary coincidence or the person who took Ollie lives in the house."

When a group of chattering women approached, Charlie drew her aside in a section of the hill path with a view over the lower gardens. "Let's wait until Lily has tested the sample before we jump to conclusions. It is possible Daisy had another bottle and was too embarrassed to admit she had taken too much, or she was simply too deeply asleep to wake up. You know what your friend Molly Ravenwood says: new mothers are so sleep-deprived that they would sleep through a brass band concert."

Grace smiled. Molly had gone into labour with her first baby at Grace and Charlie's wedding a year ago, and her second was due in four months. She'd recently found Molly asleep with her head on a pile of half-folded laundry, with mashed parsnip on her cheek, the kettle squealing on the hob, and the coalman making a fearful din outside the window. Eight-month-old Jessica Grace Ravenwood had been sitting on the floor at her feet, happily playing with the blocks Charlie had made for her. It was only when Jessica had squealed in delight at seeing Grace that Molly had woken up.

"Point taken, Charlie. No assumptions, no mistakes. It's a dreadful situation, isn't it? I fear it might tear Mr and Mrs Barclay apart if we don't find Ollie quickly."

"The one positive so far is that we're not dealing with a monster. The kidnapper turned Ollie's blanket down neatly to remove him from the cradle and snipped his hair rather than pulling it out. Nobody heard Ollie cry out, so he must have been held gently. I've yet to confirm if the kidnapper took anything else, such as feeding bottles."

"Daisy is still breastfeeding, judging from her swollen state, so Ollie may not be used to taking milk from a bottle. He is taking some solid food as well, which means he won't starve in the next few days, even if he is only given water to drink."

In their distraction, Blaze had vanished. Charlie let out an ear-splitting whistle. A moment later, Blaze reappeared from the trees and gave them a hurry-up bark. She vanished again, keeping to the path and heading around the hillside and across the rustic footbridge over the creek.

The collie slowed when they reached the lower gardens, which thronged with people. Women strolling the wide promenade with baby carriages, children playing on the grass, artists capturing the scene, a group of women bicyclists, a gentleman reading poetry to a lady – it seemed as if half the leisured residents of Dunedin had descended on the place on a perfect morning.

Charlie called Blaze to heel as they navigated the crowds, still heading towards the main entrance on the far side of the Botanic Garden. But the combined smells of wildfowl, mulch, vegetation, and crowds of people proved too much. Blaze sniffed in ever-wider circles, her drooping tail evidence she had lost the trail. Charlie called her back to retrace their steps, hoping to pick up the scent again in the maze of criss-crossing paths. The collie headed off tentatively in a new direction, towards a broad expanse of lawn with a pond beyond.

A group of children chased a ball across the grass, while their mothers watched on under pretty parasols, their light muslin gowns ruffled by the breeze. Grace gazed longingly at their serenity, wishing she could be as oblivious to the tragedy unfolding in another family's life as they were. The tranquillity was illusory, because a tussle between two boys over the ball rapidly descended into a minor brawl, complete with blood and tears. The blood was no more than a trickle from a delicate nose, so Grace left the mothers to it.

Blaze was still sniffing around with none of the certainty she had shown earlier. Charlie's shoulders slumped. "If we cannot track the offender directly to his house while the trail is fresh, finding baby Ollie will be next to impossible. We can only hope Mr Barclay is correct about Nathan Locke being the kidnapper."

"Daisy Barclay is positive Locke didn't take Ollie," Grace said. "In fact, I got the impression Daisy suspected the accusation of theft that led to Mr Locke's dismissal from the bank was fabricated by her husband. According to Daisy, the only interaction she had with the man was a spilled drink at a Christmas party two years ago and a chance encounter in the Botanic Garden three weeks ago.

Yet Daisy gave the impression that Edward Barclay was angry at her as well as Locke."

"When I talked to Barclay, his anger was directed at Nathan Locke. But it does strike me as significant that Edward Barclay sealed the nursery window three weeks ago, right after Daisy's 'chance meeting' with Locke in the Botanic Garden. Edward said Daisy requested the window be sealed for the baby's safety, but I did wonder if Edward was trying to keep his wife in, rather than intruders out, because the key to the nursery door was on the outside, not the inside."

The thought of Daisy being a prisoner in her own home added an alarming element to Grace's growing concerns about their domestic situation. "I'll ask Daisy about it. Mr Barclay dismissed the housekeeper several weeks ago, too. Daisy obviously liked her, unlike the companion, who was most definitely Edward's choice. It would be worth getting the housekeeper's view on what's going on in the household."

"We'll also have to speak to the companion, Prudence Winslow, as soon as possible." Charlie sighed. "There's a lot to do in a short time."

"We'd better get on with it then." Grace had been watching a young mother chasing after a wayward toddler, who seemed determined to taste every plant and catch every duck in the vicinity, even it meant falling into the pond. The day was shaping up as a demonstration of the perils of motherhood, as if Fate was sending them another of her cryptic messages.

The mother turned and shrieked. "Help! There's a dog savaging my baby!"

Grace followed the direction of her horrified gaze to where Blaze had her head inside a baby carriage, which had been left sitting under a shady tree. Charlie yelled, "Blaze, heel," while Grace ran to the baby carriage. A baby with a tuft of bright ginger hair gurgled at her, blowing a bubble as she smiled.

The mother ran up, dragging the howling toddler by one hand. "That dog should not be here," she snapped. "Didn't you see the signs?"

Grace had seen signs stating that dogs were not permitted, but she had also seen other dogs being walked in the gardens. "Our apologies. The dog is only here because a child is missing and Blaze is trying to find him. She's a specially trained tracking dog." Grace touched a finger to the tiny, outstretched hand, making the baby giggle. "What a lovely, happy baby you have."

The mother smiled at her adorable infant, receiving another bubble-smile in return. "I suppose there's been no harm done. A missing child, did you say? How awful. Shall I keep an eye out?"

"Yes, please. He's a boy aged around eight months old with curly blond hair."

"The only child I recall who fits that description hasn't been here much lately. It couldn't be him anyway, because his mother watches him like a hawk." She turned a knowing smile on Grace. "First-time mothers! You can spot them a mile away. Once you've had your second child, you learn to have eyes in the back of your head."

The mother glanced around and shrieked again. Her toddler, who had been by her side not a minute ago, was now teetering on the edge of the pond, reaching for a duck. Blaze pulled her leash out of Charlie's hand and dashed to the child, rounding her up like a stray lamb and herding her back to the mother, before settling herself at Charlie's feet.

Charlie ruffled the fur around her ears. "It seems Blaze hasn't forgotten her herding skill after all. Again, our apologies, ma'am. We'd best be off."

"Wait." The red-faced mother was now clutching her toddler's hand firmly, to the child's annoyance. "I have spoken to the woman with the blond baby once or twice. The boy's name is Wally, I think, or perhaps Ollie, and he looks the right age. Anyway, I thought perhaps you ought to know that I've seen a man watching the boy's mother once or twice. I wasn't sure if I was imagining it, but if the baby is missing ..."

"Can you describe the man?" Charlie said. "Tall, short? Blond, dark? Anything at all you recall."

"About average size, I think. All I saw was the outline of a gentleman in a hat on the other side of a bush. The gardens can be quite crowded, so it may be nothing, but I did get the impression he was watching her and the baby."

Grace handed her a card. "We would be grateful if you could let us know if you or your acquaintances remember anything else about the man. It could be important."

Charlie kept a firm hand on the leash as they hurried away. "Let's do a quick circuit of the lower gardens, then return to the Barclays' house before we cause any further mayhem. It's not like Blaze to mistake a scent, but I suppose all babies smell the same – fresh and new and lovely."

"You're in for a rude awakening, Charlie, if that's what you think. In the real world, babies more often smell of regurgitated food and soiled bottoms." As a middle child in a large and boisterous family, Grace had no illusions about motherhood, unlike Charlie, who was an only child.

As they passed the band rotunda, Blaze yanked the leash out of Charlie's hand again and raced towards a woman who was scanning the gardens with a worried frown. She wore heavy black garments from head to toe, which must have been fiendishly hot for the summery day, and did her insipid complexion no favours. The woman took a hurried step backwards at the dog's rapid approach, her arms jerking with the disjointed movements of a marionette.

Grace and Charlie ran after their dog, knowing that she must have picked up a strong scent, because Blaze had halted right in front of the woman, her black and white body rigid and focused on the target.

The woman threw a cross look at the owners of this unruly beast and froze, her gaze fixed on a point halfway down Charlie's body. And then she let out a scream to wake the dead.

Devotion

Grace was used to a variety of reactions to her husband. Ladies fluttering their eyelashes, criminals fleeing his intimidating bulk, babies holding their arms wide to be picked up, and the occasional pursing of lips at detecting a hint of his Chinese grandfather in his exotic good looks. But she had never heard a woman scream like that before. The hubbub in the garden ceased as people turned to stare. A baby burst into tears, a man reading poetry dropped his book, a painter splattered red paint on his smock, and a wily young bowler took the wicket of his distracted younger brother.

Charlie looked behind him for the source of the woman's fright, but there was no monster creeping up on them. He stepped towards her with a hesitant smile, gesturing at Blaze to pull back. "Miss Prudence Winslow, I presume. Don't be frightened. We are the private investigators Mr Barclay hired to find Oliver." He waved a hand at Grace. "Charlie and Grace Penrose Pyke. Our tracking dog must have picked up your scent from the Barclays' house."

Miss Winslow collapsed onto a park bench, fanning her flaming face. "Oh. You gave me such a fright when I saw the monkey in your pocket, thinking you were the kidnappers. Thank goodness you came so quickly." She reached a hand for the monkey. "Mama Monkey is one of Oliver's favourite toys. My poor, poor wee darling boy."

Charlie tucked the monkey deeper into his pocket. "I'm sorry, Miss Winslow, but I cannot let you have the toy, because our dog is using the scent to follow the kidnapper's trail."

Prudence Winslow snatched her hand back as if she'd been burned. "Then go, go! Find the beast who took our little Oliver."

Our Oliver? Prudence sounded more like a devoted mother than a companion or family friend. Calling the boy Oliver, as his father did, not Ollie, like the mother, also indicated to Grace where Miss Prudence Winslow's loyalties lay.

The sideways flick of Charlie's eyes to Grace told her he was thinking the same. "Unfortunately, the trail petered out in the gardens. May we ask you a few questions, Miss Winslow?" Charlie sat on the adjacent bench and did not wait for her assent. "What brought you here on this terrible day?"

"To look for Oliver, of course. I came straight here after I informed the minister of our church that we must rally the congregation to help with the search."

Charlie's nostrils quivered. No need to ask why. Grace's stomach lurched at the very idea of an untrained posse of well-meaning churchgoers blundering around the neighbourhood, possibly alerting the kidnapper with potentially catastrophic consequences. Once a force like that had been unleashed, there would be no more chance of stopping their search than stopping the tide rolling into St Clair beach.

"Please ask your searchers to be cautious," Charlie said, with admirable calm. "We would not wish the kidnappers to become alarmed, for Oliver's sake." He paused to let the warning sink in. "What I meant was, are you here because you suspect someone specific, who might be in the Botanic Garden?"

"Mad Aggie," Prudence said with forceful certainty. "She prowls the gardens daily, peering into baby carriages and trying to hold any child whose mother doesn't stop her. Mad Aggie has a particular fixation with Oliver. I've warned the Head Groundskeeper to trespass her, but he says there is nothing he can do if she means no harm. No harm? The man is a fool. A woman like her, desperate for a child of her own, might well resort to taking what she desires. And now look what has happened."

Grace estimated Prudence Winslow was in her late twenties or early thirties, about the same age as Daisy. But any resemblance between the women stopped there. Even in her utter despair, Daisy was attractive in a delicate, feminine way. The kind of sweet and

56

vulnerable woman men flocked to. In contrast, Prudence had uneven, heavy features and thin lips, which made her look sour, when clearly her heart was in the right place, since she was out searching for the missing boy with a mother's devotion.

"Do you know Aggie's real name or where she lives?" Grace asked.

"She calls herself Aunt Aggie, as if she's everyone's dear old auntie, but that doesn't make her behaviour acceptable. I know nothing else about her and nor do I care to."

"Age? Hair colour? Height?" Grace prompted.

"Aggie claims to be a widow, although she doesn't seem old enough, and her dress and bonnet are closer to dark grey than black. Dulled from washing, perhaps, as often happens with cheap dye on lightweight material. I think she has brown hair, which she wears in a tight chignon."

Grace couldn't blame Aggie for wearing lightweight fabric in this weather. Heavy widow's weeds, like the mourning clothes Prudence was wearing, would be oppressively hot. "We will find her, Miss Winslow. I ask that you leave her to us, because she may be unstable if she has taken the baby." Grace waited for Prudence to nod. "How did Mrs Barclay feel about Aunt Aggie?"

"Daisy saw no harm in her. She even let the woman hold Oliver, which was asking for trouble in my opinion. Aggie was besotted with him, I'm sure of it, and Daisy did nothing to deter her. I hope Edward doesn't blame me for encouraging Daisy to come to the gardens every day. I thought her health would benefit from the fresh air and seeing other mothers enjoying time with their children."

"An excellent suggestion, Miss Winslow," Charlie cut in, earning himself a smile from Prudence. "It is all too easy for a new mother to become housebound and overwhelmed with the responsibility of caring for a new child, especially when that child is so precious. Mrs Barclay had been hoping for a child for many years, I understand."

"Ever since Edward – Mr Barclay – married her. Five years is a long time for a man to wait for an heir. Edward has been a saint."

Saint was not the word Grace would have chosen for Mr Edward Barclay. Proud certainly, but with a self-righteous streak that did not sit comfortably with her. But he was no different to many men, to whom control of their wife was a moral duty. Just as a woman's duty was to bear children and submit to her husband's superior will. Grace thanked her lucky stars that she had found a man who encouraged her independence. Not that you'd think it from the sanctimonious smile hovering on her husband's lips as he nodded along to Prudence's words.

"I'm sure you're right, Miss Winslow," Charlie said. "It must have been hard on Mrs Barclay too."

Prudence nodded. "Daisy felt her failure keenly. Sometimes I think she forgets how fortunate she is to have a fine husband and a lovely home, and now a baby too. What more could a woman want?"

Love, respect, joy, and a life free of evil kidnappers, just for starters, in Grace's opinion. "May I ask how you came to live with the Barclays, Miss Winslow?"

"Mr and Mrs Barclay joined our local congregation when they arrived in Dunedin, about two years ago. We were in the church choir together. My elderly mother was still alive at the time, and I was her sole caregiver during the many years of her frailty. Mr Barclay was kind enough to advise me on financial matters, being a respected senior banker and a most welcome addition to our church community. When my mother passed away three months ago, Edward advised me on the sale of my family home. The house sold quicker than I expected, and Edward suggested I stay with them until I made plans for my future."

"How thoughtful of him," Grace said.

"It was a great relief to have his support. I shouldn't have known what to do with myself after my mother's death, but Edward showed me that by selling the house, I will have ample capital to live off and enough to buy a small cottage of my own, if necessary."

The toothy smile that accompanied this disclosure told Grace that Prudence was relieved to be free to do as she wished, especially as it seemed she now had an inheritance to tempt a suitor. "Mrs Barclay must have been grateful for your companionship and help with the baby."

"I can only hope I have repaid Edward's kindness by taking over the management of the household when that dreadful housekeeper left."

"Kind of you to take on the role," Grace said, noting that the so-called companion had once again answered the question with reference to Mr Barclay rather than his wife. "May I ask why the housekeeper left?"

"She wasn't efficient at her job, being the sort to chatter away the hours rather than get her hands dirty. Edward let her go shortly after I moved in six weeks ago."

As a banker, he would keep close watch on his pennies, Grace presumed, especially when he could get a housekeeper and companion for free. Edward had got a good deal when Prudence moved in.

"I take it you were friends with Mrs Barclay through the church, too," Grace said.

"To be honest, Daisy is withdrawn by nature and I did not know her well, but I was content to help her and, of course, I simply adore Oliver. I did wonder if she suffered from a persistent illness when she first arrived in Dunedin, because she was very thin and pale back then, and seemed weak and irritable. After a while, she seemed to regain her health, and then she found out she was with child."

"It must have been a joyful day when Mrs Barclay discovered she was with child at last," Charlie said.

"Edward was proud as punch. Daisy claimed she'd been blessed by a fairy or some such nonsense, but Edward put it down to the strict regime advised by his physician." Prudence grimaced. "Cod liver oil and cold baths. I must say, Daisy was far more tolerant than I would have been under the circumstances. But then, for all her faults, nobody can deny Daisy was dutiful to her husband's command. Edward does not tolerate quackery or ungodliness. A pity more folk do not think the same."

Grace understood the desperation to try any remedy in order to conceive a child, but she would certainly draw the line well short of cod liver oil and cold baths, or fairies for that matter. "I take it Mrs Barclay's health has remained much improved since Oliver was born?"

"I believe so, although I didn't see her very often before I moved into their home. I'd have to say she has seemed in poor spirits these past few weeks, despite having a perfectly adorable son, which is terribly sad. Edward has been kind enough to say on many occasions that he wouldn't have coped without me to look after them both."

"Did you mind, Miss Winslow?" Charlie said. "After years of devoted care for your mother, to find yourself caring for another?"

"Oh, no. I love little Oliver as if he was my own. His kidnapping has been unbearable, but I am determined to walk the streets and the parks of Dunedin until I find my little angel."

There was no doubt in Grace's mind about where the so-called companion's sympathies lay, and it wasn't with Mrs Daisy Barclay. However, Prudence appeared genuine in her desire to do her utmost to find her little angel, Oliver. Grace was about to ask Prudence if she knew of anyone besides Mad Aggie who had a grudge against Mr or Mrs Barclay when they were interrupted by a shout.

"Prudence! There you are!" A man flapped to a halt inches away from Prudence Winslow. With his beaky nose, beady eyes, and ungainly limbs, he loomed over her like a vulture landing on its prey. Although loomed was hardly the correct word, as he was the same height as her. "I thought I might find you here. Is it true? Has the Barclay baby been abducted?"

The man suddenly seemed to realise that Prudence was not alone. He slipped a pair of spectacles out of his pocket and leaned towards Grace to examine her. Grace instinctively took a step backwards. Blaze was on her feet in an instant, lunging forward and growling at the man, who fumbled his spectacles in his haste to retreat. He stumbled backwards into a bed of dahlias, his arms windmilling, but he recovered his balance, thanks to Charlie gripping his arm and pulling him out of the flowers before any damage was done.

"My apologies, sir," Charlie said. Blaze dropped to the ground beside him, her tongue lolling. "I'm Charlie Penrose Pyke, private detective. My wife and I have been engaged by Mr and Mrs Barclay to find Oliver. And you are?"

The man cast a worried glance at Blaze, before lifting his hat and giving them a tentative bucktooth smile. "Simeon Frobisher, churchwarden and choirmaster. So, the rumour is true. Poor Mrs Barclay. She must be frantic at Ollie's disappearance."

Prudence clasped his hands. "Simeon, it's too dreadful. Oliver was taken during the night and a ransom note was left in his empty cradle. I'm beside myself with worry."

"That's why I came to find you as soon as I could, to offer my full support."

"Will you help me search for Oliver?" Prudence asked.

Simeon patted her hand. "Of course. The church hall is being set up to coordinate the search as we speak. I have cancelled the practice session of the ladies' chorus and sent them to rally the troops. We will scour the streets and knock on all the doors of the parish until we find him. We can count on the support of my high school band and choir too, should we need them."

The choirmaster was certainly throwing himself into the crisis with admirable initiative, Grace thought. One might even call it excitement. All hope of keeping Oliver's disappearance a closely held secret had vanished.

"Sir, we must request you and your volunteers keep a low profile," Charlie said, "so as not to alarm the kidnapper. You must understand that if he feels threatened, baby Oliver's life will be put at risk."

Simeon Frobisher turned a worried look on Prudence.

She nodded and squeezed his hands tighter. "The ransom note warned that we wouldn't see Oliver ever again if we contacted the police. Mrs Barclay insisted on engaging these private detectives."

"You'll take our request for discretion seriously, I trust, Mr Frobisher," Charlie added.

"Of course he will," Prudence replied. "And you'll track down Mad Aggie as a matter of urgency, won't you, Mr Penrose Pyke? I'll go back to the church hall with you, Simeon."

Before he let them go, Charlie asked the name of the church, which was at the north end of the city, not far from the Botanic Garden.

Grace watched the pair walk away together. From the way Simeon Frobisher directed his full attention at Prudence Winslow, turning his body to her and leaning in as he spoke, Grace felt sure that there was at least one option available to secure the companion's uncertain future. They seemed well matched in looks and temperament and had the church in common. Grace was happy for her. The marriage market was not an easy place to navigate for a plain woman of about thirty, although Prudence now had the advantage of a substantial dowry from the sale of her family home to encourage suitors. Grace suspected Daisy Barclay would rejoice if the match came to pass, to keep the devoted Prudence away from her husband.

When they disappeared behind a grove of trees, Grace turned back to Charlie, who was bent over the dahlias. Or, more precisely, bent over the boot print Simeon Frobisher had left in the soft dirt around the flowers.

"Mr Frobisher wears the same size boot as the kidnapper," Charlie said, "but the boots he is wearing today are newer and have a different tread pattern. I ought to head back to the Barclays' house to give them the bad news that the tracking was unsuccessful. Would you prefer to stay here and look for Mad Aunt Aggie, or come with me?"

"It seems a stretch to point the finger at a woman merely because she likes to coo over babies in the public setting of the Botanic Garden, although I'd like to find Aunt Aggie before the posse from the church take out their wrath on her. But there's something off in the Barclays' household and I would like to talk to Daisy Barclay again first, if only to get her views on Aggie and other potential suspects. If you tackle Edward Barclay while I talk to Daisy, perhaps we can get to the root cause using the old 'divide and conquer' tactic."

"My thoughts exactly." Charlie slipped his arm through hers and headed up the hill path towards the rear entrance to the Barclays' street. "The Barclays don't strike me as a likely target of a kidnapping for ransom, unless the kidnapper has a particular connection to the family or they are wealthier than they appear. As Alistair is fond of saying now that he has a reputation for solving fraud cases: 'When in doubt, follow the money.'"

Follow the Money

Charlie slowed his pace as they approached the end of the street through the trees, wondering if the kidnapper had chosen this house as his target simply because it was easy to access without being seen. However, his hopes were pinned on a kidnapper with a connection to the Barclay family, if only because anyone unconnected to them would be next to impossible to find in four days.

Edward Barclay answered the door on the first knock. Daisy stood in the hallway behind him. Their identical expressions of hope collapsed when Charlie and Grace entered the house without a blanket-wrapped baby in their arms. He'd warned them not to expect a miracle, but that didn't blunt the sharp edge of their failure.

Charlie shut the door behind him and faced Mr Barclay, expecting distress but seeing anger. "Blaze tracked the kidnapper through the Botanic Garden, but lost the scent on the far side. At least we know the direction of travel. The good news is that we found several distinctive boot prints on the flower bed outside the nursery window. Once we have the offender, the prints will provide strong evidence to secure a conviction."

He was looking at Edward Barclay as he spoke, so he didn't see Daisy collapse, but Grace did. She shoved past him and lurched to Daisy's side, catching her before she hit the floor. Edward rushed to his wife's other side and helped Grace to take Daisy to the master bedroom. Charlie was left standing in the hallway, feeling helpless.

Grace ushered Edward Barclay out of the bedroom with a firm hand on his shoulder, assuring him that she would look after his wife. She shut the door firmly behind him.

"Let's talk in the sitting room, Mr Barclay," Charlie said, opening the door and waiting for Oliver's father to register his presence.

Barclay walked past him like a man condemned, his anger having drained away to despair after his wife's collapse. When they were settled in the armchairs, Charlie laid out his plan, hoping to rekindle his client's faith that all was not lost.

"Trying to track the kidnapper was always a long shot. A necessary first step in the investigation. We now have several suspects to interview and a clear path forward." The words sounded hollow to his own ears, but Barclay nodded. "I'm waiting for my team to establish Nathan Locke's whereabouts, but you can rest assured he is top of my list. However, I would like to consider other motives for the kidnapping, because we cannot afford to ignore any possibilities."

Barclay didn't respond, so Charlie continued. "One possibility is that Oliver was taken by a person desperate for a child of their own. Fairly unlikely, as one might expect such a person to snatch the child in a public place rather than breaking into a private home, but your wife's companion has suggested a suspect."

Barclay raised his head at this suggestion, but didn't ask whom Prudence suspected. Charlie wasn't sure if Barclay was in shock at their tracking failure or if he was still convinced that Nathan Locke was to blame.

"Another possibility is that Oliver was taken purely for the ransom. I'm afraid I will have to ask about your financial situation, Mr Barclay. Kidnapping is an extremely serious crime, suggesting that the kidnapper must have been sure you had the money to pay. While you have a senior position at a bank and a nice house, it is also true that there are more obviously wealthy households the kidnapper could have targeted."

Barclay grunted. "No doubt we would seem wealthy to the type of lowlife scoundrel who resorts to crime."

Charlie doubted an audacious kidnapping of a baby for ransom would be committed by your average down-and-out lowlife. For one thing, a baby would be far more difficult to look after than an adult or older child. It would be far safer and easier to burgle a shop or a wealthy home. "Do you have two hundred pounds to hand, Mr Barclay?"

Barclay squirmed, but he answered, albeit reluctantly. "I have modest savings, but it will take time to access the funds as they are invested. Frankly, it would be almost impossible for me to raise two hundred pounds by Friday, unless my wife uses the money from her inheritance. Unfortunately, Daisy has been so distraught that I cannot get her to understand she needs to act urgently to withdraw the money. I can't seem to get a word out of her on the subject. I suppose, like me, she hopes the kidnapper will be caught before the ransom deadline."

"Excuse me for asking, but is your wife from a wealthy family? A family wealthy enough to be identifiable as a potential target?"

"Not at all. Her parents had a substantial house and income, but they were by no means a notable family, even in Wellington. I doubt anyone in Dunedin would have heard of them. When her father died, the estate was shared between the two daughters, as per the father's will. The son should have inherited it, naturally, but he perished at sea. My wife's sister married a ne'er-do-well artist called James Montgomery, so her money will be gone. The sister is dead anyway, so any money she had will have passed to her husband."

"But Mrs Barclay still has her inheritance? Would it be enough to cover the ransom?"

"More than enough. Daisy put her money into a bank account and has refused to touch a penny of it so far, because she intended to use it as a dowry for her daughters. Future daughters, I mean." He shook his head. "It used to be that a husband had control of a wife's property, and rightly so, in my opinion. Women don't understand finance like men do. Heaven only knows what the government was thinking when they changed the law to allow women to keep control of their inheritance. This country is going to the dogs with all this women's rights nonsense. Giving women the vote, even. I ask you, where will it end?"

Charlie knew exactly what the government had been thinking. That far too many women were left stranded in poverty after their husbands drank or gambled away their earnings and dowries. Barclay himself had alluded to that when he mentioned the ne'er-do-well brother-in-law wasting Daisy's sister's inheritance. In Charlie's opinion, it had taken them far too long to pass the law giving women property rights, and even longer to give women the vote.

"I suppose I ought to be grateful that Daisy had the sense to put it into a bank," Barclay said, "rather than frittering the money away on clothes and fripperies. I'll talk to her again today, because time is short and Oliver's life depends on it."

"That would be for the best, Mr Barclay," Charlie said. "Although we will do everything in our power to catch the person before Friday, we must accept that our best chance of catching the culprit is when the ransom is exchanged for your son. May I ask if anyone here in Dunedin knew that your wife had inherited money? Specifically, would anyone know the amount she inherited and thus how much to ask for in the ransom demand?"

Barclay sniffed disdainfully at the question, as a bank manager might when refusing a loan to an unworthy recipient. "One does not talk about one's finances to even the closest of friends, Mr Penrose Pyke. I suppose Daisy might have mentioned her parents' death and thus an assumption was made, but she is hardly likely to be talking about the details of her financial affairs with the type of man who would kidnap a child for ransom."

"The topic can arise in the most general of conversations. For example, Miss Winslow mentioned her inheritance to me this morning while praising your kindness for advising her after her mother's recent death. It would be perfectly reasonable if you had mentioned Daisy's situation in that context. Thus, Miss Winslow might be one person who knew about Daisy's money."

Barclay rose from the chair, his face reddening. "How dare you imply Prudence might be involved in Oliver's kidnapping?"

"You mistake my intent, Mr Barclay," Charlie said, although he had asked the question in such an open way to see how Barclay would react to the suggestion. "I meant only that the subject can be mentioned innocently, but word may spread to the wrong ears. Not Miss Winslow herself, who clearly adores Oliver."

Barclay resumed his seat.

"And then there is the possibility of revenge as a motive, if the kidnapper holds a personal grudge against you or your family. Other than Nathan Locke, can you think of any such resentment, no matter how trivial the cause?" Charlie waited while Edward Barclay considered his response. From the delay in replying, Charlie guessed that Nathan Locke was not the only man with a potential grudge against his client.

"Nothing worthy of committing such a shocking crime," Barclay said.

"Debts owed? Arguments with friends or colleagues?"

Barclay bristled again, further confirming that he was a man quick to anger. "I have no debts and certainly would not allow anyone to be in debt to me. I am a senior bank clerk, living a quiet and godly life." He patted the Bible on the table beside him.

"Dismissed servants?" Charlie suggested, recalling that Grace had said the housekeeper was dismissed recently.

"We had a housekeeper, but I let her go about five weeks ago, soon after Miss Winslow moved into the house."

"Why was she dismissed? Might she hold a grudge?"

"Not at all. She can hardly have been surprised to be let go when she spent most of her time chatting to my wife rather than attending to her work, according to Prudence. Daisy insisted I let her down gently, so I simply told her we had no more need of her now we have two able-bodied women in the house. All she did was see to the laundry and cleaning, as well as the midday meal for my wife and a light supper. I eat at my club during the working week."

Mr Barclay clearly had no appreciation of how much work was involved in cleaning and doing laundry for three adults and a baby. If Barclay had been tactless in his dismissal of the housekeeper, which seemed plausible, Charlie wasn't ruling her out. "I'll need a name and address for her."

Barclay disappeared into his study, returning with a small leather-bound address book and a piece of notepaper. He wrote the name and address and handed it to Charlie. The housekeeper, Mrs Freya Marcus, lived in north Dunedin, not far beyond the main gate of the Botanic Garden. But it was not the address that had Charlie's senses on alert, nor Barclay's small, neat script, which was nothing like the scrawl of the ransom note. It was the notepaper itself: a thick creamy stock that was remarkably like the notepaper the ransom note was written on.

Edward Barclay was waiting for him to speak. Charlie didn't want to alert Barclay to this unexpected development until he was sure of his facts, so he asked the first question that came to mind. "How did you come to engage the housekeeper's services? Was Mrs Marcus recommended to you, or did she apply for the position?"

"Neither. Daisy befriended her, as she was wont to do. My wife has an uncanny ability to attract all the local waifs and strays to her because she hasn't the heart to be unkind to anyone, no matter their eccentricities. I believe the woman dabbles in art, which is an interest Daisy shares. Being an artist, I suspect this Marcus woman was dirt poor and cajoled Daisy into giving her work by playing on her sweet nature."

"If Mrs Marcus is poor, losing her income from keeping your house might have been a significant blow," Charlie said.

"I suppose so, but if you're thinking the housekeeper had anything to do with the kidnapping, you're barking up the wrong tree. The old biddy must be sixty years old at least and so tiny and feeble she could hardly lift a broom, let alone break into a house in the middle of the night. Besides, she was perfectly understanding when I let her go and showed no sign of animosity at all. Daisy was more upset by her departure than Mrs Marcus was."

Hardly a likely suspect on the face of it, although Charlie had met pint-sized Chinese laundrywomen with biceps bigger than anything Barclay was likely to have under the neat seams of his starched white shirt. "Anyone else who might hold a grudge?"

"I had a minor disagreement with a local man, Simeon Frobisher, but he scampered away with his tail between his legs when I told him his behaviour towards my wife was unwelcome."

Charlie recognised the name as the awkward man who had spoken to Prudence Winslow in the Botanic Garden this morning. He had been helping to coordinate the search for Ollie, although that act of kindness could be a clever diversion if he was the kidnapper. "Did Mr Frobisher threaten your wife?"

"Nothing so dramatic. I didn't like the way he treated Daisy with excessive familiarity. He had the darned cheek to offer her private singing lessons. Perhaps I was a little harsh on the man. Daisy has a lovely voice and I suppose Frobisher's enthusiasm to recruit her to the choir was understandable, because he is the choirmaster at our local church."

Thus, he had even less of a motive than Nathan Locke. Having met Simeon Frobisher, Charlie couldn't imagine Daisy preferring the man over her husband, at least in terms of appearance and worldly success, although the man might have hidden depths. "I'll talk to him, but I have to agree he is less likely at first glance than Nathan Locke."

They were interrupted by a knock at the back door. Barclay jumped to his feet, but Charlie gestured for him to sit. He had seen Johnny Todd sneaking around the side of the house, and Charlie wanted to talk to him in private.

Johnny handed him a telegram from Wellington, then leaned his lanky frame against the wall, waiting for further instructions. Charlie and Grace had been using Johnny's expanding range of services since he was a skin-and-bones urchin with nothing but a cheeky grin and a barrow of kindling wood to his name. He'd shot up in height and success since then to become a formidable young man.

"That was quick work, Johnny. You make the official postal service look like a bunch of middle-aged plodders."

Johnny touched a finger to his cloth cap, which was pushed back on his head rakishly, exposing a tuft of wayward hair. "They are a bunch of middle-aged plodders. Anything else, Copper Charlie?"

"Detective Charlie to you," Charlie muttered, as he always did, knowing it would never change his original nickname. "No new tasks. Keep an eye on the house around the clock, if you can. Follow any residents or visitors if you have enough lads to do so, but not at the expense of leaving the house unguarded. Don't run your lads ragged, though. Your young helpers need their beauty sleep."

"Reckon it'd take more than a few hours shut-eye to turn those toads into princes." When Johnny grinned, his eyes twinkled in a way no mother or policeman would wish to see. Too clever and too cheeky by half. "Don't worry, Copper Charlie. I've rounded up every available lad and all their trustworthy friends, brothers, cousins and grandmas to help. Half the businesses in Dunedin are chasing their tails in the absence of their usual runners."

"Don't compromise the business you've worked so hard to build for this one case, Johnny."

"Wouldn't have been no business without you and your missus." Johnny pulled an apple from a pocket and bit into it. "I don't hold with taking innocent babes neither. It ain't right. You'll find the scumbag, won't you, Copper Charlie?"

"I'll do my best," Charlie said to Johnny's fast retreating back. He could only hope his best was good enough.

Charlie opened the telegram and punched a triumphant fist into the air, only to drop it again when he read the second sentence. He headed back inside to collect Grace, wishing that, just this once, the case could be easily solved.

Fairy Godmother

Daisy Barclay curled into a ball on the bed with all her limbs tucked in and her blonde curls the only part of her head showing – a pose that made her look as defensive as a spiky hedgehog and as vulnerable as a child. Grace had expected tears at the news that the trail had gone cold, not this complete withdrawal into silence.

Grace could only imagine the hope Daisy had pinned on a swift return of her son and felt devastated that they had failed her. She took a seat on a low armchair in the corner and got her thoughts in order. There was so much to ask, but Grace feared pushing Daisy too hard and distressing her. She examined the master bedroom instead. The furnishings were heavy and dark, which suggested a man's taste. The bedside table on Daisy's side was bare of personal items, whereas Edward's side was cluttered with a Bible, song sheets, a book, a discarded cravat, a brush, and sundry other items. Daisy's possessions must be still in the nursery. Perhaps she felt as if removing them would be a betrayal of her missing son.

The wardrobe door was open, so naturally Grace got up to peek inside. Daisy's side featured a neat row of plain, matronly dresses and skirts, although Grace spied brighter colours and showier fabrics tucked at the rear. Edward's side would have done a Quaker proud. Clearly, he was a man who espoused old-fashioned values and sombre clothes. She picked up a boot off the bottom shelf. It matched the tread pattern and size of the boot prints outside the nursery window, but not the distinctive wear marks of the kidnapper's boots.

"Why are you looking at my husband's boots?"

Grace cringed inside at being caught snooping. She put the boots back. "My apologies, Daisy. Force of habit. I wanted to give you a few minutes to recover."

Daisy sat up against her pillows. "Your husband said there were boot prints in the garden."

"Made by heavily worn boots, but of a similar type to your husband's boots."

"Edward threw out a pair of old boots of the same style recently, after he bought that pair. I told him to put them in the charity box at church, because they had some wear left in them. Some of the impoverished folk supported by our parish have boots worn clear through the soles. It's a terrible state of affairs when families cannot afford to feed and clothe themselves."

Another item amongst many to follow up. Were the old boots still in the charity box and, if not, who had they been given to? Grace sat down on the end of the bed. "How are you feeling, Daisy?"

"Overwhelmed. I know I must pull myself together for Ollie's sake, but I feel his loss so deeply that the pain of it is agonising. Do you think God is punishing me?"

Suddenly, Grace saw the agony and protective curl for what it was – truly a physical manifestation of the pain of losing a baby. She could have kicked herself for her stupidity, especially as she was a medical student. Grace asked the right questions, at last, and gained Daisy's consent to examine her. Daisy wasn't being punished, she was simply producing milk that wasn't being used, and the swelling of her breasts was causing physical pain.

Grace got a bowl and showed Daisy how to relieve the swelling. Poor Daisy shed fresh tears as the milk drained away, unused, but her relief was plain to see. Grace had little doubt they were both thinking the same: without his mother's milk, how was Ollie surviving?

When Daisy was dressed again, Grace suggested a walk in the fresh air. She had to hold Daisy's arm for support and they only walked to a nearby seat with a view of trees and flowers, but it brought a little colour back to her cheeks.

"You have the healing touch, Grace," Daisy said. "And you're right about the fresh air. I used to love walking in the Botanic Garden amongst the flowers and the children at play. I would walk every day with Freya, who showed me how to capture the essence of the light and colour on canvas. Not that I had anything like her skill at painting, but it was wonderful to try."

"Freya?"

"Freya Marcus, my former housekeeper." Daisy smiled, making her look like a completely different woman from the washed-out rag doll she had seemed in the house. "Don't tell Edward, but Freya was more of a companion to me than Prudence will ever be. Freya was a better housekeeper, too, and she encouraged me to sing whenever I felt like it. We cleaned and cooked together, leaving us time to walk and talk. Freya didn't want to be paid, but I insisted, because I was taking her away from her many grandchildren and her art. It was terribly selfish of me, but I do think Freya was pleased to have the extra earnings. She'd show me a special type of paint and tell me it was thanks to our little arrangement that she could afford it."

"You must have been upset when your husband dismissed her."

"I miss her dreadfully, but it was inevitable once Prudence moved in. She and Freya didn't get along, you see, and I couldn't beg Freya to stay when Prudence was so rude to her. Freya hasn't visited me since she left, which might be because Edward wasn't very tactful in giving her notice. I hope she doesn't think I was to blame for her dismissal."

"I very much doubt it," Grace said, "when you had such a lovely relationship. I hope you still find time to paint and walk in the gardens."

"Oh, no. I loved to paint, but I'm not good at it. My best piece was a pretty scene I painted for Ollie's nursery wall, but it wasn't good enough to put up."

According to whom, Grace wanted to ask, although she suspected she knew the answer. "But you must still walk. It's important for your health and for Ollie to learn about the world." Grace wanted to bite her tongue off at her unthinking comment, but Daisy nodded her agreement.

"I go out with Prudence now. I used to walk alone on Sunday, but not anymore, because Edward doesn't like me going without a companion, and Prudence and Edward have choir practice before the afternoon service on Sunday."

Which explained why Daisy was alone in the Botanic Garden the day she met Nathan Locke. Grace assumed the "not anymore" referred to the period after Edward heard of their meeting. "Daisy, why was the nursery window sealed? I couldn't help but notice that Edward did it soon after your meeting with Nathan Locke."

"I begged him not to seal the window in case there was a fire. Edward said it was for our safety, but he was so furious with me at finding out I had spoken to Nathan Locke that I wondered if he had some ridiculous notion in his head that I was about to run away with the man."

"Why would he think that?"

Daisy shrugged with her whole body, lifting her shoulders and forearms, and rolling her eyes. "I've been faithful to Edward in every conceivable way. I never talk to men without Edward there unless the circumstances mean I cannot avoid it. I wear clothes a nun couldn't fault for propriety. I never laugh or flutter my eyelashes or speak out of turn. I even left the choir because Edward thought the choirmaster was being overly familiar when he complimented my singing and suggested private lessons."

"You shouldn't have had to do any of that, Daisy." Grace tried to speak calmly, but her words floated on a tide of anger.

"I know," Daisy said, her voice barely audible, "but it's easier to be obliging in the interests of a happy home. Edward loves me, you know. Everything he does is for my own good, and for the good of our son. Once we have Ollie back, all will be well."

They sat in silence as Grace worked out how best to respond. Daisy might well be right about her husband's love, but it didn't make Edward's behaviour any more acceptable. His version of love was crushing the very soul from his wife, despite his claim he was doing it for her good. No singing, no painting, no laughing, no walking, and now locked in a room at night. Grace fumed at the mere thought of it, but Daisy seemed to have accepted it, perhaps because the restrictions had been added one by one over time, like a dripping tap gradually eroding her self-esteem.

"Don't blame my husband, Grace. The choirmaster was excessively forward in his attentions, and I believe Prudence was … overzealous … in telling Edward about the entirely innocent encounter with Mr Locke. Prudence adores those foolish romantic tales about heroines who find their one true love and run away with him. Mr Locke, most unfortunately, has the look of a dashing hero. She was quite exhilarated by what she interpreted as a secret assignation. Prudence likes to please my husband after he helped her cope with legal matters after the death of her mother."

Daisy spoke about the close relationship between her husband and her companion without a trace of the jealousy Edward would have shown, but she must have felt aggrieved by the unfairness of it, nevertheless. It was not Grace's business to dissect their marriage, much less to advise on it, but she did wonder if Prudence or Edward could have added sleeping tonic to Daisy's cocoa to ensure they had unchaperoned time together. The very idea of a liaison between them was so dreadful she felt it was best to confirm the presence of a drug before raising it with any of them. Suffice to say that if Daisy had disappeared with the child, Grace wouldn't have blamed her.

Grace couldn't allow herself to get distracted by Daisy's plight while Ollie was missing. Nor could she afford to avoid difficult questions. "I hate to bring this up, Daisy, but there is a slight chance Ollie could have been taken by a childless woman who wanted him for herself. Or man, for that matter. It doesn't fit with the ransom demand, but we have to look at all possibilities. I understand there is a woman who frequents the Botanic Garden and has a particular interest in babies. An excessive interest, according to some."

"You must mean Aggie. Agatha Gemmel. She's a kind soul, and whoever suggested otherwise is nothing more than a gossip." The flash of anger brought spots of red to Daisy's cheeks, which died away almost as quickly as they appeared. "Sorry, I didn't mean to sound harsh, Grace, but Aggie is my saviour. Aggie really cares about mothers and their babies, and her sage advice helped me at a difficult time. If she is a little over-demonstrative in her attentions to babies, it is only because she has had a tragic past. Her husband died when she was with child, and then her baby died in infancy. Some people call her mad, but she is only struggling to come to terms with her terrible losses."

"How tragic," Grace said. "The poor woman. I will need to talk to her, but I promise to be considerate of her feelings. Do you know where Aggie Gemmel lives?"

"Somewhere between the church and the Botanic Garden, I believe, but I haven't been to her home. I expect you could find her easily enough by asking at the church or asking the other mothers in the gardens if they have seen her." Daisy struggled to her feet. "Come, Grace, enough talking. You and your husband have work to do to bring my Ollie home, and Edward will be wondering where I am."

Grace rose with her. She took Daisy's arm as they ambled down to the house. "Daisy, may I ask why you see Aggie as your saviour?"

A slow smile spread over Daisy's face, digging deep dimples into her rounded cheeks. "I was terribly thin and unwell when I arrived in Dunedin. All the doctors said it might be the reason for my failure to conceive a child, but none of their so-called cures worked. I tried them all – meat three times a day, no meat at all, electric shocks, cold baths, cod liver oil and tonics that would make a corpse gag – but nothing changed, except that my dislike for cod liver oil turned into utter loathing. Eventually, I refused to go to another doctor to be humiliated and derided as barren. The shame of it was driving me to despair."

Grace didn't blame her. The average doctor knew little about female fertility, but far too many still held the outdated opinion that it was always the woman's fault, which was blatantly untrue. Even that was better than some of the religious fanatics, who viewed infertility as a curse brought down on the head of sinners. "What changed, Daisy?"

"Somebody slipped a little red book into my knitting bag while I was in the Botanic Garden, probably while I was feeding the ducks by the pond. I don't know who gave me the book, but I had talked to Aggie that day. When I asked her, she laughed and said it must be my fairy godmother."

"Did you ever confirm it was Aggie?"

"I never inquired further, because I loved the idea that I had a secret fairy godmother waving her wand to cure me. That book changed my life. I followed its suggestions and Oliver was conceived two months later. Ollie means everything to me, Grace. Being apart from him is like having my heart torn out."

"I don't have a child yet, but I do understand." Grace hesitated to ask anything of this suffering soul, but she was alight with curiosity about the little red book. "May I ask a favour, Daisy?"

"Anything."

"Might I borrow your book? I have been married for almost a year and have similar symptoms to those you described, although not as severe. I know a year is not long, but it seems a lifetime."

Daisy stopped and threw her arms around Grace. "Dearest Grace, after what you are doing for me, nothing would give me greater pleasure than becoming your not-so-secret fairy godmother."

Grace hugged her back. "If your book works its magic on me, I shall be forever in your debt."

They walked on in companionable silence, while Grace reflected that friendship and hope could spark a light in the darkest place.

Charlie was at the front door with Blaze, waving frantically at her. She quickened her pace, determined to make him wait another minute or two until Daisy had found the little red book. Despite the dire situation they were in, Grace found herself humming and realised Daisy was smiling at her with the sort of twinkling smile that would do a fairy godmother proud.

Daisy stopped her again before they reached the house, her smile replaced with a worried frown. "It might be best not to tell your husband about the book. Men put their trust in qualified physicians, not women's wisdom. But perhaps your husband is different because he is allowing you to attend medical school."

Grace couldn't let this pass. "My career choice is mine alone, although my husband supports my choice wholeheartedly. Charlie and I both believe women and men should be treated equally."

"Long may his progressive attitude last, Grace. But the law is still against us, isn't it? Women cannot divorce without proving both infidelity and cruelty, while a man only has to prove infidelity. And the husband has all the rights when it comes to children."

The words were said with a wistful pragmatism, which suggested to Grace that Daisy Barclay had considered her options for a life away from Edward's domineering rule and found them limited and unpalatable.

Nathan Locke

After Johnny had given him the telegram, Charlie rushed inside to pass on the good news. Grace and Daisy were nowhere to be found, but Edward Barclay was in his study, shuffling papers distractedly.

Charlie waved the telegram. "I have a location for Nathan Locke."

Barclay jumped to his feet, scattering papers. "So quickly? Excellent work, Mr Penrose Pyke. I can see I made the right decision to engage your services." Edward Barclay strode across the room with his hand out for the telegram but was thwarted by Charlie, who folded it and put it in his pocket. Barclay's hand hovered in the air for a moment, before he withdrew it. "Is he nearby?"

"Near enough. We'll go immediately and let you know the outcome as soon as we can." Charlie noted with amusement that Barclay was now taking credit for the decision to employ a private detective, when he had been against the idea initially.

Barclay followed him to the front door, stopping only when Charlie suggested it would be better if he remain at home so as not to frighten Mr Locke. He called Blaze and was about to tell her to find Grace, when he saw his wife and Daisy Barclay walking towards the house, arm in arm like old friends out for a stroll. Grace must have worked miracles, because Daisy was smiling.

Grace hurried towards him, giving him the wait-a-minute signal. She disappeared into the house with Daisy, reappearing soon after with a spring in her step that reminded Charlie of their carefree time over Christmas on the Otago Peninsula. They would have to put their work aside more often, he resolved, because it was all too easy to get bogged down in the swamp of crime and forget that life should be full of joy.

"I have an address for Nathan Locke," Charlie said, when his wife was by his side again.

Grace waited until they were further down the road before speaking. "Mr Barclay is still standing on the porch, poised to run after us. It would have been pistols at dawn with Nathan Locke if he had his way. Or perhaps a more gentlemanly bout of fencing with ink-filled quills over bank ledgers. Mr Barclay certainly looks far happier than he was this morning."

"He won't be so happy if Daisy is proved right and Locke is innocent." Charlie glanced sideways at his wife, who was all but skipping. "What did Daisy tell you that made you so cheerful?"

"I like her, Charlie, that's all. She feels like a kindred spirit. Aside from that, I learned that Daisy adored both her housekeeper, Freya Marcus, and her friend Aggie Gemmel, otherwise known as Mad Aggie. They are both saints and had nothing to do with Ollie's kidnapping, according to Daisy. On the other hand, Prudence and Edward seem to be tolerated as a burden she must bear out of duty to her marriage vows. Oh, and Edward sealed the window against Daisy's wishes after her encounter with Locke in the Botanic Garden. Daisy went so far as to suggest Edward could be worried that she and Locke might run away together, which she called a ridiculous idea."

"Interesting," Charlie said. "Could there be a grain of truth in it, or is Barclay just chronically suspicious?"

"We'll see. Tell me, how did you find out our suspect's location so quickly?"

"I recruited the assistance of our Wellington branch." Charlie smiled at his wife's puzzled frown. "The manager of the Bank of New Zealand in Wellington was evidently no match for the impressive interrogation skills of our operative."

Grace stopped to allow a laden cart to cross the narrow bridge over the lower Leith ahead of them. "Our Wellington branch? Has the detective agency expanded without you informing me, my dear?"

"You may recall that a certain very astute woman offered her services if they were ever needed. I decided to take her up on the offer. Your mother, the one and only Mrs Louisa Penrose."

Grace threw up her hands. "Oh, marvellous. I'll never hear the end of it. My darling mother will be moving to Dunedin before we know it so as not to miss any of the action. She'll be solving cases during the day and lecturing me on my unladylike behaviour in the evening."

"Your mother is a miracle worker, Grace, and you don't fool me with your dramatic display of horror. I know you love her unreservedly."

"Don't say I didn't warn you," she grumbled, taking the telegram from him.

The telegram read, "NL CEMENT WORKS PELICHET BAY STOP BNZ BOSS SAID NL REHIRED INNOCENT STOP".

The cement works at Pelichet Bay were at the mouth of the Water of Leith, beyond the shallow waters of Lake Logan, not much more than a mile from the Barclays' house. Already, Charlie could detect the salt tang in the air, above the dense odour of river mud, and the harsher smells of the railway and the industrial area around the port. Even from this distance, he could see the column of smoke rising from the towering chimney of the cement works.

Grace handed the telegram back. "I assume NL is Nathan Locke, the man Edward Barclay suspects, and he is now working at the cement works here in Dunedin. What crime does the Bank of New Zealand manager think Locke is innocent of?"

Charlie took her arm again now that the cart had passed, and they crossed the bridge over the placid summer flow of the Water of Leith. "I'm not sure how much you overheard, but Locke sent Barclay a threatening letter after being dismissed over a theft from the Bank of New Zealand in Wellington. I presume the second sentence of the telegram indicates the manager at the bank now believes Locke to be innocent of the theft, and remorseful enough to offer him his job back. It will be fascinating to hear Locke's version of events, although I'd rather not be the person who has to pass the news on to Barclay."

"Then don't tell him," Grace said. "All that Barclay needs to know is whether or not Nathan Locke is guilty of taking Oliver. The two-year-old theft need not concern us, although I sincerely hope Edward Barclay doesn't jump to the conclusion that Daisy had anything to do with establishing Locke's innocence. I'm worried about her, Charlie."

Charlie squeezed her arm gently to show his agreement. "Oliver's kidnapping has caused the family understandable stress, especially as Edward Barclay cannot access enough money to pay the ransom by Friday, and is relying on Daisy's inheritance. To be honest, I hope Nathan Locke is the kidnapper. The family situation is such a horrible tangle of loyalties and resentments, I get a chill up my spine every time I walk through the door. Prudence's church friend, Simeon Frobisher, upset Edward Barclay simply by encouraging Daisy to sing in the choir. Meanwhile, Frobisher seems to have his heart set on Prudence Winslow, while Prudence talks about Edward Barclay in a way no married man should be talked about by anyone but his wife."

"Prudence worries me, too. She talks about Ollie as if he was her own baby after just six weeks living with the Barclays. As Prudence said in relation to Aggie, desperation for a child and a husband can be a powerful motive."

They had to stop by the railway line while a train chugged past, engulfing them in steam and the piercing screech of metal on rails.

When the train had passed, Grace ran a finger down Charlie's damp cheek. "Cement dust on the breeze, mingling with coal soot. We must be getting close. Not a place I would choose to work."

"Nathan Locke had little choice, because he was dismissed from his bank position with no references and Barclay wrote to other banks to warn them that he was a thief."

They arrived at the cement works via a raised embankment over the water just as a shift had ended. Ghostly figures shuffled their way out of the factory, covered in cement dust and coughing from deep within congested lungs. Cleaner figures passed in the opposite direction. A few people cast mildly curious glances at the unexpected sight of a man, woman and dog, but nobody lingered to ask their business or stopped them as they walked into the works' office.

Several people milled around the office area, but the man they were after wasn't hard to identify. He was a head taller than anyone else – and what a head it was. Tightly curled blond hair, a long straight nose, chiselled jaw, and alabaster skin. Prudence Winslow had hit the mark when she compared him to a statue of a Greek god. Nathan Locke appeared to be tidying his desk prior to departing for the day, presumably having started with the early shift. The timing was perfect, because Charlie was reluctant to make Locke's situation worse by introducing himself as a detective in front of his work colleagues. They retreated to the street entrance to wait for him.

Locke strode past them a few minutes later. Charlie hurried to catch up, leaving Grace and Blaze to tuck in behind them. "Mr Locke? May we have a word with you, please?"

Their suspect turned tired eyes on him. "What is it? I've been working since dawn, so I must warn you I am not in the mood for hawkers or Bible bashers."

Charlie knew he'd be even less in the mood for a private detective slinging accusations. He'd have to take this gently. Fortunately, he knew of a place nearby selling cups of tea and pies that boasted more meat than gristle, conveniently located between the docks and the railway station. Locke was thin to the point of gauntness and therefore unlikely to refuse an exchange of information for food. Besides, Charlie's stomach was rumbling and dinner seemed a distant prospect.

"We're neither hawkers nor bashers, Mr Locke, but we do need to talk to you about a matter of importance. The Pie 'n' Whistle isn't far. Would you care to sit for a while and join us for a bite to eat?"

Locke twisted his lips sideways, tossing up between a meal and mistrust. Hunger won. "I know it. I can spare you a few minutes, I suppose."

Charlie took their orders to the counter, adding a side of scrag ends to take to Blaze, who had been left outside. Pete the pie man, who knew Charlie by sight and remembered his usual order, was happy to oblige. Grace gave him a flutter of a smile when he sat back down with three chunky mugs filled to the brim with stewed tea. His capacity for food was a source of amusement to his wife, but a detective could not function on air alone.

"So," Locke said, "if you don't want to sell me anything, what is this about?"

"My name is Charlie Penrose Pyke, and this is my wife, Grace. We are private detectives. Your name came up regarding an investigation we are working on."

Locke's mug clattered against to the table, spilling tea. His eyelids narrowed over a jaw locked so tight it was a wonder he could talk. "Who are you working for?"

"Mrs Daisy Barclay," Charlie replied. "It's nothing to do with the unfortunate incident at the bank two years ago, which we understand has been resolved. Am I correct that you have been rehired to your former position at the Bank of New Zealand in Wellington?"

The tension eased in his jaw muscles, although Locke's eyelids remained slitted. "You seem to know a great deal about a matter that was supposed to be confidential. Did Mrs Barclay tell you she sent a letter to the bank on my behalf after hearing that her foul husband had me wrongfully dismissed?"

Charlie glanced at Grace, who raised her eyebrows fractionally to tell him that Daisy hadn't mentioned writing to the bank on Locke's behalf. "Mrs Barclay was concerned that you had been unjustifiably deprived of your livelihood. She did not know if her letter had been acted upon, so we made discreet inquiries."

"Is that why you're here? Didn't Mrs Barclay see the flower I left on the sundial?"

"Was that the white rose you left yesterday morning?" Charlie was surprised Mr Locke had admitted it so readily. Either he was genuinely innocent of the kidnapping or playing an elaborate double bluff.

"Oh, I had hoped it was a camellia. I know little about plants."

"Unfortunately, Mr Barclay saw it first and removed it."

A flash of fear distorted Locke's face. "Oh no. I hope he didn't see me put it there, because I would hate to cause Mrs Barclay any more pain. She wanted to know the outcome of her letter to the bank, but she didn't dare meet me again, so I said I would leave her a sign if my situation had improved. It was Mrs Barclay who suggested a flower on the sundial, which she could see from her window. We'd been talking about how the women's suffrage movement had shown women they could be strong and achieve amazing feats, and thus a white camellia seemed appropriate."

The admission told Charlie far more about Nathan Locke's relationship with Daisy than he probably realised. Their meeting in the gardens had covered many topics, suggesting a degree of trust and, possibly, a degree of intimacy. Locke had chosen the symbol of the suffrage movement to show her how strong she could be, suggesting he understood her home situation and was on her side. What's more, he knew Mrs Barclay might suffer pain if she was found out. Finally, and critically, Nathan Locke knew where the Barclays lived and where Daisy's window was. For her part, Daisy Barclay had gone to great lengths to get Locke his job back, despite the trouble it would cause if she was found out.

"I take it the situation with the bank has been resolved to your satisfaction, Mr Locke."

"Absolutely. In fact, I received a promotion to senior clerk. Best day of my life when I received the letter of offer, along with an apology from the bank. Another three weeks here to work out my notice and then I'll be back in Wellington with a bright future ahead of me again. If I never see another sack of cement in my life, I'll die happy. You can tell Mrs Barclay that I'm immensely grateful for her help after she discovered the truth three weeks ago. Frankly, I admire the woman's courage in defying her husband by writing the letter to my former employer. What she saw in Barclay, I'll never know."

Charlie nodded and let the silence drag while he tucked into the pie. Grace sipped tea and stayed silent. She knew his methods and anticipated his needs as if she could read his mind. With anyone else, he might have found this disconcerting, but with Grace it had always been this way, and more so now they were married. This was what a marriage should be – a merging of two like minds into a single being – not a pairing where one dominated the other. Grace had a hint of a smile playing over her lips behind the raised cup, as if she had read his mind again.

Nathan Locke picked up the knife and fork and tore into his pie as if he hadn't had a square meal in a month. Charlie could almost read his mind too, from the way his expression changed from his initial wariness, to delight that Mrs Barclay would now know how grateful he was, to growing suspicion. When his eyebrows merged into one and he put his fork down with a clatter, Charlie was ready for it.

"Did Barclay find out about the letter and send you here to threaten me?"

"Mr Barclay doesn't know about his wife's letter to the bank or your change of fortunes, Mr Locke, and I would like to keep it that way for her sake. However, a family friend told Mr Barclay about your meeting with his wife in the Dunedin Botanic Garden three weeks ago. Our client, Mrs Barclay, would be grateful for a statement from you outlining the circumstances of your meeting and your history with her to reassure her husband that it was not a planned assignation."

Locke's jaw was so tight now he risked breaking a tooth. "That blo –" he glanced at Grace, who was innocently sipping her tea. "That dratted man. Is it not enough that he destroyed my reputation once? I was down to my last few shillings when I finally secured a position in Dunedin, thanks to a friend of my sister's husband. But I suppose I owe it to Mrs Barclay. Not that there is much to tell."

Charlie poised his pencil over his notebook and waited.

"I've only met Mrs Barclay twice in my life. Once at a work party, at which somebody bumped into me, causing me to knock Mrs Barclay and spill her drink. I was mortified, of course, and fetched a napkin to mop the spill. Unfortunately, she bent over as I handed her the cloth and my hand brushed her, um, chest area, entirely innocently. Mrs Barclay was charming about it. She chatted with me briefly to ensure I understood there were no hard feelings over the incident. But Mr Barclay was furious. After that, my work was never satisfactory, my demeanour was unbecoming, my breathing was too loud for his sensitive ears … until suddenly I found myself accused of theft and fired without references. Need I add I was innocent?"

"I understand your anger, Mr Locke, but perhaps it would have been wiser not to send Edward Barclay a threatening letter."

Locke's pale face flushed scarlet. "I don't know what came over me, except that I was furious one night after a yet another rejection letter for a clerical position at another bank. My letter was regrettable. Barclay kept it, I presume, to use against me if he ever needed further proof of my evil nature. Men like him never forget a slight and never recall a good deed."

"And the second meeting with Mrs Barclay?"

"Three weeks ago, in the Dunedin Botanic Garden. I was shocked to see her there, not realising she and her husband had moved to Dunedin. She told me she visited the gardens after church on a Sunday, but I had never seen her there because I almost always spend Sundays with my sister in Port Chalmers. The one day of the week I get a decent meal and the comforts of a family

89

home. Mrs Barclay and I spoke for a short time, as one might with a distant acquaintance from the past. I mentioned the reason for my dismissal and Mrs Barclay was kind enough to promise to write a letter on my behalf, thinking there must have been some sort of misunderstanding at the bank. That's it. We parted on good terms, never to see each other again, or so I hoped. She's a charming lady, but seeing her brought back unpleasant memories."

Locke picked up his fork and finished the pie, clearly believing the issue had been resolved. As soon as he took the last bite, he rose from the table and nodded politely at Grace.

"Just one more question, if you will, Mr Locke," Charlie said. "Where were you on Sunday night? Last night," he clarified, feeling as if the kidnapping had occurred days ago, rather than merely hours ago.

"At my sister's house, as usual. I always go on Sunday morning and stay overnight, before catching the early mail train back to Dunedin in time to start work on Monday. In fact, I dropped the flower off on my way to the train early on the Sunday morning. It was intended only as a simple courtesy to let Mrs Barclay know of my change of fortune." Locke was still standing but shifting on his feet nervously. "What is this about, Mr Penrose Pyke? Why so many questions?"

Charlie set his pencil down in the exact centre of his notebook. "The matter we are investigating is far more serious than a chance meeting in the Botanic Garden. The Barclays' infant son was kidnapped last night."

Locke collapsed into the seat. "What? Kidnapped? Oh Lord, how shocking." He gaped at Charlie for long seconds, looking stunned, before the realisation hit. "Barclay is accusing me, isn't he? I had nothing to do with the child's kidnapping, nothing."

"Did you know they had a baby?"

"Only because Daisy was pushing a baby carriage in the gardens when I met her. What possible motive could I have for taking her child?"

90

"There was a ransom note, Mr Locke. And you did say that Mr Barclay's false accusation had you down to your last few shillings before you secured a position in Dunedin. Seeing Daisy Barclay in Dunedin must have brought it all back to you."

"Yes. No. I mean, yes, I am still angry at what Barclay did to me, and I couldn't swear I wouldn't break the man's nose if he stuck it within swinging distance. But no, I had moved on, especially now I have a good job in Wellington to look forward to. I would never, ever, for a single second contemplate taking a man's baby in revenge. You'd have to be a monster to commit such an evil crime."

Charlie picked up his pencil again. "I'll need to confirm your alibi with your sister. Can I have her address, please?" Locke gave it readily, even eagerly. "If we could search your lodgings, I could report back to the Barclays that you are no longer a suspect."

Nathan Locke jumped to his feet, rattling the plates and cups on the table. "Come with me. I have nothing to hide. And you can tell Barclay from me that if he uses this outrage to get me dismissed again, I will not be responsible for my actions. Against him, man to man, not his wife and certainly not his child." He stomped out of the pie shop.

"I've probably got time to get to Port Chalmers and back this afternoon," Grace whispered as they rose to follow him.

Talking to Locke's sister before he had a chance to warn her had its merits, but Charlie wanted Grace by his side on the off chance that Ollie was hidden at Locke's lodgings. He'd need Grace to grab the boy from whoever was looking after him, while Charlie took care of Locke. "I'd rather have you with me. Afterwards, could you take Blaze home and see if there are any messages waiting at the office? I'll talk to Declan Kelly as soon as we are finished with Locke and he can arrange the constable in Port Chalmers to take a statement from Locke's sister."

Grace brushed his fingers as she passed him, sending a tingle up his arm.

Nathan Locke's lodgings indicated his financial position with grim precision. A shabby but respectable boarding house, near enough to the railway station to take impoverished travellers for a night or two, while being close enough to the docks and the itinerant labour force it required to cater for pay-by-the-week residents. A dark hallway, worn-to-threads carpet on narrow stairs, but clean enough that the rats and cockroaches were kept at bay. Locke led them up to the top storey and the narrow cupboard that was his room.

Charlie might as well have sent Grace straight home. There wasn't enough space to hide a carpetbag, let alone a living, screaming infant. Blaze confirmed his assessment. She looked at him with dark, intelligent eyes, her head tilted to the side, a clear sign she was wondering why he had brought her here. Grace tipped her head at the boots under the narrow bunk. Locke's feet, in keeping with his height, would no more squeeze into the average sized boots that made the prints outside the nursery window than Charlie's would. Nathan Locke was not the kidnapper.

"Thank you for your time, Mr Locke," Charlie said. "I appreciate your willingness to help our inquiries and wish you well in your new career."

He shook the man's hand to show he meant the words. Locke had every reason to hate Barclay, after losing two years of his life and falling into such straightened circumstances. For a young man, it meant more than the loss of a job – it meant an inability to save and establish a career and thus attract a wife and start a family of his own. Charlie knew exactly how that felt, having been in the same position not so long ago. Grace had stood by him and so had his former boss and now business partner, Alistair Stewart, for which he would always be grateful.

Locke held onto his hand a moment longer than was strictly necessary, then simply nodded and stood aside so they could leave.

The silence of their departure was cut through by the wailing of a baby through the thin walls of the adjacent room. Nathan Locke's face turned the exact shade of the billowing dust around the cement factory.

Family Troubles

Grace pushed past Charlie and knocked on the door of the next room.

A girl in a heavily patched dress two sizes too small opened the door a few inches and stared at Grace with wide green eyes that had seen too much in the world that frightened her.

Grace crouched down to her level and smiled. "Hello there. May I speak to your mother?"

"Who is it?" a harried voice called from within.

"Mrs Grace Penrose Pyke. I'm from the women's free medical clinic at Lavender House, here to offer our services."

Grace pushed open the door and waved at the woman inside, who was jiggling a toddler in one arm and a baby in the other. The baby couldn't have been more than a few months old and had black hair and green eyes, like the girl and her mother. Grace shook her head at Charlie, who was guarding Locke's door with his bulk. Locke's blond head peered over his shoulder, but he retreated inside on seeing Grace shake her head.

Charlie hissed through his teeth to get Blaze's attention, then pointed to the room and circled his finger. The border collie slinked past Grace and circled the family's single room, her nose twitching but finding no familiar scent. The girl with the patched dress fell upon the dog, cuddling him like a favourite doll.

"Let the dog go, Millie." The woman turned to Grace. "Sorry. We had to give up our border collie when my husband lost his job. Fair broke out hearts, but it was a choice between the dog and food on the table. That was when we had a bigger place than this," she added.

The single room was three times the size of Locke's cupboard, but still an impossible squeeze for a family of five. Another black head peeped out from behind the only bed and Grace amended her count to six. A boy aged about five, a girl aged about seven, the toddler and the baby, plus their mother and presumably a father. Grace could see the mother had done her best, but the room had no bathroom or kitchen or even cupboards. For the working people of Dunedin, it was a familiar story – always one or two paydays away from a slippery downward slide into poverty.

Grace rummaged through her medical bag for her calling card, ignoring the one identifying her as Mrs Grace Penrose Pyke, medical adviser to the Southern Investigations Agency, and the one labelled Miss Grace Penrose, assistant to the Police Surgeon. She really must get that one updated. At the bottom of the pile was a card she hadn't used for a while: Miss Grace Penrose, medical assistant, Lavender House Women's Free Medical Clinic.

Grace handed the woman the card and took the toddler, who squirmed out of her arms and toddled over to wrap his arms about Blaze.

"Don't worry about the dog, ma'am," Charlie said from behind Grace. "She loves children."

The baby reached out a pudgy fist towards Charlie, who reached out his much larger fist to touch knuckles. The crying stopped, and the baby gurgled happily.

"Well, our Jonty likes the look of you, sir. Happen you look a little like his father." The mother looked Charlie up and down, her smile vanishing. "You wouldn't be a policeman, would you? If you've come to take my children away from me, you can think again. We may be poor, but we look after our own."

"I can see that, Mrs –"

"Mrs Guthrie."

"We're only here paying a social visit to your neighbour, Mrs Guthrie, but my wife heard the baby crying and –"

"Thought you might like a little help," Grace finished. "Lavender House runs a free medical clinic for women and children. Our volunteers keep a stock of clothes and food for any family in need."

"We don't need charity," Mrs Guthrie declared, unconvincingly.

"Not charity," Grace replied, "just a little helping hand until you're back on your feet. With so many good men out of work these days, it's only right that a community rallies around to see them through it, as others have done for them in the past."

"I'll leave you to it, Grace," Charlie said. "You and Blaze go home. Hopefully, I won't be long."

When Charlie was gone, Grace took the baby from Mrs Guthrie to give her a few minutes of rest while the older children played with the dog. The baby needed changing, which gave Grace an excuse to linger.

Mrs Guthrie sank into the only chair and propped her swollen ankles on the end of the bed, letting out a long sigh. "Oh, lass, you're an angel. And what a lovely husband. I expect it won't be long before you are just like me – knee deep in children, surviving on a couple of hours of sleep a night. Not exactly the home I dreamed of, but I cannot complain when I have my wee lovelies around me. Mind you, I live in fear of finding out I've another on the way."

Grace mumbled a non-committal 'mm', thinking she ought to be careful what she wished for. A baby seemed like the perfect addition to their busy lives in theory, but four children under the age of seven in a space not much bigger than their bedroom at home wasn't her idea of heaven. The classic baby problem – some families with too many, while others were desperate for any.

"We came by yesterday to see the man who lives next door to you," Grace said as she unwrapped the foul-smelling cloth covering the baby's bottom.

"That would be Nathan. He's a right sweetheart. Lovely with the children, especially young Billy, and always bringing us the odd bit of bread or carrots, pretending he bought too many by mistake. A right gentleman who ought to have a family of his own, but I reckon he's seen hard times too. Yesterday, you say? Nathan's never here on a Sunday, love, because he goes to stay with his sister. He offered us the use of his bed for Sunday nights, and we take it in turns to get one good night's sleep a week. Well, to be honest, I let my husband have it mostly, because he has to be up early to see if he can pick up a shift at the docks. I could have done with the sleep last night, but I didn't regret it when I saw my husband whistling on the way to the docks this morning."

Grace rocked the newly changed baby in her arms until his eyes shut. With exaggerated care, she handed him back to Mrs Guthrie. "I ought to be on my way."

"Water tap is out in the backyard if you want to wash your –"

Her sentence was cut off by the stomp of boots on the stairs, followed by a bristly face at the door. "Who was that man I saw leaving just now? Had the look of a copper about him."

Mrs Guthrie sprang to her feet and wrapped a protective arm around her baby, but it was too late. The man's loud voice had woken the baby, who protested this indignity with a wail. "Just a friend of Mr Locke's, Mr Battersby, not a copper."

"Is that a dog in your room, Mrs Guthrie? You know I don't allow mongrels inside. And, for the love of God, can you stop that baby screaming? I've had that many complaints from the other residents, I've a mind to give you your marching orders."

"Please don't, Mr Battersby. We've nowhere else to go." Mrs Guthrie jiggled the baby, but he wasn't about to forgive the interruption to his sleep. She tried to plug the boy's mouth with her little finger, but the baby screamed louder, setting off the toddler.

The landlord clamped his hands over his ears. "Right, that's the last straw. I want you out as soon as your week's rent is up. Day after tomorrow. I'm sorry to be so strict, but you knew I had a no-family policy from the start." Battersby exited before Mrs Guthrie could plead her case.

Grace took the baby again, patting his back and shushing him until he dropped back into a doze.

Mrs Guthrie spent a minute with her head in her hands, her shoulders heaving with silent tears, before she wiped her eyes and stood up, smiling. "Right then, children. Who wants to play a fun game? First one to pack all their things wins a hug."

The children looked at her with doleful eyes that said their mother had tried this trick before.

"How about a hug and a bright, shiny sixpence?" Grace said.

The children switched their gaze to Grace, still not convinced. The five-year-old boy broke first, but only when Grace produced a coin from behind his ear, as Charlie had taught her to do. He seized a flour sack and stuffed his meagre possessions into it. Millie took the toddler's hand and set about her task with the resignation of an adult who has seen it all and doesn't expect it to end well.

The task was finished in a heart-achingly short time. Grace dished out sixpence each to the two older children. As she handed the baby back to Mrs Guthrie, she whispered, "I'm sorry for bringing our dog into your room and causing trouble for you, Mrs Guthrie."

"Never you mind, love. Did the children good to hug a dog again, and we'd have been evicted anyway, because we've no money to pay next week's rent. Besides, the landlord did us a favour allowing us to stay in the first place, because they don't allow children here. It was only supposed to be a week to get us back on our feet."

"Where will you go?"

Mrs Guthrie shook her head. "We'll have to pray that Joe got a few hours' work today. I've a distant relation up the coast who might take us in for a few days if we can afford the train ticket. Otherwise, we'll be on the street."

"I'll see what I can do," Grace said, although she knew Lavender House was full and didn't take men. "What line of work is your husband in?"

"He was a wheelwright before we had to move to Dunedin, but my Joe can turn his hand to anything."

"He could try Mr Campbell at the carriage works on Walker Street." Grace knew Mr Campbell was already struggling to find work for the men he had, but he had always gone out of his way to help her after she assisted during the breech delivery of his first son. "Tell Mr Campbell I sent you."

With a last wave to the children, she took her leave, being careful not to look back, because she couldn't bear to see their miserable, resigned expressions. She told herself they would find somewhere to live, knowing that her attention needed to be focused on the kidnapped baby, but her heart was leaden.

After a brief stop at the single outside tap to wash her hands, Grace plodded home with Blaze at heel. Working men plodded the street alongside her, heads bowed after a long day. It was too late now to go back to the Botanic Garden in search of Mad Aunt Aggie, so Grace heeded Charlie's instruction to take Blaze home.

Baby Ollie had now been missing for at least twelve hours and the ransom was due in three and a half days. Grace tried to picture Ollie tucked up in a warm blanket, clean and fed, but she couldn't shake the image of him screaming and screaming, with no mother running to comfort him.

Discreet Help

Charlie left the Guthries' room in the boarding house with his mind on the next steps in the investigation, now that Nathan Locke had put up a convincing case for his innocence.

He bumped into a man on the stairs, who gave him a surly glare. The landlord, presumably. Charlie didn't stop, because he still had a lot to do as the afternoon faded. He hesitated at the exit, worried that the Guthrie family might get into trouble for having unauthorised visitors, but decided Grace could charm the man out of his surly mood better than he could. He had his own devil to face in breaking the news to Edward Barclay that Nathan Locke had an alibi and Oliver was still missing.

Barclay reacted, as expected, with equal parts disbelief and anger. "How can you be sure Locke isn't lying?"

"I will check his alibi, of course," Charlie replied, "but our dog did not react to his smell and there is no way he could have Oliver hidden in his spartan room at a boarding house."

Charlie resisted the temptation to say that Nathan Locke no longer had a strong motive, as he had been exonerated of theft and offered his job back, because that would only add to Barclay's fury and put Daisy at risk. If Barclay got a whiff of his wife's involvement in helping Locke, Charlie feared what he would do to her. Daisy sat in the corner, listening to the conversation, showing no emotion that Charlie could discern. He wasn't surprised she had learned to wear a blank mask to conceal her thoughts from her jealous husband.

Barclay paced the sitting room, coming to terms with the unwelcome news. "If not Locke, then who?"

"We have other potential leads, Mr Barclay. If you will excuse me, I must continue my investigation. Time is tight, as you will appreciate." That much was true, but Charlie's real reason for cutting short the interview was that he feared Barclay might fire him for rejecting the man Barclay suspected.

As soon as Charlie was back in the street, Johnny Todd appeared from nowhere and told him Mr and Mrs Barclay hadn't left the house, but the companion had been out most of the day. She had returned with a man, but he had left her before he came within sight of the Barclay house. The description matched Simeon Frobisher, the choirmaster at the church and organiser of the search.

Charlie's next stop was the home of Detective Sergeant Declan Kelly, a trusted friend and a first-rate policeman. Charlie didn't need reminding of the threat in the ransom note – *No police if you want to see the boy again* – but Declan could be relied on to investigate with the utmost discretion. Family meant the world to Declan, and a kidnapped child would have him champing at the bit to help. He'd have to inform his commanding officer, Detective Inspector Wallace, but Wallace was a doting grandfather with a soft spot for children and a policeman's loathing for anyone who hurt them.

Declan's six-year-old son answered the door to the Kelly's cottage. "Uncle Charlieee! Papa let me eat three cheese rolls because Billy Watts pushed me over and I knocked out my tooth and now I can't eat my supper! Look!" Patrick bared his teeth to show the gap at the front.

Charlie bent down to inspect the hole. "That must have hurt, Patrick."

"Not much. It was wobbly anyway. Papa says a new tooth will grow, but only if I'm nice to my sisters and sit up straight during Mass."

"That's true," Charlie said, trying not to laugh, "but you only get one chance for a new tooth in that spot, so you'd better be careful."

The Kelly family was clustered around a small table that took up most of the kitchen area of the cottage. Kathleen, who would be two years old in a few months, was on Declan's knee, waving a spoon in her father's face and giggling. Declan was encouraging her to eat mashed pumpkin, peas, and stew, but the flecks of orange and green on the faces of both the man and child indicated he had only been partially successful. Declan's wife, Moira, was buttoning up after feeding the baby.

"Welcome to Bedlam, Charlie," Declan said.

Moira rolled her eyes and handed Charlie the baby, who was his goddaughter. He patted her back until she burped, slopping a milky drool down his shoulder. Declan handed him a cloth without comment, while Moira went to the stove to retrieve a dish of rice pudding.

Patrick took up his spoon and licked his lips.

"No pudding for you, young man, until you eat your supper," his mother said. "You know the rules."

"Can't Uncle Charlie eat mine just this once?" Patrick asked. "Papa says Uncle Charlie's always hungry and when he's hungry, he'll eat the horse out from under you."

"Patrick! Your father was pulling your leg." Moira cast an apologetic grimace at Charlie and pushed Patrick's barely touched plate in front of him. "Just this once, and only because Uncle Charlie looks like he needs it more than you."

"For the record, I don't eat horses," Charlie said. Hunger overcame his reluctance to eat a child's supper, especially as Patrick was grinning as he sucked down a small helping of rice pudding. Nobody took the baby from him, so he tucked her in the crook of one arm – such a tiny bundle – and ate with the other hand. He bent down to inhale the sweet scent of a newborn baby just as the sweet little angel expelled gas and a noxious substance from her rear.

Moira put her pudding down half-eaten and took the baby from him. "In one end, out the other," she sighed. "Send the children to me once they've eaten, Declan, so you can talk to Charlie."

"My apologies for arriving unannounced when you're busy, Moira," Charlie said.

"Never anything but busy around here and you're always welcome."

Five minutes later, Declan showed him through to the sitting room and poured him an ale, before collapsing into a faded armchair with a groan. "Feels like I haven't had a decent night's sleep in six years. What can I do for you, Charlie? If it's parenting advice you're after, my only suggestion is to sleep in separate beds until you can afford to hire a nanny."

After the day he'd had, Charlie was ready to believe it. It was all too easy to see children as bundles of pure joy, but a dose of reality never hurt. The thought of a child being kidnapped or injured, or even running off unsupervised for a few minutes, was enough to turn his stomach. He couldn't begin to imagine how much worse he would feel if it was his own child.

When Charlie explained the situation and showed him the ransom note, Declan reacted with the expected combination of outrage and practicality. Declan agreed he would make the case his top priority, as long as Detective Inspector Wallace agreed. The first task would be to check Nathan Locke's alibi with both the sister and the railway staff at Port Chalmers, which was about ten miles away by train.

"It helps that the suspect is distinctive," Declan said. "Tall, blond, and handsome is sure to stand out. I'll also order a check of police files for any criminal with a history of kidnapping or extortion, and put word out amongst the beat constables to investigate any incidents involving crying babies. I'll ask them to check abandoned buildings, too, and put out a watch notice at the railway and port. Anything else?"

"Could you use your police powers to have a quiet word with Mr Barclay's manager at the Bank of New Zealand? Ask if he has been acting strangely, and see if you can find out how much is in the bank accounts of both Edward and Daisy Barclay. Edward says he hasn't the money to pay the ransom and Daisy appears to be reluctant to use her inheritance."

"That's odd. If my son was kidnapped, I'd be pawning every item of value and begging for a quid or two from everyone I know. If Barclay is a senior clerk at a bank, wouldn't he be able to arrange a loan or an advance on his pay in such extreme circumstances?"

"Good point, Declan. I don't need to say it to you, old friend, but urge the beat constables to be discreet in their inquiries. Even with your help, it'll be a miracle if we find Oliver before the deadline."

Declan picked up on his meaning straight away. "We'll have a plan in place by Friday noon to have plainclothes officers ready to watch the ransom drop and surrounds. Any idea where the exchange will take place?"

"My best guess would be somewhere near the north end of the city, around the church or Botanic Garden, but we should be ready for any possibility." Charlie rose and held out his hand. "Thanks, Declan. I know this is a large favour to ask."

Declan punched him lightly on the shoulder, which was still sticky with baby drool. "I may not get the big payday like you fancy-pants private detectives, but I want to see the little fellow back with his parents just as much as you. Good luck, Charlie, and thanks for trusting me. Why don't we meet here at noon tomorrow to exchange information? Moira will have a pot of soup simmering."

Charlie dispensed with the obligatory slap on the back and instead pulled Declan into a quick, manly embrace. "How can I thank you both?"

"Reckon me and the missus could do with decent sleep sometime soon, if you want to have the little troublemakers at your house for a night. I'd say it would be good practice for you, but I suspect it might put you off children forever."

"Consider it done. I can always get Grace to sedate them."

Little Red Book

Grace must have looked as weary as she felt when she arrived home, because Mrs Brown, their housekeeper, took one look at her and said she'd run a hot bath while Grace talked to Lily Stewart, who was waiting for her in the drawing room. Mrs Brown knew that in this house the investigation always came first.

Grace entered the drawing room with her nerves on edge. Lily Stewart was a dear friend and the wife of Charlie's business partner, Alistair Stewart, but she was also Charlie's aunt and would have heard about this morning's argument over taking the case. Most people who looked at Lily didn't see past her tiny stature and the Chinese features inherited from her father, but she was a tiger when it came to defending family.

"Lily, how lovely to see you."

Lily kissed her cheek. "Likewise, Grace. I won't keep you long because I know you will have had a gruelling day, but I wanted to stop by with the results of the cocoa analysis. It contained a significant amount of chloral hydrate, probably enough to knock out an average person, assuming the person drank it all. The cocoa and sugar would have disguised the taste."

"Ah, I thought that might be the case. Thank you for testing the sample so quickly. I know how busy you are." Lily was a herbalist with a growing skill in laboratory work, who also worked as a medical assistant at Lavender House when she wasn't out and about doing charitable work in the Chinese community.

"Alistair told me a baby had been kidnapped from his home," Lily said. "We both want you to know we will do everything we can to help, Grace. Such a shocking thing to have happened in our city."

"We may need extra hands when the ransom money is exchanged for the baby on Friday at noon, if we don't get him back before then."

"I'll let Alistair know." Lily seemed uncharacteristically hesitant. "Alistair said Charlie didn't want to take this case. To be honest, we thought he would have refused to let you join the investigation."

"Better to be helping than helpless," Grace replied. "There's no need for you and Alistair to worry, but I would like you to know that Charlie and I are looking to our future with hope, come what may."

Lily rushed to gather Grace into an embrace. "I'm so glad. It's not my place to interfere, but Charlie has been miserable lately because he fears you blame him."

Grace gaped at Lily for a long moment, wondering if she had misheard. "Why would I blame Charlie?"

"Charlie worries the issue lies with him, because our family line has not been blessed with many children, unlike yours. I can see this has come as a surprise to you, Grace. I truly hope I haven't added further upset by speaking so frankly."

Grace would have laughed if it hadn't been so serious. All this time, she had been worried that her husband blamed her for her inability to give him the child he so wanted, while he had been blaming himself. "Thank you, Lily. Honestly, you've been a great help."

When Lily left, Grace sank gratefully into the hot bath. By the time she'd worked through her thoughts and emotions, the water was cool and opaque with soap suds.

It wasn't until she had dried herself and put on her silk robe that Grace focused on the drugged cocoa. Unless she had drugged herself, Daisy Barclay was not to blame for sleeping through the kidnapping. That left Edward Barclay or Prudence Winslow as the most likely people to have given Daisy a knockout dose of chloral hydrate. Did that mean one or both of them had also taken Ollie?

107

Or did they have another reason for wanting Daisy to sleep soundly? Prudence Winslow presented herself as a strait-laced churchgoer, but it wasn't difficult to see she had committed the sin of coveting Daisy's husband. Likewise, Edward showed more regard for Prudence than his wife.

When Grace dragged her wrinkled body out of the bathroom, she found Blaze asleep on her blanket in the drawing room and another blanket spread over the sofa for Grace, complete with a plumped cushion against the armrest. Blessed be the housekeeper who anticipates one's every need. After the chaotic scrum of her childhood battling for food at a table with five hungry brothers, living under the tender care of Mrs Brown still felt like an extraordinary privilege.

Right on cue, Mrs Brown entered the room with a tray of fragrant food and a carafe of water. "Is Mr Penrose Pyke expected?"

"He'll be late. Thank you, Mrs Brown. I'm starving." Grace had given up trying to get Mrs Brown to use their first names. Their housekeeper was an indispensable part of their household, as she had been to Grace's great-aunt over many decades, but she had her standards.

Mrs Brown poured a large glass of water. "Any leads on the kidnapped baby, Mrs Penrose Pyke?"

"None that look promising at this early stage. It's going to be a challenging week." Grace hadn't spoken to Mrs Brown about their latest investigation, but nothing got past their housekeeper. In fact, she had often proved essential to their investigations. "No whispers below stairs?"

"Not on the subject of Oliver Barclay, although plenty of gossip I'll not waste your time with." Mrs Brown laid a linen napkin, starched stiff, across Grace's torso before putting down the tray so gently, not so much as a pea moved. "One or two leads for potential future business for the detective agency, which I'll keep a watch on."

"The Barclays have no housekeeper or maid, but I'm going to talk to their former housekeeper tomorrow. A Mrs Freya Marcus." Grace raised an eyebrow, needlessly, because their housekeeper picked up hints faster than a magnet picks up iron filings.

Indeed, Grace had to be careful about what she said, because incautious words, even mumbled under one's breath, led to action. A simple "I really must search for the old whatsit in the attic", for example, would have the contents of the attic turned upside down. On the plus side, Mrs Brown would simultaneously undertake a thorough cleaning of the attic whilst she searched, resulting in the reemergence of several useful items thought lost. She was a treasure beyond compare.

"Mrs Freya Marcus? I don't believe I have heard the name." Small pink dots flared in Mrs Brown's cheeks, a sign of mortification at having failed in her self-imposed task of knowing every servant, shopkeeper, delivery boy, and rumour in the city.

"She may be no more than a family friend who helped for a while, rather than a proper housekeeper," Grace said, before changing the subject. "Dinner smells divine, as always."

Mrs Brown took the hint and left her to eat. The very fact that she had served the meal on a tray in the drawing room, rather than at the dining table as decorum dictated, indicated that Mrs Brown understood Grace had had a tough day.

Grace settled her back against the cushion to eat. When she had scraped the plate down to the pattern, she pulled Daisy Barclay's little red book out of her medical bag, knowing she ought to be thinking about the kidnapping, but intrigued by Daisy's recommendation of the book. It wasn't mere curiosity. Daisy, who had been childless for five years before she read the book, had suffered symptoms that were all too familiar to Grace.

In fact, the book was only red under the pretty paper that had been attached to it to preserve the cover, as something treasured. Grace opened the book to see who the author was, but the woman's name looked foreign and meant nothing to her. The book was old and showed signs of significant use. She read on eagerly. The text was in English, but the slightly stilted wording suggested a translation.

Grace's excitement increased as she realised the listed symptoms matched her own with an eerie exactness. *Tiredness, even after a full night's sleep.* Tick, although Grace had always put that down to being constantly busy and thus having insufficient time to sleep.

Inability to put on weight, no matter how much food is consumed. With Charlie in the house, lack of food was not the problem, yet she was still thin. When people commented on it, Grace liked to say that some of us are born to be greyhounds, while others are born to be bulldogs or lapdogs. Quite often, the people who had the temerity to comment on her weight fell into the yapping, ankle-biter dog category, but Grace refrained from saying so to their faces. Her thoughts drifted to what type of dog Charlie would be. Blaze looked up from her blanket bed and woofed, as if she could read Grace's mind and was voting for Charlie to join the noble ranks of border collie. Intelligent, agile, faithful, adorable – Grace had to agree it was a good fit in terms of character.

She moved to the next symptom listed in the book. *A longer and weaker monthly cycle than normal.* Definitely, although she'd always thought that an advantage until now.

Irritability. Grace snorted. Am I really that irritable? But her response carried with it a ring of irritability even in her head. She could see she was going to have to make some changes, starting with saving her tetchiness for people who deserved it. There were certainly plenty of those in her life.

Grace kept reading, devouring words that seemed to have been written specifically for her. Daisy Barclay must have felt the same, because she had written notes and exclamation marks in the margins. *Yes, that's me!!* was the common theme.

A closer examination of the handwriting reassured Grace that the writing bore no similarity to the ransom note. The possibility of Daisy Barclay staging her son's kidnapping had occurred to her, but Daisy was far from the top of her suspect list because it would have made more sense for her to have run away with her baby. Besides, Daisy had been locked inside the room and in a deep sleep, so she could not have broken the outside seal on the window.

When Grace got to the suggested treatment, Daisy's notes were more extensive and included barbed comments such as *exactly the opposite of what the stupid doctor said!* Again, Grace felt the same. If this book was correct, she had been harming rather than helping herself. The book recommended a strict diet, eliminating seafood in particular, although eating river fish was encouraged. The list of foods to eliminate included dairy and bread, while the foods to strictly limit included sugar, alcohol, tea, and coffee. Grace groaned. All her favourite things, and most of the foods she had been encouraged to consume to increase her weight.

Grace almost gave up reading at the thought of life without bread and cheese. Besides, she was already up to her gullet in advice on how she needed to gain weight to match the maternal ideal of a rounded body and rosy cheeks. She had reached the point where she couldn't bear to look in a mirror anymore. Her body, which had merely seemed slim before, now seemed gaunt and unnatural. Ironically, Grace always received compliments on her lovely slim waist when she donned a fitted gown and ventured into society. Society's double standards for women were logically impossible, but it had never mattered to her until the many doctors she had talked to all agreed excessively thin women sometimes found their fertility was compromised.

She kept reading, because this book was different. It set out a sensible schedule for eight weeks on an elimination diet to test the effect on her own body, because every woman's reasons for infertility were unique. After the test period, she could gradually reintroduce restricted foods, while monitoring her symptoms. The book also offered positive suggestions, such as drinking lemon balm tea, eating oats instead of wheat, and substituting chicken for fish. Grace read about the importance of daily exercise and exposure to sunlight, especially in the morning and during winter, as well as suggested techniques to overcome negative thoughts and seek time for quiet reflection.

The avoidance of negative thoughts might be a stretch in the current circumstances, or indeed at any time in her busy life, but Grace felt buoyed by new hope and determination to try the regime. She had tried everything else, apart from the bogus remedies such as the cod liver oil and cold baths recommended by Daisy Barclay's doctor. One had to draw the line somewhere. At least this book seemed to speak to her condition like nothing else she had read.

Grace reached the end of the short book and saw that Daisy had scribbled notes on the blank end papers, noting her improvements over the eight weeks. When she flipped over to the inside back cover, she saw Daisy had filled the space with tall, elaborate, joyful letters: *I'm having a baby!!* The words were surrounded by flowers.

Daisy's utter joy sang from the page, leaving Grace with two overwhelming desires. The first was to commit herself to the same path. The second, and even stronger, desire was a fierce determination to rescue Ollie, because Daisy had been through so much to conceive him and she deserved better than to be terrified for the life of the son she cherished. Grace would barge her way into every house, shed, warehouse, and cave in the city if she had to.

The sound of a key turning in the front door lock interrupted her excessively ambitious plan. She expected the light dance of Charlie's footsteps down the hall, but heard shuffling feet and the thump of a cane. Great-Aunt Anne had arrived.

"Come in, Mrs Drummond," Grace called. "I'm in the drawing room."

When Anne entered a room, everyone noticed. Although she was in her mid-seventies, gaunt and stooped with age, her commanding presence could stop the most garrulous of self-important officials in mid-sentence. The women she helped at the Lavender House refuge and medical clinic revered her, her family adored her, but most other people were terrified of her. Grace modelled herself on Anne but had yet to reach the terrifying stage, although some of her medical colleagues might beg to differ.

Anne pierced her with a steely glare, which no longer had any effect on Grace. "Mrs Drummond, indeed. Since when did you stop calling me Auntie Anne?"

Grace rose to kiss her cheek. "Since you shocked Dunedin society by finally accepting one of Kenneth Drummond's many proposals. I thought the poor old dear would have a heart attack when you agreed. I hope he hasn't regretted it."

Anne had recently married again after several years of being a widow, and she had moved into her new husband's house. Grace and Charlie still lived in Anne's old home, where she had lived for most of her life with her first husband, Gordon Macmillan.

"Cheeky monkey," Anne grumbled.

"To what do I owe the honour of this visit, Auntie Anne?" Grace asked.

"Can't I visit my own house?" Anne brushed down the armchair that had been hers for decades. "There's dog hair on my chair. I've only been gone for three months, and the place has gone to rack and ruin."

Grace smiled. She was well used to her great-aunt's ways, knowing Anne would move mountains to help her when needed. "Blaze is shedding hair because she is pining for you."

Blaze perked up at the sound of her name and came over to pay homage to Anne by letting Anne pat her head. When their border collie had first arrived in Dunedin, there had been protracted negotiations with Anne, who was the top dog in the house, before Blaze and Anne had come to an understanding. To wit: no running under the feet of elderly ladies, no snoozing in Anne's favourite armchair, and no slobbering. Blaze had gradually wormed her way into favour, until most evenings had ended with Anne and Blaze curled up together in the armchair nearest the fire, both slobbering, but only slightly.

Not that Grace would admit it, but her great-aunt's absence had left a deep hole in her daily life, even though Anne and Kenneth Drummond lived close by. "I could use your advice, Auntie Anne."

"It's hard to think with a parched throat."

Sure enough, their housekeeper, Mrs Brown, chose that moment to appear with a trolley bearing a teapot, cups, and her famous ginger cake. "Nice to see you home, Mrs Macmillan. Oh, I mean Mrs Drummond."

"Jolly annoying isn't it, all this changing of names. Kenneth flatly refused to change his surname to Macmillan. Men can be so unreasonable. It comes from getting their own way all the time." Anne scooped up a slice of cake and licked her lips. "Mrs Brown, you are a culinary goddess. I do miss you, you know, but there are only so many changes a man will allow to his household, and Charlie wouldn't survive without your cooking."

"Always a pleasure to have a man with a hearty appetite under my care." Mrs Brown rattled the trolley away.

Anne raised the teacup to parched lips and followed it with a bite of gingery deliciousness. "Ah, as mouth-watering as ever. Aren't you eating, Grace?"

"I've just finished dinner." Grace still had a ginger cake sized hole in her stomach but resisted in deference to her vow to follow the guidance of the little red book. Lemon balm tea and carrot sticks didn't have the same appeal, but they would have to do for the next eight weeks.

"In fact, I am trying a new eating regime." Grace held out Daisy's book. "I've never heard of the author of the book or the methods she advocates, but our new client found the advice helped her. I know what you are thinking – that I ought not to be swayed by an unqualified quack out of desperation – but Daisy Barclay had the same symptoms and it worked for her."

"Desperation, Grace? I know you are eager for a child, but a year is still a drop in the ocean of your life, no matter what the so-called experts say."

"I know. It's just that I seem to be surrounded by babies. Lavender House is overflowing with new life, Molly is pregnant again, and Declan Kelly and his wife have had their third child. Charlie had a letter recently from his newly married friends, Hamish and Etta MacEwen, announcing their pregnancy. This time last year, Hamish and Etta hardly knew each other and already they have a child on the way."

"How does Charlie feel?" Anne asked.

"He longs for a child, although he is also stoic and unwavering in his support."

Anne didn't waste her breath on platitudes. "Tell me about the book."

Grace launched into a brief summary of the recommendations of the book, while Anne tapped her cane on the floor and murmured an occasional "mmm". "What do you think, Auntie Anne? Am I being foolish?"

"Actually, I believe there might be something in it. It reminds me of a woman I met on the voyage to New Zealand all those years ago. A lovely woman, but very weak and thin when we first met, to the point of finding it exhausting to walk. Your grandfather, the first Doctor Penrose, had come across a similar case and recommended she exclude bread from her diet. She was a different woman after that. It was a joy to witness her transformation before our eyes over the following weeks."

Grace had heard many stories about that epic voyage from England to New Zealand. Anne put her own lack of children down to her severe illness on the voyage, which had taken her to the edge of death. Every woman had her story, and no two stories were the same, just as The Book said. Grace cringed at the realisation the little red book had taken on capital letters in her mind, as if she was already thinking of it as gospel. As a trainee doctor, she ought to know better. "I don't suppose you know if the woman from the ship ever had children?"

"Six of the little blighters. You would remember her as a friend of your grandmother's in Wellington, Mrs Charlotte Templeton."

Grace had a vivid memory of Mrs Templeton at her grandmother's seventieth birthday party. Two elderly women, still as fun and lively as ever. "I do recall her. In fact, I went to school with several of her grandchildren. Thank you, Auntie Anne. I can always rely on you to bring me hope and good advice."

"Talk to Charlie, Grace. He needs to understand what you are going through. Talk to him about the fact that it is entirely normal for some women to pop out babies whether or not they want them, while others take years to conceive, for whatever reason. But don't hide from him the possibility that for some, like his Aunt Lily and me, it never happens. Lily and I have built wonderful lives, regardless. It is not the end of the world, but simply a chapter in your life story that you might not have expected."

"Daisy Barclay took several years to conceive, as do many other women. There's always hope. But you're right. I'm coming to accept that I can be around children in other ways, as a doctor, a friend, and an auntie."

Anne pulled her into an embrace. "Of course there is always hope. Grace, my dear, you are young, healthy, and loved. Let that be enough for now, for it is far more than most people have. In fact, be grateful you are not stuck at home with a swarm of snivelling brats under your feet." Anne released her and settled back into her chair. "Now, tell me about this kidnapping while I finish your share of this delicious cake. What can I do to help?"

"We've been told about a woman who has a particular fondness for babies, especially the kidnapped boy, Oliver Barclay. Her name is Aggie or Agatha Gemmel. Does the name mean anything to you?"

Anne closed her eyes and consulted her mental filing system of contacts, which encompassed a fair proportion of the city. Just when Grace thought she had fallen asleep, Anne's eyes opened, and she shook her head. "I don't recall anyone of that name."

"I could also use your help with checking for eight-month-old blond baby boys where they ought not be. Could you ask Miss Newland at Lavender House if the description matches any recent arrivals in case some deluded woman had taken the baby and sought shelter amongst the other women at the refuge?"

"I'll do it now. I'll pass the word discreetly around my contacts too."

"You're the best, Mrs Drummond. Or should that be Mrs Anne Godwin Macmillan Drummond in honour of your many past lives?"

"Cheeky monkey," Anne grumbled, as she pushed herself out of the armchair with her trusty walking stick. "There's no cause to disrespect your elders just because you're a married woman now." A wave of the stick in Grace's face, a cackling laugh, and she was gone.

Talking to Anne always left Grace with a warm glow inside and helped her to focus on what was important. Anne was right, Grace needed to count her blessings. She had a wonderful husband, friends and family she loved, a comfortable home, and she was a godmother to two lovely children. Her problems were trivial compared to what Daisy Barclay was going through right now. And Prudence Winslow, so desperate for marriage and children that she was blinded by the faults of the men around her. Or Mad Aggie, who had had a husband and child and suffered the tragedy of their loss. Not to mention poor Mrs Guthrie, living in a boarding house with four children in one room and about to lose even that.

Grace realised belatedly that she hadn't asked Anne if there was room at Lavender House for another desperate family, but that would have to wait until tomorrow. She wanted to have an early night so she could be up at dawn for a busy day. If only Charlie was home to hold her in his strong arms and tell her everything would end happily ever after.

Old Boots

Night had long since fallen when Charlie pushed open the gate to their home.

The utter silence, aside from the relentless tick of the hall clock, had him on tiptoes to avoid waking Grace. The shrivelled, lukewarm dinner in the oven still tasted fine, thanks to Mrs Brown's legendary culinary skills, and it filled a spot the child-sized portion of stew at the Kelly's house had not. After a cursory wash, he crept upstairs.

Grace must have heard him come in, because she had shuffled over to his side of the bed to warm it. She was nine-tenths asleep when he slid in beside her and wrapped his cold arms around her warm body. Bliss. To think a mere four years ago he was sleeping in draughty barracks under a too-thin blanket after a night shift separating brawling drunks and chasing pickpockets down seedy alleys.

"I love you," he whispered into her hair.

"Mm-hm."

"I hope you know you're all I will ever need to be happy, Grace. After today, I'm not sure babies are worth the heartbreak."

Grace turned over and held his head in her hands, kissing him gently to avoid the sharp bristles of a long day. "We'll find Ollie, my love."

He needed to hear it, even if he only half believed it. "One day gone already. Three and a half days until the ransom drop. We'd better get some sleep." Charlie didn't add that it would only get harder from here, as the hope of fresh leads died and the trail went cold. Besides, Grace was already curled against his chest, asleep.

On Tuesday morning, Charlie wolfed down a quick breakfast. He was delighted to see the old Grace back again, as if she had reached deep within herself and found a new purpose. She had risen early and was now briefing him on what she had found out yesterday and her plan for the day ahead, starting with Mad Aggie.

"Take Blaze with you, Grace, while I track down the Barclays' former housekeeper." His hand was reaching for the last piece of toast when he realised Grace had not had a single slice and was drinking a lemony concoction rather than her usual tea. "You'll fade away if you don't eat, my love."

"You have the toast, Charlie. I've already had breakfast." Grace paused, as if deciding whether to say something else. "I'll be eating a little differently for a while. Daisy had the same symptoms as me and was kind enough to lend me a book that helped her. No expectations, but worth a try."

He put down the toast and reached out to take her hand. "Whatever you want, as long as it's not electric shocks and ice baths." Charlie withdrew his hand and reached for the butter, because it was a shame to waste the toast, especially as a private detective never knew when his next meal might be. "Alistair agrees that the kidnapping is unlikely to have been the work of a criminal gang, but Declan is checking local criminals to be thorough." His hand hovered near his mouth, but his hunger had left him. "I don't mind admitting that I feel helpless. Even Alistair, with all his experience, has never been involved in a kidnapping for ransom. He warned me it might not end well."

"How do you mean?" Grace asked.

"It's not unknown for kidnappers to take the ransom and kill their victim. I'm not saying this to be cruel, but because you should know what we may have to face. Grace, I meant it when I said you don't have to be involved, especially now we can rely on the full resources of the police."

"Don't you want me on the team?"

"Of course I do, but not if it's going to cause you distress."

"Charlie, you need to know that I can still function as a normal human being, even if I can't conceive a child. Unless you cannot bear to be around me anymore." Grace gave him a look that demanded his honesty.

"Don't be absurd. I will love you until my last breath, no matter what. Unless you cannot bear to be with me. After all, it's my family who lacks children, while your family is abundantly fertile. Five brothers, two sisters, and uncountable cousins for you, and me an only child with not a single cousin I know of. It's only logical that the fault lies with me."

His wife nodded sagely, as if she'd expected him to say that. Had he been right to worry that she blamed him? Lily had advised him to talk to Grace, but he hadn't found a way to bring it up before now.

Grace dotted a line of kisses down his face and freshly shaved jaw. "Charlie Penrose Pyke, I can honestly say that thought never crossed my mind. Lack of vigour in the bedroom is not a problem you suffer from. Let's not worry about it anymore for the moment. Right now, we have more important matters to deal with."

"More important matters? Grace, I cross my hand over my heart and say there is nothing – nothing – more important to me than you."

Their tender moment of reconciliation was interrupted, inevitably, by a hammering on the front door. Grace gave him a last lingering kiss, returning moments later with a telegram. "From my mother. We might have to start paying her a commission."

Charlie swung his wife onto his lap so they could read the telegram together. "BIL V WORRIED SIL STOP BIL COMING SOUTH STOP."

"Delightfully cryptic. I hope it means something to you, Charlie."

"Edward Barclay mentioned they had no relatives in Dunedin, but Daisy had been very close to her sister before she died. I asked your mother to see if she could track down Daisy Barclay's brother-in-law to see if he had heard from her lately."

Grace reread the telegram. "The brother-in-law is very worried about his sister-in-law, Daisy. He's leaving Wellington to come to Dunedin, so he must be seriously concerned. Do you think my mother told him about Ollie being kidnapped or hinted at problems in the marriage?"

"Definitely not. I only told her to ask if Daisy had been in contact with him."

"He's not the only one who is worried about Daisy," Grace said. "Daisy excuses Edward's behaviour as a husband's natural concern for his wife, but her reactions suggest to me that she fears what he would do to her if she doesn't obey him."

"I agree, but Edward Barclay seems to think his behaviour is entirely warranted, as a traditional husband who feels it is his duty to protect and correct his wife. It's hardly uncommon, even in this age of women advocating for more rights. But I get an itchy feeling around my neck when I hear him talk about her."

"Itchy feeling?" Grace snorted. "He makes we want to slap some sense into him. Barclay is excessively controlling of his wife, ridiculously jealous of her talking to other men, and arrogant as well. Daisy feels he blames her for the kidnapping, and everything else that is not right in his own self-centred world. The worst of it is that I think she believes him and doubts herself. If I were Daisy, I would have walked out on him before they left Wellington. Did you know Edward wouldn't let Daisy return to see her sick sister before she died?"

Grace stopped to take a deep breath. "I'm so fortunate to have a husband like you. Forgive me if I do not say it more often, but you are everything to me, Charlie."

"As are you to me." Charlie leaned closer so he could kiss her forehead. "Although good fortune has nothing to do with it. You would have joined a nunnery before marrying a man like Edward Barclay."

121

Grace snorted again. "The nuns wouldn't have me either. What do we know about the brother-in-law?"

"According to Edward Barclay, he is a ne'er-do-well artist called James Montgomery. His motive for rushing down here to Daisy's aid might be entirely selfless, but I suppose he could stand to gain if he separated Daisy and her inheritance from her husband. He cannot have kidnapped Ollie because he was in Wellington, unless he paid someone else to do it. But why would he? If he did come to rescue his sister-in-law, he'd take both Daisy and Ollie."

"Legally, he'd have no right to separate Ollie from his father," Grace said. "Daisy knows she has to stay with Edward if she wants to see her son. Are you finished toying with that toast, Charlie? I'm eager to get to the Botanic Garden and talk to the people who might know Aunt Aggie."

Blaze, who was lying on the floor under Charlie's chair in the hope of bacon ends, jumped up and ran to fetch her leash. As an associate detective, the dog's enthusiasm was unbeatable.

"I'll come with you, at least until we establish that Mad Aggie isn't truly insane."

Grace suggested they stop at the church on the way to see if anyone remembered Edward Barclay dropping a pair of old boots in the charity box. The church hall was open but empty. The charity box sat unattended near the door, and thus readily accessible to anyone who wanted to help themselves.

Like all church halls, the place was a testament to the many activities undertaken by the parish. One corner housed a bookcase of children's Bible stories and a pile of cushions, presumably used for Sunday school. A makeshift stage at the front had been partially dismantled after a Christmas production, with cut-out pieces of wood painted as two sheep, a cow and a donkey still gathered around an empty manger. Two ancient bath chairs stood in another corner under a poster advertising free nursing care for the elderly on alternate Wednesdays.

"Can I help you?" said a voice behind them. The elderly lady had to look up at them awkwardly, because her curved spine was bent low over a walking stick.

"Good morning," Grace said. "We'd like to talk to the person in charge of the charity box, please."

"You're looking at her, young lady."

Charlie stepped forward and handed her his card. "We're investigating a break-in where the intruder wore an old pair of boots, similar to a pair we believe may have been donated to your charity box."

The old lady looked him up and down. "You'll be the detectives working for the Barclays, I suppose, despite your youth. Mind you, everyone looks young to me these days. Who brought the boots in, Mr Penrose Pyke?"

All hope of discreet inquiries now dashed, Charlie admitted the boots had belonged to Edward Barclay.

The old woman shook her head with painfully slow movements. "I don't recall any boots. We usually sort the box once a week, which means it is possible they were there, but were taken before we got around to sorting them. Folks in need are welcome to take items as needed, no questions asked. I hope it isn't vital evidence. We're all praying for the wee bairn."

"We're doing our best to find him," Grace said. "Thank you for your help."

"You might want to ask Mrs Agatha Gemmel. She was rostered on for sorting last week when I was laid low with my rheumatism."

"Do you know where Mrs Gemmel lives?"

"On Duke Street, near the gate to the Botanic Gardens. The white house with the Calvary crosses above the door. You can't miss it."

Mad Aggie

Grace parted company with Charlie at Duke Street, because time was short and she had convinced him that she could handle Mad Aggie on her own, while he searched for the housekeeper.

Agatha Gemmel's house was a sizable family home, showing the first signs of slipping down the slippery slope to disrepair. An overgrown hedge, vegetables unpicked and going to seed, a broken latch on the gate, a few flakes of peeling paint on the window frames. Grace wondered how long ago Aggie's husband had died and whether she lived alone inside this home, which was made to be filled with children and laughter.

She had imagined Aunt Aggie as a middle-aged woman who liked to spend her time looking out for young mothers after losing her own child in infancy, and her husband before that. However, the woman who answered the door under the Calvary crosses was probably in her late twenties, although her lack of vivacity made her seem older. She was encased in shades of black and grey from head to foot, with only the sparkle of a silver cross around her neck to break the uniformity. Grace mentally readjusted her assumptions to a more recent bereavement than she had supposed.

"I'm looking for Mrs Agatha Gemmel," Grace said, handing the woman a card.

The woman studied the card, before examining Grace. "Are you the wife of the detective looking for Ollie? Oliver Barclay, I mean. Who hired you? Daisy or the husband?"

"Daisy Barclay," Grace said firmly. "May I come in and talk to you?"

Aggie showed her through to the parlour, which was scrupulously dusted and tidied, but smelled of nothing in particular, indicating it was little used.

Grace sat on an overstuffed chair. "Daisy says you have been a good friend to her since she arrived in Dunedin. I gather she was quite unwell and didn't know anyone here."

The compliment earned her a smile. "Thin as a stick she was, though you'd hardly think it to see her now. I saw her sitting by herself in the Botanic Garden after church one Sunday and I said to myself, Aggie, you can't let that poor lost soul look so miserable. We used to chatter away together every Sunday after that and other days as well. I like to think I helped her."

"You did," Grace said. "Indeed, she credits you with her recovery after reading that little book you gave her."

"What book? Oh, you mean the book she found in her knitting bag. It wasn't me. I told her it must be her fairy godmother, and that seemed to please her. Daisy seems to think the book helped her to conceive a child, but it's not true. What happened to her after so many years of childlessness was nothing short of a miracle from God."

Grace hadn't failed to notice the cross on the mantlepiece, nor the needlework sampler on the wall, which read: *Jesus said to her, I am the resurrection and the life.* She wasn't sure how to ask the necessary questions about the kidnapping, so she went for an indirect approach. "Ollie's kidnapping has come as a terrible blow to Daisy, as you can imagine. We're asking for the help of family, friends, and people with connections to the local community. Anything you may have seen or heard that struck you as unusual. Questions about the Barclays or Oliver, for example."

"Believe me, Mrs Penrose Pyke, when I say that I would have come forward straight away if I knew anything relevant. Daisy Barclay is like a sister to me. She helped me too, you see, when my son passed on to heaven. After his death, I lost my way for a time, until Daisy assured me God had a higher purpose for me."

Grace wanted to know about the death of Aggie's son, but decided it would be better to request the details through official channels. Working for the police surgeon had its uses.

Aggie was still standing, which indicated she was as yet unsure of Grace's intentions. Grace regretted taking a seat without being asked, both because it had been impolite and because Aggie was on the tall side for a woman and held the back of the chair with what looked like a powerful grip. Not a woman to be underestimated, especially as her feet looked about the same size as the boot prints in the garden.

"I've just come from the church, Mrs Gemmel, where I was inquiring about a pair of worn men's boots of average size that may have been deposited in the charity box. It may seem an odd question, but it could be important. The elderly lady who directed me to your house suggested you might know, as you have been in charge of sorting the donated goods while she recovered from a bout of rheumatism."

At last, Aggie took a seat, apparently satisfied that Grace hadn't come to accuse her. "Oh, I see. The answer is no. I haven't seen any boots in the charity box for several weeks. To be honest, most donations are of items that are not practical for the people who need them. Flimsy shawls bought on a whim and hardly worn, for example, rather than sturdy working clothes."

"That's helpful to know. I understand how difficult this must be, Mrs Gemmel, and I do appreciate your help. There is one favour I would like to ask you. May I be permitted to bring my dog into your house? We are requesting this assistance from every household we speak to, because it is the quickest way to rule out places where Ollie might be staying. Blaze is a trained tracking dog."

Aggie drummed her long fingers on the armrest as she looked at Grace. "I'm not stupid, Mrs Penrose Pyke. I know some mothers call me Mad Aggie. Somebody has told you that I lost my child and thus jumped to the conclusion that I might be lunatic enough to steal another woman's baby, which I most certainly did not. And if you're wondering why I'm staying inside my home instead of going out searching like the rest of the church congregation, you should know that my life has become impossible since Ollie's

126

kidnapping. A malicious gossip opens her mouth and whispers my name and now every person I pass stares at me as if I am the devil incarnate."

Prudence Winslow, for one, had been quick to point the finger at Aggie and had been instrumental in spreading the gossip. Grace hoped her visit to Aggie would not add fuel to the fire. "I'm sorry to hear you do not feel safe in your own community, Mrs Gemmel, but allowing us to search your house would help to establish your innocence to those gossips."

Aggie stood up and went to the door. "Bring your dog in. I have nothing to hide. All I ask is that you treat my son's bedroom with the dignity it deserves, and don't judge me for keeping it as it was when he passed on."

"You have my word."

Grace called Blaze in. The collie made quick work of the parlour and hall but perked up as soon as she entered the larger sitting room. With nose quivering and tail extended, Blaze ran across to a knitting bag sitting on a side table. Grace glanced at Aggie, who looked puzzled rather than worried. Grace bent down to praise their clever canine, leaving Aggie to make the next move.

Aggie picked up the bag, her frown clearing instantly as she drew out a stuffed giraffe, which had the slight lop-sidedness of the set of animal toys Daisy had made for her son. "I must say, I am impressed by your dog. Ollie dropped this toy at the park the last time I saw Daisy. I picked it up and have been meaning to return it, but I haven't seen her since."

Grace held out her hand for the giraffe to return to Daisy. "How long ago was that?"

"About three weeks, from memory. I must admit, I have been worried about Daisy. Her husband can be quite … overbearing at times. I don't think she was happy." Aggie was still holding the giraffe. She handed it over when Grace showed no sign of withdrawing her hand, but not before clutching it to her heart. "Ollie is very dear to me. Such an adorable wee boy."

127

"Daisy will be grateful to have the giraffe back to give to Ollie when we find him," Grace said gently. "Getting back to the day the toy was lost, did you happen to see Daisy talking to a tall, blond gentleman?"

Aggie blushed. "As a matter of fact, I did. I was talking to another lady at the time, but I did note that Daisy was surprised to see him. Not an organised assignation, you understand, although they talked for some time. Daisy seemed very upset by the meeting and hurried away, leaving Ollie's beloved giraffe behind. Unfortunately, her so-called companion saw her too. More like a wardress, if you ask me, escorting poor Daisy like a prison guard and watching her every move with those covetous eyes of hers. That's why I have been worried about Daisy."

Grace was left with the impression that Aggie and Daisy were close and loyal friends, assuming that Aggie hadn't just been befriending Daisy to get access to her son. Finding the stuffed giraffe was a concern, but Aggie's explanation for having it was plausible. Even so, Grace wasn't about to leave the job half-finished. She sent Blaze on her way with a flick of her finger and watched as the collie circled around every open room at speed, with not a flicker of interest. Even though it was a sizable house, the search was over in seconds.

She called Blaze to heel for the last door, which she presumed was the deceased son's room. The door opened on well-oiled hinges. The nursery was a shrine – there was no other word that came close. Shelves stacked with baby paraphernalia, a box of brightly coloured toys, a cot neatly made up with pure white sheets and a soft blue blanket. Grace's heart broke to see it. On top of the dresser, a candle burned between a picture of Jesus on the cross and a framed quote from the Bible. *John 3:16: For God so loved the world that he gave his one and only Son, that whoever believes in him shall not perish but have eternal life.*

Blaze didn't move from her side, as if she too recognised the need for solemnity. Grace blinked back tears as she shut the door. Aggie stood behind her, head bowed.

There was nothing Grace could do but hold the grieving mother's two hands between her own and thank her for permission to come into her sanctuary. Grace's footsteps down the hallway to the front door echoed in the silence. Loneliness must have driven Aggie to visit the gardens and chat to the young mothers as if she was still one of them. In Daisy, it seemed, Aggie had found a way of redirecting her grief into helping another lost soul.

Grace stopped at the door as a crazy idea popped into her head. She spoke without thinking. "Mrs Gemmel, I know of a family who is desperate for a roof over their heads, if only for a few nights while they find themselves somewhere to live. Their names are Mr and Mrs Guthrie and they have four children aged between newborn and about seven years old. I don't know them well, but I believe they are decent folk who have fallen on hard times. I have no right to mention it, but I fear my visit to their room in a boarding house caused their tenancy to be terminated. The landlord didn't appreciate a dog on his premises."

It was like watching the sun rise after a bleak winter's day. Aggie made a show of thinking about it, but the answer was never in doubt. "I'd have to meet them, Mrs Penrose Pyke, but I do love to help a family in need."

Grace scribbled the address on the back of one of her cards. "Tell them I sent you. They have to be out by the end of tomorrow. You are under no obligation. I simply thought –"

"I know what you thought, and you're right. That I'm a lonely woman who needs a good cause to drag me out of my misery. I'm heartily sick of people treating me as either mad or pitiful."

"That's not –" Grace began, but she was swamped by an unexpected embrace.

"God bless you, Mrs Penrose Pyke. And don't hesitate to call again if I can do anything to help Daisy and Ollie."

"Thank you. And God bless you too, Mrs Gemmel."

Aggie bustled Grace out of the house. Her mind was clearly miles away already, no doubt making lists of what would be needed. Grace hoped she hadn't thrown the Guthrie family into the maw of madness, but she doubted Aggie was mad, and the Guthrie family probably wouldn't care anyway, as long as they were under one roof.

However, Grace wasn't entirely sure that Agatha Gemmel was as innocent as she seemed when it came to baby Ollie. The missing baby was not in her house, but the glow on Aggie's face whenever she mentioned his name had hardly been reassuring. And then there was the issue of the slightly unnerving shrine to her deceased son. Losing her own son had hit Aggie to the core of her being. Had Ollie been snatched to fill that aching void?

Grace headed towards the Botanic Garden, reassuring herself she had done the right thing for both parties. If nothing else, she would have an excuse to visit Mrs Guthrie to see how they were settling in. If Aggie had hidden Ollie elsewhere, her absences would not go unnoticed.

The Housekeeper

Sideways glances and giggles followed Charlie as he walked through the Dunedin Botanic Garden on a Tuesday morning without either a wife or a dog by his side. A lone man was clearly an object of interest and amusement. Charlie wondered if this was how Grace felt every time she walked into a roomful of male doctors, but decided it was far worse for her because it would be disapproval rather than amusement on many of the faces.

A group of lady cyclists watched him openly as he passed by. He suspected they would lose interest if they knew he was not an enthusiast of bicycles, which he considered a poor cousin to riding a horse. Cheaper to run, certainly, and available in an instant, but far less dignified. More to the point, he adored horses and despised metal monstrosities that hurt his rear end and refused to stay upright.

Charlie had heard about the women's bicycling group from Grace, who admired them for their determination to pursue their own paths in life. According to her, they were mainly women who pursued feminist and intellectual goals, or physical challenges, over the more usual female activities. All power to them, as far as Charlie was concerned. Many people were appalled by their radical clothes, which they called 'rational dress', but their detractors disparaged as unfeminine and scandalous. Personally, he was not opposed to a glimpse of leg, although he had struggled to contain his laughter on first spotting knickerbockers on a woman.

He doffed his hat to the foremost woman, who looked vaguely familiar. "Excuse me ..." he faltered as he tried to decide the right term to use: Ma'am, Miss, Citizen, Suffragist. "Excuse me, do you happen to know a lady by the name of Mrs Freya Marcus?"

"Depends on what you want with her, Detective Penrose."

"Art lessons, Miss Halbrook." Her reply helped him put a name to the face. Felicity Halbrook, notorious for her opium smoking salons, had provided an important piece of evidence in a previous case. He hadn't met her, but Grace had pointed her out once. She was not a person one could easily forget, nor a person who valued the company of men.

Felicity laughed a raucous, open-mouthed laugh – a laugh that was unapologetically joyful. "Art lessons? You're no more a budding artist than I am the Prince of Wales."

He bowed low. "Your highness."

Felicity hopped over the herbaceous border around the lawn the group was sitting on, making the jump effortlessly in her knickerbockers. "Grace said you were that rarest of beasts – a man worth marrying. I heard you helped collect signatures for the women's suffrage petition again last year."

"That was indeed my honour and pleasure." Charlie forged on, hoping he'd passed her test of acceptable male behaviour. "I'd like to talk to Mrs Marcus about an investigation. She is not a suspect, or no more than anyone else in Dunedin, but she knows the family who have been the victim of a dreadful crime. To be honest, Grace and I need all the help we can get."

"I don't know where Mrs Marcus lives, but she often paints in the garden on sunny days. She's been in the flower gardens recently. Tiny body, big personality, long plait of grey hair. We call her Madame Miniature. If you do want art lessons, she would be a wonderful teacher. Oh, and you might want to talk to Aggie Gemmel as well. Rumour has it that a few of the mothers who frequent the gardens believe she wants to take their babies. I heard one woman asking the Head Gardener to warn her off a few weeks ago. Mad Aggie, some call her, although she looks as sane as you or me."

Not much of a recommendation, given Felicity Halbrook's reputation for flamboyant clothes and outrageous behaviour.

"Thank you, Miss Halbrook. Grace is talking to the potential madwoman as we speak."

"You're a lucky man to have lured a woman like Grace Penrose into the outdated patriarchal straitjacket called marriage."

"I couldn't agree more at my luck, Miss Halbrook, although I like to think of our marriage as an equal and cooperative arrangement in which Grace has the last word." He said it to make her laugh again, which she did.

But her laugh stopped abruptly. "We're all hoping you find the little lad alive."

Charlie lifted his hat again, then hurried away, shaking his head over the unstoppable spread of news about the kidnapping. On the positive side, almost everyone would do their utmost to help.

Freya Marcus was right where Felicity Halbrook had suggested she might be, and as unmistakable as her description. The artist's easel was taller than she was, meaning all he saw as he approached was a swirl of bright shawl around an indigo skirt, and a pair of feet in shoes that could only be described as child-like. The idea of this woman wearing man-sized boots and breaking into a house was laughable. She'd need an entire week's worth of the *Otago Daily Times* to stuff the boots to stop her feet from sliding out.

Once around the side of the easel, she looked no more likely as a suspect. Apart from her diminutive size, Freya Marcus was at least sixty years old, if not older. A single plait of hair, more white than grey, reached down to her waist.

The painting propped on her easel was both a shock and a delight. "Oh! That's beautiful!" Charlie's words came out unbidden, and he was about to apologise for distracting her when she turned bright blue eyes on him and grinned. Charlie fought against an odd compulsion to hug her. Freya Marcus radiated the mischievous twinkle of the sort of favourite grandmother who let you stay up late while reading you fantastical stories. He recovered his poise and said, "My apologies for distracting you, but your painting is unlike anything I've ever seen."

"Perhaps you ought to visit more exhibitions, young man. Several of us are following France's lead in embracing Impressionism." Freya's vocabulary and pronunciation could almost pass for an educated native speaker of English, but for a persistent European accent and her unusually expressive use of her hands to emphasise her point.

"I've seen works by Petrus van der Velden and James Nairn, but, impressive as they are, they are nothing like this." Charlie waved a hand at the almost-finished painting, which was alive with vibrant colour and the very essence of the place, without depicting the scene in photographic detail. Up close, it looked like nothing more than splodges of paint, but from a distance, the splodges became a lively bustle of people amongst the summer flowers. "May I ask where you learned to paint?"

"I grew up in a small fishing village in Denmark and married a young man with his eyes on the horizon. After a successful career at sea, he was offered the command of a merchant ship out of Le Havre in France. With our children at school or out making their way in the world, I was fortunate to be able to immerse myself in the new impressionist movement of painting. It was … exhilarating."

"I can see that. How did you come to move to the far side of the globe, Mrs Marcus?" Charlie knew he ought to be asking more pertinent questions, but the artist's worldliness and talent fascinated him. She reminded him a little of Grace, pursuing her passion against the tide of conformity.

"Mrs Marcus makes me sound ancient, young man. Do call me Freya. Everyone else does. As for how we came to be here, we visited family and never left. My son came first, as crew on one of the first steamers. He married here and encouraged his siblings to come. I loved my life in France, but painting can be done anywhere and the thought of missing my grandchildren's lives was too appalling to contemplate. I'm a widow now, so I need my children around me all the more. Are you an artist too?"

"I sketch in an amateur way," Charlie said, "but I have never tried painting. Is that Daisy Barclay on the bench seat next to the baby carriage, Mrs Marcus ... Freya?"

"It is." Her arms had crossed her narrow chest. She might as well have asked if he was friend or foe.

"I'm acquainted with Daisy Barclay, but only because the Barclays have hired my services to find her missing son. I presume you know Ollie has been kidnapped?" He offered a card. "Charlie Penrose Pyke. I have been hoping to speak with you, Freya."

"I know who you are, Mr Penrose Pyke. A tall, dark-haired, young detective asking questions of an insignificant old lady does rather give you away. What I want to know is, who are you working for – Daisy or her husband?"

"I'm working for Oliver Barclay." When this didn't satisfy her, he said, "but I confess my sympathies lie mostly with Daisy Barclay, although both parents deserve my utmost efforts. They both love Ollie, and that is enough for me."

Freya nodded. "Ask me whatever you wish. I will choose how I answer."

"First, may I ask about your painting? I couldn't help but notice the darker tangle of bushes looming over Daisy Barclay, which stands out from an otherwise joyful scene."

Freya cleaned her brush and closed her paintbox, before retreating to a nearby bench seat in the shade, where she used her floppy straw hat to fan her face. Sitting back on the seat, her feet barely touched the ground. Only then did she speak again. "You're the first person to notice the darkness, Charlie. In fact, I'm not sure I was aware of it myself until you pointed it out. I paint from the heart rather than simply transferring what I see to the canvas. In this modern age, we have cameras to record the physical, but only paintings can capture the essence. I must have been in a gloomy mood that day. I will paint over it."

A gloomy mood? Charlie was more inclined to believe the darkness around Daisy expressed Freya's concern for her former employer. "I hope you will forgive me for asking, but why are you painting when the beloved baby of a friend has been kidnapped?"

Freya's smile told him she was amused rather than offended. "Perhaps you ought to have watched me before you talked to me. I have been walking the gardens every ten minutes or so, talking to anyone I see and recording who is present – and who is not. I am a member of the local congregation, so I know they are busy knocking on doors and talking to people who know the Barclays. It seemed to me that nobody was taking account of Daisy's love of the Botanic Garden and the acquaintances she has made here, and thus I assigned myself to the task. Unfortunately, with no results. The only people missing amongst the usual garden visitors are a woman called Aggie and a few perfectly ordinary women who come irregularly. Nobody has seen Ollie or any baby fitting his description or heard any unexpected baby crying in the area."

"I retract my question, with apologies. If you ever want a job as a detective, I'd hire you in an instant."

Freya beamed at the praise, but only for a moment. "Shall we move on to more important matters, Charlie?"

To Charlie, the conversation was beginning to feel like a consultation with a fellow detective rather than the interview of a potential suspect, which freed him to get to the heart of the issue. "I'll be honest with you, Freya. The relationships in and around the Barclay household concern me. I don't believe Ollie was kidnapped by a stranger for the ransom alone. As Daisy's housekeeper for much of the past two years, you know the household better than anyone."

"It's true I know Daisy, or I did until five weeks ago. However, my work as a housekeeper only took me to the Barclays' house for a few hours during the day. I hardly knew Daisy's husband, because I always arrived after Mr Barclay had left for work and left well before he returned. My job ended rather abruptly soon after the companion moved in, so I cannot claim a close acquaintance with her either. Nor would I wish to."

"I would value your views as Daisy's close friend."

"The views of a foolish old woman who sits around chattering about nothing all day rather than doing her job?" Freya had an unexpected gift for mimicry. It could almost have been Edward Barclay speaking.

"Perhaps if Edward Barclay knew the older women I have in my life, he would have understood the value of wisdom and true friendship, rather than worrying about a trace of dust on the mantelpiece."

Freya's laugh was the tinkle of crystal meeting crystal. "Perhaps Edward Barclay understood all too well the relationship between me and Daisy. Once Miss Prudence Winslow was foisted upon us, the end was inevitable."

"Daisy misses you. My wife, Grace, who works with me, said Daisy was disappointed you hadn't visited since you were dismissed."

The lightness vanished from Freya like a candle being snuffed. "You can tell Daisy that it was not by choice. Edward Barclay made it very clear I had to stay away for Daisy's sake. His words were sugared with concern for his wife's delicate state, but I know him well enough to understand his words were a threat. You're no fool, Charlie Penrose Pyke. I suspect you already know that Edward Barclay is a master at creating the impression of caring for his wife, while keeping his cruelty behind closed doors. If Daisy puts a foot out of place, if she so much as glances in another man's direction, he'll make sure she regrets it."

"Physical abuse?" Charlie asked, the words acid on his tongue.

"Amongst other punishments, such as locking her in her room without supper like an errant child or banning her from going out. But yes, his favourite torment was pinching her arm underneath the sleeve where it wouldn't show. I've seen the bruises, and they were not trivial. In fact, I have recorded each instance in a logbook, in case Daisy should ever need an independent record as proof of abuse. To be honest, it was the reason I agreed to be her housekeeper, because I sensed an unhappiness in her that compelled me to help. I am the mother of four lovely children and more grandchildren than I can count, but one never loses that protective instinct a mother has from the day they discover there is a new life growing within them."

While Charlie wasn't entirely surprised by the abuse, the stark truth sickened him. "Did you encourage Daisy to go to the police or seek a divorce?"

"That was a choice only Daisy could make after weighing up the risks. I made sure she knew she had many options open to her to remove herself from her husband's completely unacceptable behaviour. She knew she could move in with me, even if she was unwilling to inform the authorities, but Daisy said she had made her marriage vows and would not waver from them over a few bruises. Like many women in her position, she came to blame herself for being an imperfect wife."

"No doubt helped along by her husband constantly listing her failings." Charlie knew it was a common theme amongst the women Grace helped at the Lavender House refuge.

"Exactly so. Once Daisy had Ollie, she had no choice but to stay, in her own mind at least. Besides, she knew her husband could simply claim she was clumsy, and the bruises came from walking into a door. He was careful not to hurt her too much. Just enough to control her."

Even without resorting to lies about clumsiness, Edward Barclay was within his rights to discipline his wife. No judge would condemn him, especially if he claimed his wife was disobedient or unfaithful. And nothing short of the most severe forms of abuse would convince a judge to award custody of a man's much-loved son and heir to the mother.

Charlie wanted to know if Freya knew about Nathan Locke, who had supposedly only seen Daisy after Freya had left her housekeeping position. "Did Daisy give her husband cause to be jealous? I'm thinking particularly of two men, a former bank colleague of Edward's, Nathan Locke, and the churchwarden, Simeon Frobisher."

"I don't know the first man," Freya said, "but Daisy is an attractive woman who draws men's attention merely by entering a room. I do know Simeon Frobisher. Edward Barclay had cause for concern about his behaviour, but not Daisy's response. Have you met Simeon?"

"Briefly." Charlie recalled Grace's instinctive step backwards when the man leaned towards her, but all he had seen was an awkward but earnest man of the church.

"Simeon Frobisher, who is the choirmaster at the local church, is a gifted teacher of music and singing. A good Christian man and a hard worker, but also rather childlike in his eagerness and lacking an awareness of acceptable behaviour. If he admires a woman, he stands too close, for example. With Daisy, Simeon was captivated from the moment he heard her voice. His angel, he called her more than once in front of other people. Daisy told me that Simeon left pressed flowers in her hymnbook and hid song sheets in her knitting bag to encourage her interest in music. For a single girl, it might have been charming, but for a married woman it was recklessly inappropriate, especially when her husband is the jealous type. Fortunately, Daisy found the unwanted gifts before Edward saw them. Naturally, she told Simeon to desist. In fact, she left the choir, thus sacrificing another of her few pleasures because of a man's inconsiderate actions."

While Charlie didn't condone Simeon's actions, he did understand that a man who admired a woman often left common sense at the door in his desire to please her. But not so blatantly, and never to a married woman. Edward Barclay had good reason to be angry at Simeon Frobisher's attentions to his wife. Charlie would certainly have had stern words with anyone who was that forward with his wife, in the unlikely event that Grace hadn't dealt with the matter first. The critical difference, Charlie hoped, was that he wouldn't have taken his anger out on Grace. Although he conceded it might be different if she had encouraged the attentions.

"Did Edward Barclay know of Simeon's attentions to his wife?"

"*Everyone* knew, or at least they did after Edward found out and yelled at Simeon in front of the entire congregation. Simeon was fool enough to ask why Daisy wasn't in the choir that day, and that he hoped his offer of private singing lessons hadn't upset her. Honestly, I wonder about Simeon's ability to comprehend basic human feelings at all sometimes. It never occurred to him that Daisy wouldn't have told her husband about the offer of private lessons."

"Edward must have been furious when he found out," Charlie said.

"The minister had to intervene to prevent it from coming to blows. Simeon was mortified at being attacked in front of the parishioners who mean the world to him, but I think he never quite understood what he had done wrong." Freya's eyes glistened with tears, which she swiped away with a paint-splattered hand. "Daisy had a burn on her hand the next morning. She said she had been careless around the stove."

Charlie closed his eyes and counted to twenty. One man too insensitive, the other too sensitive. A recipe for disaster, and Daisy paid the price. Charlie was beginning to see that Simeon had strong reasons to hate Edward Barclay, and perhaps even Daisy too, for being the cause of his disgrace. As the churchwarden, his reputation as a moral man would be vital to his position. Simeon had kept his position, suggesting the sympathy of the church lay with him rather than Edward.

"If the disagreement almost came to blows, surely Edward would have left the choir." It didn't make sense to Charlie, because he knew Daisy's solo walks on a Sunday were only possible because Edward was at choir practice.

"Edward Barclay has the hide of an elephant. Daisy left the choir at the first hint of Simeon's professional interest in her, but Edward wasn't about to be forced out of the choir when he felt himself to be in the right. He tried to get Simeon fired as the choirmaster, of course, but Simeon has been valued part of the parish his whole life. The local folks understood he meant no harm in encouraging Daisy's singing, because to hear her sing was pure joy. To a choirmaster, she was a gift from heaven. Simeon was drawn to Daisy like sailors to the Sirens of Greek myth."

Charlie wished he could hear her sing. A sweet face, blonde curls, and the voice of an angel. No wonder the choirmaster let his enthusiasm overcome common sense. "Am I right in thinking Simeon Frobisher has switched his attentions to Prudence Winslow?"

"Switched *back*," Freya said. "Simeon Frobisher and Prudence Winslow grew up together. When Simeon was appointed as churchwarden, he asked Mr Winslow for Prudence's hand in marriage, but her father refused because he didn't think Simeon's prospects were sufficient for his daughter. Prudence doesn't have a fraction of Daisy's attractiveness, but her family was well to do and Simeon was as poor as a church mouse. A shame, as they were well matched. All the gossiping ladies of the parish hope Prudence will accept him now that she is older and still unmarried, because it would be in everyone's best interests to have Prudence Winslow out of the Barclay house."

Which confirmed Charlie's impression that the tangled relationships between Edward, Daisy and Prudence were causing problems. It seemed there wasn't much that passed beneath the notice of the ladies of the parish. Except the two pieces of the puzzle vital to the investigation – the identity of the kidnapper and the location of the missing baby. So far, each person interviewed had nominated a most likely suspect, but none had suggested the same person, and not a trace of baby Ollie had been found.

"Do you have any suspicions about who took Ollie, Freya?"

"None at all, but I wouldn't be surprised if the culprit or culprits share a table with Daisy Barclay." Freya pressed wrinkled, paint-splotched fingers against his hand. "Tell Daisy she only needs to get a message to me and I will be there for her. That girl has the makings of a fine artist. She's a wonderful mother and friend too, if only she could be convinced to believe it. You are seeing her at her worst, Charlie. When she is away from her husband, she is a joy to be with."

"Daisy will be grateful to have your support, Freya." He rose and tipped his hat to her, feeling a lingering tingling on the back of his hand as if he had been touched by magic. "I am grateful for your perceptive comments. I only wish I had talked to you sooner."

"I keep a spare key under the carved troll around the rear of my cottage." Freya gave him a mischievous grin, reminding him of the pixies of folklore. "Just in case you had me down as a fiendish kidnapper of innocent babes." She gave him the address, not far from the Botanic Garden, and went back to her easel with a swish of her colourful shawl.

Charlie almost wished she was the kidnapper, partly because she would be a worthy opponent, and partly because Ollie would be in the best of company. Maybe he should take some time away from work and learn to paint, he thought, as he watched her take up her brush again.

He made a quick circuit of the main gardens before heading to Freya's cottage, just in case her jest was a double bluff. The cottage comprised three small rooms with barely room to swing an easel amongst the furniture and stacks of canvases facing every free wall. He didn't bother to go inside, as there was nobody at home and nowhere to hide a baby. Besides, Freya would not have spent the morning painting and snooping in the gardens if she had an eight-month-old infant under her care. But he did check that the key was under an ugly creature in the back garden, made less fearsome by decades of moss and tiny flowers springing from his troll feet.

Charlie glanced at his pocket watch, which told him it was time to meet with Declan Kelly and enjoy a bowl of Moira Kelly's excellent soup.

Suspect Soup

Grace stirred the hearty soup Moira Kelly had prepared for them, while Moira cut the loaf of bread Grace had bought as their contribution to the meal. The two older Kelly children were unnaturally quiet as they sat at the table, slurping their portions of soup and eyeing up the stack of currant buns Grace had added to the bakery order. Their mother had warned them the buns would only go to children who behaved themselves during an important meeting.

Moira returned the bread knife to a high shelf out of reach of little hands. "I wish I'd known that a currant bun was enough to get a little peace in the house," she whispered to Grace.

Outside the kitchen window, Blaze dropped the soup bone she was gnawing and fled down the road with her tail madly wagging. A minute later, Grace heard the approaching sound of Charlie and Blaze sharing their barks and words of mutual devotion. Charlie came inside, greeted Moira, dotted a kiss on Grace's cheek, and stuck his nose over the soup pot, sniffing deeply.

She waved the wooden spoon at him. "Honestly, husband, you lavish ten times more affection on your dog than your wife."

"Is that so?" Charlie's arms slid around her waist and his lips went to her earlobe. "Would you like me to scratch you behind the ears and command you to sit outside with a bone while I devour this delicious repast?"

Moira smiled as she laid the table. "Honestly, Charlie, you're as bad as Declan with his little jokes."

Grace rolled her eyes, but didn't push him away. As the investigation drew on, she found she needed his embrace to keep her from collapsing under the weight of her fears. "You seem inordinately cheerful, Charlie. Please tell me Freya had the key to this mystery. Freya Marcus is the Barclays' former housekeeper," Grace added for Moira's benefit.

"She's as lively and clever as a pixie," Charlie said, "as well as a wonderful artist and promising detective. I learned a great deal about the players in this drama. Freya doesn't know who took Ollie, although she has good reasons for mistrusting Edward Barclay and disliking Daisy's so-called companion, Prudence Winslow. But I also learned that Simeon Frobisher has cause to hate Barclay, who humiliated him in front of the church congregation."

"Which means we're going around in a circle," Grace said, "because Prudence is sure Aggie is the kidnapper and Aggie thinks it is Prudence. Aggie is in hiding because she has been so openly accused of the crime, but Blaze found no trace of Ollie at her house, except for his toy giraffe. Aggie said she picked it up after Daisy dropped it in the Botanic Garden while meeting Mr Locke."

The front door opened, followed by the distinctive tread of a policeman's boots down the hall.

Charlie continued to gaze into the swirling soup as if mesmerised by it. "Edward suspects Nathan Locke, but he also doubts his wife's loyalty and dislikes Freya, while Daisy isn't saying who she suspects, although I'd wager she worries about both Prudence and her husband. It's a little like this soup, isn't it? The ingredients are there, all mixed up together, but with no clear pattern emerging as the accusations swirl. And, unlike most of our investigations, time is strictly limited."

"We can only hope the Barclays have the ransom money ready by Friday," Grace said.

"I believe that is my cue," Detective Sergeant Declan Kelly said from the doorway. His two older children ran to him, grabbing a leg each, while Declan made a show of struggling to move across the room under their dangling, giggling weight.

Moira gave the children a currant bun each and told them to play outside, while Grace handed around bowls of soup and plates of bread. The bowls were barely on the table before the two men started scooping up the soup as if they hadn't seen food in a week.

Grace caught Moira's eye and received an eye-roll of recognition. "It's not a race, gentlemen." When they ignored her, Grace added, "your cue, I believe, Detective Sergeant Kelly."

Declan put his spoon down reluctantly. "First the bad news. Nathan Locke's alibi is almost unbreakable for the night of the kidnapping, and his sister has no knowledge of Oliver."

"Almost unbreakable?"

"He was definitely at his sister's house in Port Chalmers. The family had neighbours over for supper and they stayed late. Nathan Locke was seen by the railway staff early the next morning, boarding the first train to Dunedin. He's known there, because he leaves by the same train every Monday morning, after arriving on Sunday to visit his sister. His sister does his laundry, including every item of clothing he has, except his Sunday best, which he leaves with her for the next visit. Unless he borrowed a fast and fearless horse and rode through the early hours to Dunedin and back with the baby, all without rumpling his best clothes, Nathan Locke is not our man."

Charlie stopped slurping long enough to let out a grunt. "Any word from the beat constables?"

"Not a peep, Charlie. It's as if every hardened criminal in Dunedin has taken a summer break from their wicked ways. No reports of crying babies or anything else suspicious either."

"Johnny tracked me down after I left Aggie," Grace said. "He and his lads have talked to their contacts on the wilder edges of society but come up with nothing. Johnny said the lad watching the Barclays' house reported nothing of significance either. Prudence left the house again at an early hour, while both the Barclays have remained at home, as we requested. There's been no message specifying the ransom drop location."

"*Somebody* must be looking after Ollie," Charlie said. He left a fractional pause, which Grace interpreted as her husband mentally adding, *if he is still alive.* Charlie flicked a glance at her and continued. "Freya, the former housekeeper, hasn't got him, and neither has Aggie. The Barclays have hardly left the house, and Nathan Locke is no longer a plausible suspect. Of the people we have considered so far, that only leaves two people unaccounted for: Prudence, Daisy's unwanted companion, and the choirmaster, Simeon Frobisher. Of course, we've hardly begun to look at other suspects and motives, so Ollie could be anywhere."

"Or with a trusted friend of any of the current suspects," Grace said.

"Or paid conspirators," Declan added.

Moira took her seat at last. "If Edward Barclay or the companion took Ollie, why would they bother to break in through the window?"

"For the same reason the ransom note was left," Charlie said. "To make Oliver's disappearance look like a kidnapping for ransom rather than a child abduction. I'd very much like to know where Miss Prudence Winslow has been spending her days, because she is out from dawn to dusk."

"I know where she was for part of the morning," Declan said, grinning with the relish of a gossip about to share a tasty morsel of news.

Spoons hovered in midair while they waited for him to go on.

"Edward Barclay's manager at the Bank of New Zealand was far more helpful than I expected once I explained the urgency of the situation, probably because he has children of his own. He provided me with information on the bank accounts of both the Barclays and Miss Winslow. Edward Barclay has no more than a few pounds to his name, Daisy has almost twenty pounds in her account, and Prudence Winslow withdrew the sum of two hundred pounds this morning, despite the teller advising her against walking around the city with so much cash."

"Very interesting indeed," Charlie said. "It doesn't particularly surprise me that Edward convinced Prudence to lend him the ransom money, especially as his wife was unwilling to provide it. And now we know why, if Daisy has less than twenty pounds left of her inheritance. I wonder where the rest went?"

"Mrs Barclay took the bulk of her considerable funds from the bank in a single withdrawal early last year," Declan said. "Without telling her husband, it would seem. No wonder she is reluctant to discuss the ransom with him."

"I will ask her next time I see her," Grace said. "The odd thing to my mind is why a senior clerk at a bank in his late thirties only has a few pounds to his name. In his position, I was sure Edward would be able to raise the money from the bank as a short-term loan, even if he didn't have cash on hand."

Declan leaned forward with a gleam in his eyes as he laid down his final ace. "Ah, now, that might have a little something to do with the fact that Edward Barclay was dismissed from his position at the bank last week."

Soup dripped from Charlie's spoon onto the table. "Don't keep us in suspense, Declan. Why was he dismissed?"

"The Dunedin branch of the bank received a letter from the Wellington head office notifying them that Edward Barclay had lied about a theft two years ago. The manager I spoke to gave me the impression that they were not sorry to see him go. Edward Barclay was not well liked amongst his peers and less so amongst the junior staff I talked to on the way out. His boss also showed no surprise that he had so little in his bank account, which rather suggests that Edward Barclay was known to be living beyond his means. And we all know that desperation for money is a powerful motive."

"Edward never admitted to me, or to his wife, that he had been fired. I suppose the humiliation would be too much for a man who has such a fine opinion of himself." Charlie reached over to punch his friend on the shoulder. "Not a bad morning's work for a flat-footed copper."

Declan parried the blow. "Worth a couple of nights of child-minding, I reckon, if a lowly drawing-room detective is tough enough to cope."

"A couple of little children? How hard can it be?" Charlie ignored Declan and Moira's snorts of laughter. "If Edward is out of work and broke, he might have viewed Daisy's inheritance as his last hope. All the more reason to wonder if he staged the kidnapping to force his wife to hand over her money."

Grace pushed her bowl away, unable to stomach another mouthful. "Daisy is going to be in serious trouble if Edward finds out that she wrote a letter of support for Nathan Locke. I doubt she realises her letter has indirectly cost her husband his job, since Edward hasn't admitted he is no longer employed. We cannot let Edward find out about Daisy's role in his downfall. In fact, I wonder if we should find Daisy a safe place to stay."

"I'm sure Edward doesn't know yet," Charlie said. "Taking Daisy away now might be more suspicious than leaving her at home, at least until the kidnapping is resolved. However, it might be best if we keep a watch over Daisy tonight. Johnny's boys could use a break."

Grace nodded, but her mind churned with Declan's revelations. "This kidnapping is very much in Edward's favour. If Daisy still had her money, she would have paid it over in a heartbeat, giving Edward the money and the freedom to divorce her and marry another woman with a tempting inheritance. Even now, he gets Prudence's money, without having to divorce Daisy and marry Prudence. And he gets to keep his precious son. I'm only surprised he didn't set up the kidnapping to implicate Daisy. Perhaps he never thought about the marks in the dirt left by his boots, which presumably never made it to the charity box."

"We're not sure the boots are his, Grace."

"You only have to look at the way he walks to see he must wear out the inside edge of the tread," Grace replied, "like the prints in the garden. His knees will give out in another thirty years if he does nothing about it."

"I agree that the weight of evidence is beginning to point at Edward," Charlie said, "but he would have to be an extraordinary actor to be so convincing in his role of the grieving father. The man is so arrogant, I suspect he'd struggle to conceal his delight at fooling us all. And he's barely left the house, which means he must have a trusted accomplice to look after Oliver. We need to talk to Prudence Winslow again urgently. Simeon Frobisher, too, because he has two reasons to hate Edward Barclay: the humiliation over the choir incident and Edward's dishonourable intentions towards Prudence, who Simeon may see as his intended wife."

Moira gathered up the bowls. "If I was Mrs Daisy Barclay, I would run a mile from her odious husband. Could she not have arranged for her child to be moved out of reach of her husband, while she prepares to leave or divorce him? Might she have taken her inheritance and moved it to another bank to be further beyond his grasp?"

"Much as I like Daisy," Grace said, "I think Moira makes an excellent point. Fear for her child's safety can drive even the sweetest woman to desperate measures."

"Freya confirmed that Edward Barclay is physically abusive," Charlie said, "but Daisy couldn't risk leaving him because she would lose custody of her child. If she arranged for an accomplice to take Ollie and leave the ransom note, then she could have taken the chloral hydrate to give herself an alibi."

"Clever, but also highly risky," Grace said. "Edward strikes me as the type of man who would stop at nothing to hunt her down to get his son back."

The soup shrunk to a lead weight in her stomach as an overwhelming fear engulfed her. A fear that the worst was yet to come.

The choirmaster

After taking their leave of the Kelly family, the world seemed a more ominous place. Doubly so, because dark clouds had rolled in while they were eating, threatening rain. The clouds hung so low over the high hills around Dunedin that Charlie was sure it would already be raining in the headwaters. Not a night to be out keeping watch on the Barclay house. Charlie wondered, as he often did at such times, whether he could cope with working in an ordinary job, but the thought was fleeting. There really was no contest between detective work and doing the same boring work every day until either his body or his mind wore out.

Charlie had insisted Grace go home, because she looked drained by the strain of the investigation and he needed her to stay awake all night, keeping an eye on Daisy. He doubted anything would come from his investigations this afternoon but still clung to the hope that tonight would be the night the kidnapper delivered the ransom instructions. If so, he would be waiting. That is, if the ransom drop was still part of the plan and the kidnapper did not already live in the house. Too many ifs for his liking.

Once Charlie talked to Prudence and Simeon, he resolved to go home and join Grace in taking a nap. After all, he couldn't leave his wife with the feeling she was less important than his dog, even if it had been said in jest.

Fortunately, Simeon Frobisher was easy to find. Charlie went to the church, and there he was, sitting at a trestle table. He was bent over an unfurled map of the local neighbourhood, peering at it with spectacles perched on his nose and protruding teeth pinning his lower lip. All the awkwardness Charlie had seen in him at the gardens yesterday had vanished, as he coordinated the house-to-house search. The choirmaster might be as poor as a church mouse and not blessed with the skill of diplomacy, but he was dedicated to his work and very well organised.

As each new volunteer group of searchers arrived, Simeon took their list of houses, ran his finger down it for any suspicious activity, and then crossed the houses off the map, which was already a sea of red crosses. The police could never have mounted an operation of this scale with the number of men they had to spare. But here, every available person in the parish had been mobilised. If there was ever a war, Simeon Frobisher and his ilk would be vital.

Charlie watched as an elderly man hobbled up at tortoise speed using a walking cane and put down a list of six houses, which was probably all the old fellow could manage. Behind him, a giggling contingent of children reported no sightings of a blond baby in any of the local play areas and parks. Then an efficient-looking young lady approached and handed over a list of boarding houses, homes for unmarried mothers, and similar institutions. She departed again with the speed of a woman on a mission. All very impressive.

Simeon glanced up to see who was next. The hall had emptied, so Charlie stepped forward.

"List?" Simeon said, holding out his hand. He took a second look. "Oh. You're the detective fellow, aren't you? Mr, ah …"

"Charlie Penrose Pyke. You're doing a splendid job, Mr Frobisher."

Simeon blushed. "Thank you, although I would be a great deal happier if I had something to report to you. To be honest, I fear the boy could be well beyond our reach by now. In a day and a half, Oliver could have been taken hundreds of miles away."

"Let's hope not," Charlie replied. "I find it especially commendable that you have dedicated your organisational skills to the search, given the strained relationship you have with the parents."

The blush deepened to crimson. "I'm doing it for Oliver, not his father. Even a man like Barclay does not deserve to suffer the loss of a son." His tone suggested that Barclay deserved to suffer just about any other punishment.

"Even worse for the mother, I should imagine," Charlie said. He gave the words no special emphasis but received a sharp glance from Simeon, anyway.

"Of course. Mrs Barclay must be terribly distraught. I wouldn't know, naturally, but Miss Winslow could tell you what a fine mother she is."

"Has Miss Winslow been in this morning to assist?"

Simeon consulted a list. "Miss Winslow is talking to railway staff, I believe. Ticket sellers, porters, conductors, and so forth, in case anyone has noticed a person travelling with a baby matching Oliver's description. One can always hope, although I doubt many people would recall a single baby on a busy day. The kidnapper would be foolish to travel in public without concealing Oliver and his distinctive blond hair. Is that all, Mr Penrose Pyke?"

Charlie needed to find out if Prudence had an accomplice looking after Oliver. A family member or a friend with a baby of their own, such that the presence of a crying baby would draw no attention. But, how to ask without offending Simeon, her potential future husband? "Miss Winslow's dedication is astonishing, given how distraught she must be feeling about Oliver. Does she have a sister or friend locally she can rely on for support?"

"She has no family locally, but she has me for support. Mr Penrose Pyke, I seriously hope you're not entertaining any thought that Prudence is involved in Oliver's kidnapping. She is a fine Christian woman, who is still young enough to have children of her own. If she adores Oliver, it is only because she loves all children, as is entirely natural for a woman of her sensibilities."

"Of course, Mr Frobisher. I meant nothing more than to inquire after her wellbeing at a dreadful time."

Simeon let it pass, if only because another group had arrived clutching a list. He waved them forward, which Charlie took as a dismissal. He couldn't think what else to ask the choirmaster, anyway, as Charlie already knew of his dislike of Edward Barclay, and he suspected Simeon was too clever to give anything away if he did have some involvement in the kidnapping.

Charlie drifted around the hall, quietly chatting to the few people present. The general feeling was that Mr Frobisher was a worthy young man who worked hard for the parish, especially when it came to raising the standard of music through his work with the church choir and high school bands. Prudence received similar praise for her work with the Sunday school, while Daisy was little known but liked. In contrast, Edward Barclay received grudging praise as a respectable man, a banker, and a good Christian, but nobody admitted a liking or admiration for him. More than a few garnished their faint praise with the curled-up nose and lips of a person sniffing an unpleasant odour.

The heated exchange between Edward Barclay and the choirmaster was brushed off as an unfortunate misunderstanding by those who commented on it at all, although three ladies expressed their embarrassment on behalf of dear, kind Mr Frobisher, and were quick to insist his position as choirmaster was never in doubt. When Charlie casually mentioned the importance of having somebody close to lean on for support in a crisis, he received only general agreement in response. Not a single person mentioned a specific parent, sibling or friend to whom Edward, Daisy or Prudence might turn in their hour of need, beyond those persons Charlie and Grace had already spoken to.

The minister, who was in the church next door to the hall, gave him much the same story, except that he had more praise for Daisy than any of the ladies Charlie had spoken to. "A charming lady with the voice of an angel, our Mrs Barclay. It's a pity we do not see more of her. She used to do such fine work with the women's committee when she arrived in Dunedin, but now she's been blessed with a child, we rarely see her apart from Sunday services, when she scarcely raises her eyes or her voice. Tired, I expect, as young mothers often seem to be. Miss Winslow is quite the opposite. I scarcely know what I would do without her to arrange the tea for the church committee, organise jumble sales, and take Sunday school for the littlest of God's lambs. How she loves children. A great shame she has not married, although it has been fortunate for us."

Time was ticking on, with little to show for it.

As Charlie walked the short distance to the tram stop, he cursed himself for forgetting to get an address for the choirmaster. A small matter, as he would not be so foolish as to hide a baby within the house of a bachelor. As churchwarden, he probably lived within a short distance of the church, which placed him in the direction the kidnapper had gone with Oliver, but then every other person they had talked to also lived in this direction, aside from Nathan Locke.

Charlie was beginning to feel as if he deserved a decent clue, but it was not to be had at the railway station either, because he didn't find Prudence Winslow there. None of the railway staff recalled a woman asking questions about a baby, which left Charlie feeling uneasy, but not unduly so. The porters and ticket sellers were always busy, and not one of them spared him more than a weary glance when he asked about her.

Acutely aware of a long night ahead, Charlie took a hansom cab home. He stopped by the kitchen to let Mrs Brown know that he and Grace would be resting for two hours, before taking an early supper and leaving again for the night.

Mrs Brown took it in her stride, well used to their erratic hours. "I put word out through my informants in the serving classes, Mr Penrose Pyke, but haven't heard a peep about a baby boy where he oughtn't to be. Mrs Macmillan stopped by earlier to say the same. Oh, Mrs Drummond, I mean."

"We have had no luck either." Charlie smiled to himself at her use of the word informants for her extensive contacts amongst the serving classes. Between Mrs Brown, Anne Macmillan Drummond, Declan Kelly and Johnny Todd, there wasn't much that happened in Dunedin that could be concealed for long.

Except for one small, blond-haired baby boy, who seemed to have vanished without even the faintest puff of smoke. Bile rose in Charlie's throat as he tried to push aside the one appalling possibility he hadn't allowed himself to dwell upon – that Oliver Barclay had been stolen to sell to a couple desperate for a healthy child of good parentage. It would be naive to think it didn't happen, for where there was money to be made, there were vile scoundrels willing to do whatever it took. The adoptive parents would no doubt convince themselves they were saving an unwanted orphan from a terrible fate.

What he needed right now was his wife in his arms, telling him everything would be fine in the end. He found Grace in the drawing room, dozing on the sofa in her dressing gown, with her long, dark hair flowing to the floor and Blaze across her feet. Her eyes opened as he picked her up. The collie considered him with soulful eyes, but went back to sleep when he told her to stay.

Grace must have sensed his mood, because she didn't ask about the investigation. Upstairs in their bedroom, she helped him undress, before gently pushing him backwards onto the cool sheets. He pulled her down beside him and wrapped his arms around her.

"Grace?"

"Mm?"

"I was wrong to have suggested taking the case without your help. Not only for your skills, but because I would not have coped without you by my side. Remind me that I'm an idiot next time I forget we're a team."

"You can count on it, Pyke."

Breaking Point

The evening sky bulged with ominous black clouds and rumbled with distant thunder as Grace walked arm in arm with her husband towards the Barclays' house for their night of surveillance.

As they passed Aggie Gemmel's house, the sound of children's laughter drifted across the garden from behind a newly trimmed hedge. Mr Guthrie was putting his broad back into digging the vegetable patch, while Aggie supervised the two older Guthrie children, who were picking silverbeet and pulling carrots with squeals of delight. Aggie had the baby in her arms and a look of utter bliss on her face as she laughed along with them.

Mrs Guthrie waved from the kitchen window. She was outside a moment later, embracing Grace and thanking her profusely. Mr Guthrie came over to shake Charlie's hand and add his thanks, but Aggie just waved and stayed with the children.

"We won't overstay our welcome with Auntie Aggie," Mrs Guthrie promised, "but, my goodness, I can't tell you what a relief it is to have a roof over our heads. The children couldn't believe their luck when they found out they could have a bed each and a room to themselves. Your friend, Mr Campbell from the carriage works, is willing to meet with my Joe tomorrow and maybe give him a chance to show what he can do. It's as if all our Christmases have come at once."

Grace glowed with warmth as they walked away, despite the chilly wind and the first splatters of rain. From the look of those clouds, it would soon pour with rain. The river rushed past between its steep banks, a far cry from its usual summer saunter. The rapid rise of the water meant it had already been bucketing down with rain in the headwaters. Fortunately for Grace, she would be inside the house, while Charlie drew the short straw, sheltering in the garden shed to watch the front door from the outside.

Charlie wore a grin the size of a watermelon slice. "Trust you to come up with a solution to the Guthries' housing problem, Grace. A double solution, in fact, as you have cleverly arranged a guard for one of our suspects."

Their mood soured as they approached the Barclays' house, where angry voices drifted from the sitting-room window. Charlie put his finger to his lips and pointed to the garden bed under the window. Squatting under an open window, eavesdropping on clients, wasn't exactly the most noble of enterprises, but needs must when a child's life was at stake.

"Don't try to deny it, Edward." The normally soft-spoken Daisy had a razor edge to her voice. "You made up the theft and had Mr Locke dismissed out of sheer spite."

"Money did go missing, Daisy, and I resent your implication that I lied. Perhaps I was wrong to accuse Locke, but I was sure it was him. Why are you so concerned about him if Locke means nothing to you, as you claim?"

"For the love of God, Edward, can't you see what's in front of your nose? Mr Locke did nothing more than apologise for a spilt drink at that party and I never saw him before or since, except for a single brief meeting purely by chance in the Botanic Garden."

"Do you expect me to believe that? I saw the way he leered at you at the party, and you did nothing to stop him."

A sharp squeal followed. "Edward, stop that. You're hurting me."

Charlie rose to a half-crouch, ready to dash to the rescue.

"Tell me the truth, Daisy. Were you planning to run away with that man? I swear to you, if I find out Locke has Oliver, I will tear him limb from limb. And don't think I won't do the same to you if you had anything to do with Oliver's disappearance."

Daisy must have wrenched free, because the next thing they heard was a resounding slap. "How dare you say such a terrible thing? Of course I didn't take Oliver. How could I have? All I want is to have my son back in my arms again."

"Then you'll have to find the money for the ransom, Daisy, because I cannot."

"How is that possible? You have a good salary and savings, don't you?"

"I have expenses, Daisy. Now more than ever, I must keep up the appearance of a successful banker."

"But you *are* a successful banker."

The room went quiet. Grace would have given anything to see the glares man and wife must be throwing at each other. It was Daisy who broke the silence.

"You've been fired from your position at the bank, haven't you? Why didn't you tell me, Edward? Who did you upset this time? Now I suppose we are going to have to move to another city and start over again."

"I didn't upset anyone, and a little more loyalty and understanding from my wife would be appreciated. It was Locke's fault. He convinced my former manager in Wellington that he was innocent and once again I have been the one to suffer the consequences." After another extended pause, Edward's voice cut through the silence, his voice dripping with suspicion. "You wouldn't have had anything to do with Locke getting his job back, would you, Daisy? It wasn't long after you met Locke in the Botanic Garden that I heard my services were no longer required at the bank."

"Don't blame me if you've been found out in your lies and wrongful accusations."

Grace waited for another cry of pain from Daisy Barclay, but it never came.

"I'm sorry I lost my temper, my dear." Edward Barclay's voice had dropped to a soft croon. "Forget about my position. It's Oliver's life we have to focus on now. I need your inheritance money to pay the ransom."

"I don't have it anymore," Daisy said. "My sister needed it to pay for medical treatment when she was gravely ill last year. Don't you think I would have given whatever money I had to you already to save Ollie?"

"What? You gave your inheritance away without consulting me? To a sister who died anyway? How could you, Daisy? That was our money to build a solid future."

Seconds ticked by while Grace wondered who would erupt in fury first. Daisy's voice, when it came, was a low snarl. "Is that what Ollie's kidnapping is about? Have you spirited my son away yourself to force me to give you the money left to me by my family? Where is Ollie, Edward?"

The sickening sound of a fist striking flesh, followed by Daisy's cry of pain, seared into Grace's heart. Charlie was already sprinting for the front door.

"That is the last time you hit me, Edward. Ever. Why don't you ask your precious Prudence to pay the ransom, since you are so clearly lining her up to be your next victim? Or is she helping you to hide my son?"

"*My* son," Edward shouted, "or so you tell me. How dare you accuse me of hiding Oliver? Why would I?"

"I notice you don't deny you are after Prudence's inheritance too. Well, you can have her and her money for all I care. As soon as I have Ollie back, I will start divorce proceedings. I was a fool to marry you just because my father demanded it, but I don't mean to be a fool forever."

"You're still a fool, Daisy, if you think you can divorce me without just cause. But I can divorce you for infidelity. Prudence will swear to it."

"I have never been unfaithful, unlike you and your obedient little lapdog." Daisy cried out again. "You can hit me all you want, Edward, because the more bruises I have, the easier it will be to prove you are a violent abuser as well as an adulterer. Enough evidence to divorce you, and good riddance."

"Go on then, just you try it if you can stand the shame you will heap on yourself. But I promise you that you will never see Oliver again. Never!"

Charlie burst into the room, bellowing, "Stop!" and hauling the warring parties apart. "Mr Barclay, if you ever raise your fist to your wife again, I will hand you in to the police myself. Now calm down, both of you, and remember why we are here. Mr Barclay, did you have any role in the disappearance of Oliver?"

"Absolutely not."

Grace didn't want to miss a second of the revelations, so she scrambled through the half-open window, thankful for her slenderness for once. Fortunately, no one noticed her, because they were too intent on glaring at each other, while Charlie held them apart.

"Mrs Barclay," Charlie said. "Do you know where Ollie is?"

"No. I wouldn't be standing here if I did. I demand you show me the ransom note. Edward cannot disguise his handwriting from me."

Charlie handed her the ransom note, which had already been checked for fingerprints with no result, aside from the prints Edward Barclay had left on it when he picked it up. Daisy stared at it with eyes narrowed. Then, her eyes widened for an instant before her face became a blank.

"You recognise the handwriting," Charlie said, stating it as a fact.

"No," Daisy said, still staring at the note. "It's the notepaper that is familiar. My husband uses it. Is that why you refused to show me the note, Edward?"

"Anyone can buy that notepaper from the stationer," Edward said. "I swear to you, I did not write that note, and I had absolutely nothing to do with Oliver's kidnapping. Why would I have hired your services, Mr Penrose Pyke, if I was the kidnapper?"

"Because I was the one who insisted on hiring a private investigator," Daisy replied in an icy voice. "And you are so arrogant, you thought you could get away with it, because nobody would suspect a distraught father who prides himself on being seen as a pillar of the community."

"It's getting late," Charlie said. "Oliver's kidnapping has taken a terrible toll on you both, and taking it out on each other is not helpful. Let's just try to be civil and work together until this is over. When Oliver is back, I hope you will forgive and forget."

After the vicious exchange, Grace knew there was no going back for the Barclays and she knew Charlie knew it too, but he had to do what he could to keep the peace for a more important cause.

"Grace, please take Mrs Barclay to sleep in the nursery while you go to your own bed, Mr Barclay. I will be outside the house, keeping a watch in case the actual kidnapper leaves a note about the location of the ransom drop."

Charlie crossed his arms over his broad chest and planted his feet wide to make his point. Edward Barclay's face was still a fiery red and taut with clenched muscles, but he did as he was told, pausing only to grab a decanter of port from the sideboard as he left. Daisy Barclay grabbed a bottle of whisky and two glasses as she stalked out with a stiff spine and a rapidly swelling eye.

When they were alone, Grace let out a long breath. "Remind me of this whenever I feel sorry for myself for being childless."

Charlie took a moment to wrap her in his comfortingly powerful arms. "These last two days have showed that we are a couple who pull together in a crisis, Grace, rather than tearing apart. I'll be in the shed. Can you manage in the armchair in the nursery?"

"It's far more comfortable than the shed, my love."

"It's not the comfort I'm worried about. I want you as a barrier between the Barclays if their anger flares up again under the influence of alcohol. Shout if you need help. Jump out the window if you are in danger."

Grace headed for the nursery, glimpsing a white face through a crack in the door as she passed by Prudence's room. She didn't blame the woman for staying out of the altercation. Grace wondered if she had heard Daisy's comment about Prudence being the next victim. If the companion packed her bags and left tomorrow, Grace wouldn't be surprised. If she stayed, it would only be out of concern for baby Oliver.

Daisy was already under the bedcovers in the small side room off the nursery when Grace arrived. "I'm sorry you had to witness that disgraceful spectacle, Grace. Your husband is right. We have let the horror of the situation get to us. A stiff whisky and a good sleep are what we need. Will you join me in a dram?"

Daisy picked up one of the two glasses of whisky she had poured and pushed the other towards Grace. Daisy tipped her head back and drained the glass in a single swallow. Grace hesitated, then followed her example. Drinking on the job was not ideal, but she needed it tonight.

Daisy's eyelids were already sagging. "Good night, Grace. Your support has meant the world to me."

Grace took the candle and retreated to the main room of the nursery. The candlelight threw a ghostly flicker on the white muslin over the baby's cradle. She couldn't bear to look at the empty spot where Ollie ought to have been sleeping, so she blew out the candle. It was going to be a long night without sleep.

Despite her earlier nap, Grace soon felt too sleepy to think anymore, especially as the patter of the rain on the roof had the same effect as a lullaby. She had meant to ask Daisy more questions about the sedative that had been given to her in her cocoa on the night of the kidnapping, but that would have to wait for the morning. Daisy's reaction to the ransom note had been interesting, too. Did she know who had written it, or had she been right in suspecting her husband?

A jagged bolt of lightning lit up the sky behind the thin curtains. By the time she reached the nursery window to close it, a deluge of rain had made the shed a blur against the dark shapes of the trees beyond.

Grace settled into the armchair again, knowing this case would haunt her for the rest of her life if they failed to get Ollie back.

A Dark and Stormy Night

Charlie tried to find a comfortable spot in the shed to rest, but he was large and the shed was small and filled with sharp implements. He propped himself just inside the shadowed doorway where he would be unlikely to be seen by an intruder intent on getting to the house, resting his back on what felt like an instrument of torture, but was only a stack of gardening equipment. The only consolation was that the floor was strewn with straw. He doubted it would stay dry for long, with the rain now pouring down, forming an expanding puddle around the lower sill of the door. Perhaps it was just as well he couldn't get comfortable, because he was tired enough to sleep anywhere. The nap he'd intended to have earlier had been delightfully shortened when his wife joined him in bed.

The rain grew steadily heavier until it felt as if the heavens had ruptured, pounding the corrugated iron roof over his head with what sounded like a month's worth of rain, drumming loud enough to hurt his eardrums. Within minutes, a stream of water trickled inside, threatening to soak his rear end. Worse, he could scarcely see a yard ahead into the deluge. The front door of the house had faded to a blur. The kidnapper would probably be tucked up in bed on such a night if he or she had any sense, while Charlie sat shivering and damp, waiting for nothing.

He lit the dark lantern he had brought with him. After a few minutes of shuffling spades, rakes, hoes and slashers into a pile, he had cleared a space where he could sit more comfortably by the open door, with a view of the approach to the front door on his left and a narrow view down the nursery side of the house on his right.

Charlie was about to sit down on an upturned pot when he glimpsed a familiar shape, which had been hidden behind a spade. A pair of boots. Muddy, well-worn boots, he realised, after inspecting them more closely. The type of old boots one might consign to gardening, as attested by a few stray strands of straw inside the boots. Edward Barclay's old boots, he surmised, since they were the same size as the boots in the house, and thus the same size as the boots that made the marks around the nursery window. The uneven wear marks matched the pattern made by the kidnapper's boots too.

Charlie's pulse hammered. Mustn't jump to conclusions. Daisy could be right about her husband setting up the kidnapping to gain access to her inheritance, but the boots were not definitive proof. It was possible somebody had stolen them to implicate Barclay, since the shed could be accessed by anyone who knew the boots were there. This didn't get him much further ahead, as Charlie was sure by now that someone in the family or in their circle of acquaintances had taken Oliver.

The one positive was that such a person would not wish to harm the child. Unless fresh evidence unmasked the kidnapper's identity, Charlie would have to wait for the ransom drop to catch their man, or woman. Assuming the kidnapper was after the money and not the child. Too big an assumption as far as Charlie was concerned, because the ransom note might have been nothing more than a blind to distract them from the real motive for taking the child.

He huddled in his overcoat, damp in both body and spirit, and watched the hypnotic stream of water descend.

When Charlie jerked awake, his ear had slipped sideways onto the prongs of a rake and the rain had eased to a light drizzle. His feeling of guilt at dozing off vanished when he realised a dark figure had stepped off the porch and was making its way towards the street. A heavy oilskin coat disguised the outline of the person, but the gown flowing from the bottom of the coat and the feminine sway to the movement indicated a woman. Prudence, he presumed, because Daisy could not have escaped with Grace on guard.

Charlie waited a moment for her to move out of sight, while he decided whether to follow her or stick with his vigil. He had seconds to decide before she disappeared into the darkness. Was the companion fleeing the chaos of the Barclay household ... or was she sneaking out for a more sinister reason?

Just as Charlie had decided to follow Prudence, another figure left the house at a run. Edward Barclay had stopped to pull on boots and trousers, but his braces were bouncing loose around his thighs with a pale nightshirt flapping around them.

When Charlie got to his feet to join the chase, his legs wobbled under him. Needle stabs of pain warned him his legs had gone to sleep from the uncomfortable position he'd been forced into. He pushed himself onward, only to trip on the uneven edge of the path in the dark, losing precious seconds as he dragged himself off the ground. The gate cost him another three seconds of fumbling for the latch. The two figures had rounded the corner by the time he reached the street, and he hadn't seen which way they went.

Darkness lay thick about him, slowing him down as he stumbled over potholes and slipped in gravel. He turned right, towards the city and church, catching a flash of pale nightshirt ahead. He was gaining, but also holding back and attempting to move quietly, to see where Prudence was heading. Charlie cursed himself for leaving Blaze at home. He had worried that Blaze might growl and alert the kidnapper during their night-time vigil. What an idiot he'd been. Blaze had been better trained than that.

Barclay caught up to the woman on the Dundas Street bridge. Charlie could hear the faint sound of shouting, but the words were indistinct over the roar of water thundering down the streambed. Their waving arms suggested an altercation.

Charlie sped up. As he approached, he saw a flash of pale hair where the hood of the oilskin had fallen off. Daisy, not Prudence. His heart contracted when he realised Daisy must have disabled

166

Grace to get past her. He shut out the image of Grace lying bleeding in the armchair and prayed that she had only fallen asleep. It would only take a few more seconds to reach the bridge and pull the Barclays apart, and then he would go back to Grace, even if he had to handcuff his clients to achieve it.

But those few seconds were too long – far too long – for what unfolded before his eyes. Edward lashed out, knocking Daisy against the side of the bridge. Charlie raced towards them, bellowing at them to stop.

Edward must have heard him, because he lunged forward, knocking into his wife, who teetered on the railings of the bridge. Both Barclays screamed. Charlie wasn't sure if Edward reached out to grab his wife or reached out to push her over the edge, but the effect suggested the latter. Daisy gave one last heart-wrenching scream as she tumbled over the rail into the river. Edward flung a glance behind him at the person sprinting through the darkness towards him, before fleeing in the opposite direction.

At the end of the bridge now, the full horror punched Charlie in the gut. The usual gentle flow of the Water of Leith had been transformed by the heavy downpour of rain into a raging torrent.

Miraculously, Daisy was still visible, clinging on for dear life to one of the support pillars of the bridge with only her head above water. The floodwaters gushed around her, pummelling and pulling her. She wouldn't last a minute.

Charlie wrenched off his heavy boots and coat, and waded into the torrent, the pressure of the water punching into him like a herd of charging bulls. He got to within inches of Daisy – close enough to see the terror on her face – when she made a fateful mistake. She let go with one hand so she could reach out to him. The pressure of the water sucked her off the pillar and flung her into the wild flow.

Charlie's frantic lunge to grab Daisy was his undoing. One second, his toes were scrabbling on the riverbed. The next second, he was in a swirling, tumbling nightmare, unable to breathe, not knowing which way was up.

The jagged end of a snapped tree trunk rammed into his back, but also gave him something to cling to, allowing him to force his head above the water. That first breath of air tasted like nectar.

Off to his right, he caught a flash of white between the pressure waves. Daisy had grasped a branch too and was kicking for the riverbank but making little progress against the racing water. Charlie cut across the river at an angle, kicking against the current for all he was worth. As he reached out to grab Daisy, her branch foundered, and she went under, leaving him with the hem of her nightdress in his fist. He reeled her in, holding her head above the torrent with one arm, while clutching his bucking tree truck with the other.

As they raced downstream between steep banks, branches and logs crashed into his body. All he could too was hang on and try to shield Daisy from the worst of the onslaught. He nearly lost his grip entirely when a projecting branch swung upwards and slammed into the side of his head, but when he surfaced again, spluttering, Daisy's arm was still locked within his numb fingers. The cold water helped to keep him conscious, but Charlie knew it was only a matter of time before he chilled down to the point where he could no longer hold on. That's if he didn't get knocked out first or dragged under by the churning current.

Ahead of him, approaching at speed, was a sharp bend in the Leith, where the outward force of the turning current might propel them onto the riverbank. The plan almost worked, until he made the mistake of putting his foot down to thrust them out of the water at the bend. His left foot caught between two unyielding objects, sending a wave of pain to his faltering brain as his lower leg and ankle twisted in a way nature never intended. The log he'd been holding shot out from beneath his hands. The last thing he remembered before he passed out was scrabbling with his hands to drag them up the steep bank.

Flotsam and Jetsam

Grace jerked awake at the rattling of the window in its frame. A sharp wind whistled through the narrow gap at the bottom of the window, billowing the curtains in ghostly waves. She had left it open just a little, so the cool air would keep her awake. So much for that theory. She only hoped that Charlie hadn't looked in and seen her asleep. It was still raining, but not nearly so hard as it had been earlier. With heavy eyelids and even heavier limbs, she pushed herself out of the armchair to check on Daisy Barclay.

The bed was empty. Grace shook her head in case her dulled senses were playing tricks, but there was no mistaking her failure. Daisy had sneaked past her and left.

As she ran from the house to find Charlie, she realised that no ordinary sleep could have left her brain so foggy. Daisy had drugged her whisky and Grace had been foolish enough to gulp it down without thinking.

Charlie was no longer in the shed. Instinct sent her stumbling towards the trees, following the same route the kidnapper had taken two nights ago. Grace hadn't gone ten yards when she slipped in the treacherous mud. On her hands and knees, with a sharp stick through her sleeve, she came to her senses. Daisy would not have come this way dressed in her nightdress. If she was fleeing the house, she would take the road.

Grace pushed herself up, the bottom of her dress and boots clogged with mud, and staggered to the road. At the intersection, she wavered, before turning right along Dundas Street towards the homes of their suspects and the church that linked them. Under a streetlamp, she paused to scrape the bottom of her boots, registering a dark streak flowing down her arm from a cut. Grace felt no pain, and the blood was only oozing, not pumping, so she ran onwards into the night along the road.

Sheer panic cleared the drug haze from her brain, leaving her jittery and frantic, but with a growing awareness that the roaring sound was not coming from within her head. It was coming from the bridge ahead, or rather, from the stream under the bridge. Grace ran to the bridge railings, unable to comprehend how the placid Water of Leith had transformed into a raging torrent. Logic told her the heavy rain had been gathered by the hilly surrounds and channelled between narrow banks, but the reality of the flood left her dumbstruck. Racing, swirling water, tumbling and thrashing with many-pronged tree branches and even entire trees, surged high up the steep banks of the stream.

Grace was about to stumble onwards when a sixth sense registered something out of place. A pair of large boots sat on the bank near the end of the bridge next to an overcoat. Charlie's boots and coat. And there was only one reason he would have taken them off in that spot. Grace stared in horror at the churning water and called Charlie's name through an acid-filled throat.

No reassuring answering cry reached her eardrums over the thundering water. She slashed a wet hand across her eyes to clear the tears away. It made no difference. She couldn't see more than a few yards ahead, and those few yards were completely devoid of large and much-loved human flesh. Damn the man for being a hero. Couldn't he have assessed the situation rationally and realised that no one could survive this watery death-trap?

Grace scrambled down the bank to retrieve the discarded boots and coat – heaven knows why, but it seemed important to her addled brain. She swiped another hand over her face, adding a layer of mud from the boots to the tears, and ran along the riverbank. Every few yards she spied a large piece of flotsam churning in the rapids or caught in vegetation at the side of the river, but each time it proved to be a false hope.

She was almost at the university when she spotted a constable walking his beat, hunched into a heavy oilskin and rubbing his hands to keep warm. Goodness knows what he thought of the rabid mudlark who appeared from the storm and shrieked at him, but he responded with commendable good sense. After blowing three long blasts on his whistle to gather any available reinforcements, they set off together to scour the banks.

When they passed the sharp bend at the far side of the university, not three blocks from the hospital, the constable blew his whistle again and broke into a sprint. Grace dashed after his solid back, towards a large piece of jetsam on the steep bank of the river. Two bodies, she saw, as she raced closer. One large, one small. Neither moving. The constable was already crouching by the smaller body, with its mass of blonde curls shimmering in the light of his night lantern. Her face was ghostly pale, the lips unmoving.

For a ludicrous instant, an image of the old lady walking to the cemetery flashed through Grace's mind. Smiling at a young couple kissing in public, passing on wise words: *Make every moment count, my dear, for life may be short and love is precious.*

Grace threw herself down beside the larger body as a second constable ran towards them. "Get help," she yelled. "We need to take them to the hospital." She didn't waste time checking to see if the constable had obeyed. Her fingers went to her husband's pulse point, his skin deathly cold under her shaking fingers. She couldn't feel a thing.

By the time a clattering behind her heralded the arrival of help several minutes later, Grace's arms were pulsing with warm blood from pumping Charlie's arms back and forth. She checked the pulse point again, feeling the longed-for flutter of life. Her beloved husband spewed up water over her sodden, filthy dress. Grace had never been so happy to be spewed upon, although her medical training warned her it was only a reflex. He was unconscious, but at least he was alive. Later, she knew, she would feel guilty for abandoning Daisy to her fate, but she also knew she would never regret the decision to tend to Charlie first.

The older constable she had waylaid squatted down to grab Charlie's legs, while the other constable grabbed his shoulders. Grace had time to note that the second constable had fluff instead of whiskers on his upper lip, before they lifted Charlie's body onto a co-opted milk delivery cart, placing it between Daisy's body and the milk churns. Grace jumped aboard next to him for the short ride to the hospital, while the older constable sat beside the milkman and the young constable, his eyes alight with excitement, hung onto the side of the cart.

At the hospital, the waiting orderlies pushed her aside in their haste to rush the victims inside. Grace tried to follow, but the older constable placed his bulk in her path and insisted she give a statement. He cleared his throat with slow relish and drew a notebook out of an inner pocket with all the haste of a man casting a line for a fish on a sultry summer's day. Frustrated by the delay, she gave him the victims' names and addresses and assured him she would give a full statement to Detective Sergeant Kelly as soon as she saw to the patients, one of whom, she emphasised with rising ire, was her husband.

The constable nodded to the young policeman, who hurried away, before turning a sceptical frown on Grace. "Now then, Mrs," – he consulted his notebook – "Mrs Pyke. I'd not be expecting a detective sergeant to turn out in the early hours of the morning for a fall into the Leith, however tragic the consequences. I understand that you're worried about your husband, but it'd be best to leave the doctors to do their work while I record your full statement for my report."

Grace tossed up whether to explain she was within months of graduating as a doctor herself, but that would only waste more time for no gain. "I can assure you Detective Sergeant Kelly will come immediately when he hears what has happened, Constable. The incident is more likely to be an attempted murder than an accidental fall and the victim is vital to a case DS Kelly has been investigating, alongside my husband, who is also his best friend. However, I understand you have a duty to do, so perhaps we could achieve both objectives if you accompany me while I check on my husband's condition."

She ducked around him and strode off before he could reply. After a gruff harrumph, the tread of heavy boots followed her rapid steps through the maze of hospital corridors. A nurse directed her to the correct ward, addressing her as Doctor Penrose Pyke, which generated a further harrumph from her constabulary shadow. Grace smiled to herself at his incredulity. The nurses had taken to calling her "Doctor", even though she was a final year medical student, because it was the only way they could convince reluctant patients that "that slip of a girl" had the proper medical training to tend them.

When they reached the right bed, Charlie was all but invisible behind the attending doctor and two nurses bearing trays of equipment. When Grace slotted herself into a gap at the head of the bed, she almost wished she hadn't. Stripped of clothes, her husband's body was a patchwork of cuts and contusions, and the severe swelling of his left lower leg and foot indicated a severe sprain or worse.

"Any fractures?" Grace asked the doctor. She examined her husband's eyes, which had opened at the sound of her voice, but remained unfocused. Charlie mumbled something that might have been "I'm fine", before his eyes fluttered shut.

"You won't get much sense out of him, Grace," the doctor replied. "We've given him morphine. He's been fortunate, considering the circumstances. No fractures of the major bones. We'll have to wait for the swelling to go down to see if there are any cracks to the smaller bones of the foot, but there will certainly be damage to the tendons and ligaments." The doctor paused his examination long enough to send a wry grin at her. "You ought to take better care of your husband, Grace."

"Believe me, I try, but King Canute had more chance of holding back the tide. Anything else of serious concern?"

"He took a knock on the head, but nothing too serious, as far as we can tell. His vital signs are encouraging, but he'll need several days of bed rest at the very least, followed by several weeks of restricted activity."

Grace didn't like her chances of keeping Charlie restrained for weeks, but she would certainly ensure he stayed in bed for the next few days, under strict supervision. The bruising and leg injury would heal, but a knock to the head was a concern, because concussion was always a fickle beast, and he might have internal injuries that would only become apparent later. And then there was the possibility that filthy water had entered his lungs, containing who knew what infectious diseases and noxious substances. Once he was well again, he'd get a piece of her mind about reckless heroism – again – but for now he needed her tender loving care, whether or not he wanted it.

"You have my permission to restrain or sedate him if he attempts to get out of bed," Grace said.

The nurse picked up a particularly fearsome syringe and waggled it. "Understood. We've had Detective Pyke in here before."

The constable's eyes widened in horror at the syringe and he excused himself, promising to alert Detective Sergent Kelly to the situation immediately.

Grace allowed a nurse to take her into a cubicle and press a towel on her, but only because she understood that getting pneumonia would not help Charlie or Oliver. By the time she had stripped and dried, the nurse had deposited dry clothes beside her, before hurrying about her business. The clothes, doubtless left behind by a larger, older woman who no longer needed them, may she rest in peace, fell about her body in comical folds. Grace secured the voluminous dress with a length of bandage and went to check on Daisy Barclay, their client, but also on the cusp of becoming a friend.

Daisy's pale face glowed in the lamplight as if she was half ghost already, but Grace took it as a good sign that there was no doctor at her bedside. One of the hospital's most experienced nurses, Nurse Dawson, updated Grace on the patient's condition, which was battered but stable.

"She's semi-conscious but hasn't said anything yet," Nurse Dawson said. "We'll need a name for the records. Do you know her?"

"Mrs Daisy Barclay," Grace replied. The figure in the bed, who had showed no signs of life so far, reacted to the sound of her name. The doctor inside Grace wanted to leave her to rest and recover, but the police would need to know the circumstances of Daisy's near drowning as soon as possible.

Daisy's eyes fluttered open. "Grace?"

Grace sat by the bedside and took Daisy's trembling hand. "You're safe now, Daisy."

"He pushed me."

Grace took a second to process the words, which came out as a hoarse whisper with an ominous gurgling undertone, before looking up into the nurse's startled eyes. "Nurse Dawson, could you please witness Mrs Barclay's statement?" Grace squeezed Daisy's fingers. "Can you say that again please, Daisy, stating names if you can."

"My husband, Edward Barclay, pushed me off the bridge into the river. Deliberately, with the intention of killing me." Daisy sank back into the pillow, exhausted by the effort.

Nurse Dawson wrote the words in the notebook every nurse carried. Recording messages for loved ones was a task they were honoured to perform when all else failed. From the sickly hue of the nurse's face, this was the first time the patient's words had been an accusation of attempted murder.

Daisy's eyes flickered open again, her voice weaker. "Charlie?"

"Don't you worry about him. I swear that man could walk through the fires of Hades and come out smiling."

"He held my head up. Protected me. Thank him." Her words were now barely a whisper.

"I will." Grace was sure Daisy had slipped into unconsciousness again, having achieved her goal, but a faint squeeze of her hand told her Daisy wasn't finished.

"Ollie ..."

The faint squeeze dropped away as Daisy faltered. Grace waited in case Daisy had more to say, but the only sound she made was the rasping of laboured breath. Despite her yearning to return to Charlie, the revelation that Edward Barclay had tried to kill Daisy changed everything. When Edward found out Daisy was still alive to testify against him, he would be frantic.

"Nurse Dawson," Grace said, "can I ask you to refrain from registering the patient's name until the police have conducted their investigation? I'll stay with her until Detective Sergeant Kelly arrives."

Fortunately, Nurse Dawson saw the risk and readily agreed, before hurrying about her other duties. Edward Barclay wasn't Grace's only concern. If word got out that Edward had been arrested and Daisy was incapacitated in hospital, the kidnapper might cut his losses and kill Ollie, fearing that no ransom would be forthcoming.

In the dim glow of the nightlights, Grace kept vigil, her pulse quickening at every clatter of a bedpan or shuffle of approaching feet. Even in the dead of the night, a busy hospital never rested. Daisy slept on, mostly deathly still, but occasionally tossing and turning or crying out. Grace could only bathe her brow and pray that Daisy's condition wouldn't worsen into an acute fever.

About half an hour later, the approaching feet took on the solid stomp of a policeman's boots. Grace turned to see Detective Sergeant Declan Kelly, his hair wild under a skewed hat and his shirt flapping where he had failed to tuck it in completely. Not that she could criticise his sartorial elegance, given the over-sized sack of a dress she was wearing. She put a finger to her lips and gestured for him to follow her to a quiet corner in the shadow of a cabinet beyond the last of the sleeping patients.

Grace quickly summarised the events of the evening, handing Declan the notepaper on which Nurse Dawson had recorded and signed Daisy's accusation of attempted murder by her husband.

"It was good thinking on your part to get an independent witness, Grace," Declan said. "Even so, no court is going to accept the testimony of a wife against her husband, especially when Edward Barclay challenges her account, as he surely will."

Grace shouldn't have been shocked by this, because she understood the harsh reality of Daisy's situation. Edward Barclay would argue that the fall from the bridge was self-inflicted, given his wife's depression and the added stress of her missing child, and that her accusation against him was due to her delirious condition. An accidental fall was so much easier to believe, perhaps with Edward heroically lurching forward to try to stop her.

"It's a shame Charlie can't corroborate her account," Declan said.

"You talked to Charlie?" Grace resisted the urge to dash off to see her husband. He could wait another few minutes until Declan took over from her, and then she would glue herself to Charlie's bedside until he was out of danger. "What did he say, Declan?"

"He was extremely groggy, but he asked after you first. Charlie was worried that you might have been incapacitated by Daisy Barclay when she escaped the house."

"Daisy drugged me." Grace still felt like a fool for falling for such an obvious trick, so she moved on quickly. "Wasn't Charlie there when Edward pushed his wife off the bridge to her likely death?"

"He saw it happen, but it was dark and drizzling. Charlie said it looked like a push, but he couldn't swear to it in a court of law.

Barclay knows somebody witnessed the altercation, but Charlie was in the shadows, so he doubted Barclay knows who saw him. At the very least, Barclay's actions caused his wife to tumble into the water, and he didn't stop to try to save her, which gives me cause to take him in for questioning. It's about time he faced an official interrogation over his son's disappearance, anyway. If Edward Barclay is still in Dunedin, that is."

"Why wouldn't Edward be in Dunedin, Declan? If he didn't wait to see Charlie dive to the rescue, then he would have assumed his wife was dead and his role in her demise would never be proved."

"Because the senior constable sent that wet-behind-the-ears new recruit to inform Edward Barclay of his wife's 'accident', before ascertaining if it really was an accident. The young idiot didn't even know for sure if Daisy was alive or dead at that stage, but he did tell Barclay his wife had been taken to the hospital. Barclay must be terrified that his wife had lived to tell the tale."

Grace recalled giving the policeman the victims' names and addresses so she could escape his persistent questions. Too late now for regrets. Even now, the new recruit might be knocking on their front door and informing Mrs Brown that Charlie was on his deathbed. Their housekeeper would tell Alistair and Lily Stewart, but at least she would pass on the news with due caution and common sense.

"Can I leave Daisy's security to you, Declan? After I've checked on Daisy again, I'd like to look in on Charlie."

"A doctor arrived on the ward a few minutes ago. Why don't you let him see to Mrs Barclay?" Declan pointed to the man in a doctor's white coat, who was now leaning over Daisy's bed, adjusting her pillow. Declan let out an oath and took off down the ward at astonishing speed.

Grace took half a second longer to realise what had alarmed him, before she hurtled after him, yelling, "Help! Doctor!" at the top of her lungs.

The man beside Daisy jerked his head towards them, the nightlight silhouetting his profile. Edward Barclay kept pressing the pillow to his wife's face for another few precious heartbeats, before he flung the pillow aside and ran for his life. How long had Edward been there before they noticed him? Suffocation only took minutes and Daisy was ominously still.

In the long seconds it took for Grace to reach her side, floundering in the overly long borrowed clothes she had been given, Edward almost made it to the door. A doctor running in the opposite direction caused him to hesitate long enough for Declan to launch himself at Edward, tackling him to the floor with the devastating precision of a seasoned rugby player. No ifs and buts this time – the fiend had been caught red-handed.

Daisy lay absolutely still. Grace's fingers shook so much she struggled to detect a pulse. She fought her panic and tried again, but she was pulled aside by the doctor who had rushed to her aid.

For once, Grace was relieved to have the responsibility taken off her, but it didn't help to hear the infuriating whine of Edward's voice in the background telling Declan that Grace was the one responsible for letting his mentally unstable wife leave the house during a storm, leaving him to dash heroically to his wife's side in her hour of need.

The worst of it was that Edward was right. Grace had failed to keep Daisy Barclay safe. If Daisy died, she would never forgive herself.

Impatient Patient

Charlie drifted back to consciousness when he felt the familiar sensation of soft fingers on his wrist. "Grace?" he rasped, before opening his eyes to the reality of the hospital bed and a uniformed nurse taking his pulse.

"I'm Nurse Rowley," she said. "Your wife left a message to say she will be back as soon as she can, and that you're not to leave until she has talked to you. I understand she was involved in a medical emergency during the night."

"What happened?" Charlie said.

"I wasn't on the night shift and the staff have been instructed not to say a word until the police investigation is completed."

"Please, I have to know."

The nurse must have seen his distress, because she relented. "I truly don't know, but the rumour is that the woman who was brought in with you last night was attacked in her hospital bed by her husband. Don't worry, Mr Penrose Pyke, your wife is unharmed, although I heard she was drugged last night by the woman victim. It seems that both of you had quite the exciting night, even by your standards."

Charlie didn't think he could feel much worse than he already did, but he also had that dreadful sinking feeling in his gut. "Did the woman survive?"

"I really can't say."

"It's very important, Nurse Rowley. The woman is central to an urgent investigation."

"I truly don't know for certain and nobody is talking. But an orderly told me he was called by your wife to take a body to the mortuary in the middle of the night and I know the woman's bed

180

was empty this morning." She leaned closer to whisper. "The husband was caught in the act and arrested. Matron is threatening to dismiss anyone who breathes a word about it, so please keep the news to yourself."

Daisy dead, Edward arrested. The case Charlie had been reluctant to take on had turned into a poisoned chalice. He tried to push himself upright, only to be gently but firmly pushed down by Nurse Rowley.

"Rumour also has it you plunged into raging floodwaters to save the woman, Mr Penrose Pyke. Don't you think that's enough heroism for one day? You're in no fit condition to get up, let alone to dabble in the police investigation."

Charlie's memory was hazy, but he did recall trying to hold Daisy Barclay's head above the water and shielding her from the swirling debris. His whole body felt as pummelled as a boxing bag. He shut his eyes against the painful glare of daylight. "What time is it? In fact, what day is it? I feel as if I have been asleep forever."

"It's half-past nine on Wednesday morning. You've only been asleep for a few hours. Right now, you need to rest and recover. The doctor said you need to remain here under observation for a few days."

"I don't have time to sleep," Charlie grumbled.

"Doctor's orders, I'm afraid. Your wife made it very clear we were to give you another sedative if you tried to move."

Charlie could ill afford to sleep given the critical state of their investigation, but he had no choice, because the nurse was already fitting a syringe with a wickedly sharp needle. "Nurse Rowley," he said with a brightness he didn't feel, "I'm much recovered thanks to the excellent care of the hospital staff. Whatever my wife told you, I don't need to be knocked out with a strong sedative, although a mild painkiller would be appreciated."

The nurse looked at him with old eyes in a youthful face. She filled the syringe, her smile never faltering. "Doctor Penrose Pyke warned me you would try to charm your way out of it. She was most insistent."

Charlie pointed at the pile of fresh clothes on the cabinet beside his bed. "My wife also brought me clothes, which means she didn't expect me to obey."

A drop of liquid squirted from the end of the needle. "I believe an elegant older gentleman with a moustache brought the clothes in this morning. He must have been told of the accident but been unaware of the severity of your injuries."

If Alistair Stewart had brought clothes, he would surely go home to report the injuries were more severe than he had expected. Alistair would tell Lily and thus his aunt must be even now racing down to the hospital to mother him. And then there was Grace, who would come up here as soon as she could to personally ensure that he was out for the count for several more wasted hours.

Charlie kept his arm tucked under the blanket and a pleasant smile fixed on his lips. "I believe I am within my rights to refuse treatment, as long as I sign a form to show I have knowingly acted against medical advice. My wife will understand."

The nurse looked dubious, but the needle didn't come any closer.

"A mild painkiller is all I need, I promise. It's not the first time I've taken a knock on the noggin." Charlie rapped his knuckles on his head to prove his point. "Tough as a brick wall," he gasped, as pain lanced through his brain. Too late, his fingers felt a lump the size of a baby's fist on the left side of his head.

"It only takes a tap from a sledgehammer to knock down bricks," the nurse said. "However, I'll give you a mild dose of painkiller if you promise to stay in bed until the attending physician does his rounds. He can decide."

She returned with the promised painkiller, which Charlie took obediently. He burrowed down in the bed and closed his eyes, knowing nurses were always run off their feet with patients to see. She was gone before he spat out half the dose. It was a sad fact that

Charlie had been injured often enough now to judge the dose perfectly. If he'd taken the full dose, he'd have been pain free but unable to function. With half a dose, he could manage to fight through the pain to get the job done.

As he waited for the medication to take effect, he took a quick inventory of his injuries. The one part of his body he could see – his arm – looked like a swollen and mottled sausage against the white sheet. Charlie lifted the sheet to assess the extent of the damage. Being churned down a river amongst a flotsam of logs and other debris had left bruises and gashes aplenty, but they would fade soon enough. No stitches or broken bones that he could discern, which was a miracle. However, his left foot and lower leg were heavily bandaged and sporting a lively shade of deep purple around the edges. When he tried to flex his leg, pain shot through his body, leaving him dizzy and queasy. But not dizzy enough to stop him.

All in all, his condition was not as bad as it could have been. It would have been worth it if Daisy Barclay had survived. Dead or alive, he owed it to her to continue the search for Ollie, which meant he had to escape the hospital before Grace came back and sedated him. Not that Charlie didn't trust Declan Kelly to take over the investigation, but because it would eat away at him for the rest of his life if he didn't do everything he could to help find the baby boy.

He shifted his attention to his surroundings, spotting a pair of crutches beside the bed of a snoring man. A distance of a mere twenty yards or so, although it might as well have been a mile. Crawling was an option, although he doubted that would do his ankle any favours.

Charlie swung his protesting body out from under the bedclothes, biting back a curse at the stab of pain. Getting dressed proved challenging. He slid and wriggled his underclothes on with a tolerable level of agony, but the stretching required to put his shirt and waistcoat on left him sweating and trembling. The bulbous purple swelling of his foot under a thick bandage made putting on his trousers impossible, which he only discovered after getting his right leg in one trouser leg and his left leg stuck when his foot wouldn't pass through the lower end of the other trouser leg.

Charlie was teetering with his trousers at half-mast on the edge of the bed – and on the edge of his dignity – when he was rescued by a passing orderly, who produced a pair of sharp scissors and snipped the trouser seam open at the bottom.

"If you don't mind me saying so, sir, you don't look well enough to leave. Are you sure the doctor signed you out?"

"It's not as bad as it looks," Charlie said cheerily, although the sweat was pouring off him as he struggled to sit upright, despite the painkiller. "I don't suppose you'd retrieve my crutches for me. Somebody's left them by the wrong bed. Thank you for your help." The orderly looked doubtful, so Charlie gave him an encouraging pat on the shoulder. "I'm only leaving because it's an emergency. A child's life is at stake."

"If you say so."

The orderly attached a line of safety pins down the trouser seam to stop it flapping and then retrieved the crutches while Charlie put on his right shoe. The left shoe proved to be an insurmountable hurdle, because there was no way it would fit on his swollen foot. No matter, he could hail a hansom cab and hobble the rest of the way.

Charlie waited until the orderly hurried about his business before attempting to stand with the crutches. The best he could say was that he was upright, just, and the pain was bearable, just. That was all that mattered. He was surprised Grace still hadn't come to check on him, but that was for the best. He tentatively shuffled the crutches ahead of him while balancing on his good leg. After an alarming wobble, a trip over a stray end of a blanket, and a crash into a bed-end, Charlie made it to the exit, cursing under his breath at the ridiculous crutches. All the wonders of the great age of invention and mankind couldn't come up with anything better to support an injured man than a couple of sticks.

He stopped briefly at the reception desk on the way out, where the clerk denied anyone named Daisy Barclay was registered at the hospital. When he asked about deaths in the last few hours, the clerk refused to give him the information.

Fortunately, there was a hansom cab directly outside the hospital. Unfortunately, it didn't prove much easier taking the cab, as mounting the high step into a narrow space with the unruly crutches was near impossible. The cabbie took pity on him and helped to hoist him in, with enough cursing from both parties to make a passing group of ladies give them a wide berth. He thanked the cabbie with ill grace – weakness made him grumpy – but resolved to make up for it with a generous tip at the destination. Generous enough that the cabbie wouldn't mind waiting to take him home.

He escaped in the nick of time, because Lily and Alistair were striding towards the hospital as the horse leant against the traces and whisked him away.

Charlie gave the driver the Barclays' address. Now was his chance to talk to the elusive Prudence Winslow without the Barclays in the house. Daisy's unwanted companion seemed the most likely accomplice if Edward took his son. And Prudence was still a suspect in her own right, because she was besotted with Oliver and had the opportunity to take him, as well as the means to care for him. It was time to put the companion under pressure.

The Barclays' house was resoundingly silent. Charlie took the broom from behind the door and waved it, but none of Johnny's lads appeared from out of a bush with a cheeky grin and an offer of help. Charlie thumped up the hall, getting a crutch caught on the end of a carpet and crashing into the wall. His agonised yelp went unanswered.

By the time he reached Prudence's room, he was not surprised to find her absent. The room smelled of her cloying scent and was crammed with furniture, presumably treasured items from her family home. However, the drawers and armoire had been emptied to the last stocking. Daisy's companion, or Edward's confidante, had fled the roost. Charlie sank down on the bed, which had been stripped of sheets, with the blanket neatly folded at the end.

A note to Edward Barclay lay on the pillow. Edward had long since lost his right to privacy, in Charlie's opinion, so he didn't hesitate to read it: *E, Don't try to follow me. I know you lied to me. P.*

Short but not sweet. Charlie tried to recall if they had a sample of Prudence's handwriting, but his brain still felt like a boxing bag after an intense training session. Her writing featured sharp spikes and narrow letters – the very opposite of Daisy's feminine hand – but not a clear match to the ransom note either.

Charlie wasn't surprised Prudence had left after witnessing the argument between Daisy and Edward last night, although he was eager to find out exactly what lies Edward had told Prudence. He contemplated his options. Traipsing about town trying to find Miss Prudence Winslow didn't appeal, while returning home to his own bed was a temptation he couldn't afford. If lying down on her bed and waiting would further his investigation, he would have done it, but he doubted Prudence would be back.

Instead, he searched Barclay's study, starting with the locked drawer of the desk. Right at the bottom, in an unmarked envelope, was a letter from Barclay's solicitor confirming that Edward could not gain legal access to Daisy's inheritance without her agreement unless she was declared mentally incompetent to manage her affairs. The letter went on to outline the requirements for filing a divorce petition with the court, including the specific nature of evidence required to prove infidelity. The letter ended with a sternly worded paragraph advising Edward not to remarry immediately or to make his intention to remarry known until the divorce was finalised.

Had Daisy known what Edward was planning? Or had her accusation against her husband, that he was lining Prudence up to be his next victim, merely been a guess? A stab of regret swamped all other thoughts, as Charlie realised he would never have the chance to ask what Daisy had been thinking. He would blame himself for her death for the rest of his life, but right now, he had the living to attend to.

So many questions, but only one that he should be focused on: who had Ollie Barclay? Charlie could only speculate, and it was driving him crazy. He went outside to sit on the porch in the fresh air, hoping that Grace would appear in a puff of smoke, wearing the dimpled grin that always signalled a crucial piece of evidence.

Instead, he saw Johnny's lad trotting up the road, puffing like a miniature steam engine.

"Copper Charlie, am I glad to see you. The companion woman hightailed it with suitcases early this morning. I wasn't sure what to do, but I reckoned you'd want to know where she went, so I followed her. She went a short way up the Leith Valley to a small cottage. A man let her in and she didn't leave again." He proudly held out a grubby scrap of paper with an address scrawled on it in a childish hand. "Johnny's teaching us our letters."

"Very impressive, Grubber. You've done well." Charlie didn't recognise the address, but his bet would be Simeon Frobisher. "What did the man look like?"

"Kind of gawky and thin. He kissed her on the cheek."

Undoubtedly Frobisher. Charlie flipped the boy a coin. "Get yourself a hot feed and some rest, Grubber. I don't expect there will be much to see here for the rest of the day, because nobody is home and they'll not be back anytime soon."

Grubber threw him a mock salute and scarpered before Charlie could change his mind. He watched the lad enviously as his fully functioning legs propelled him down the road at speed. He wished he had asked the lad to bring him back a serving of the hot food that Grubber would soon be scoffing. A pie and mash would go down a treat. Charlie tried to remember the last time he had eaten, but could only recall the distant memory of last night's early supper. On the other hand, it was probably just as well he hadn't eaten, because his stomach was still cramping from the filthy water he'd swallowed.

He wrestled the crutches into obedience and thumped his way back into the house. The obvious next step was to call on Prudence to find out why she had fled the Barclay residence, but Charlie couldn't resist the lure of a soft armchair to take the weight off his aching foot for a while and give himself a chance to think.

Charlie had no sooner collapsed with a heartfelt sigh when a caller thumped on the front door. He levered himself out of the chair, cursing under his breath, and crutched his way to the door.

A dishevelled, red-eyed man stood on the porch with a suitcase and a determined jut to his jaw. He dropped the jut at the sight of Charlie and hazarded a half smile. "I'm here to see Mrs Daisy Barclay."

"You'd better come in, Mr Montgomery." Charlie wished he'd left with Grubber. He might be enjoying a pie right now, which would have been far preferable to breaking the news of Daisy's death to her brother-in-law on this miserable day. Presumed death, he corrected himself, since the facts were as yet unconfirmed.

Montgomery didn't take a seat until he had helped Charlie to sit, found a stool and a cushion to prop his leg on, and poured him a glass of water and a slug of brandy from the bottle on the sideboard. Charlie liked the man already.

"If you don't mind me saying so, sir, you look as if you ought to be in hospital," Montgomery said, after tossing back his own glass of brandy. "Tell me, how did you know my name?"

"You have a smudge of soot on your face, a suitcase with a New Zealand Rail tag from Wellington to Dunedin, and an artist's calling card of paint under your fingernails. My mother-in-law, Mrs Louisa Penrose, sent a telegram to say you were coming." Charlie held his hand out. "Charlie Penrose Pyke."

"James Montgomery, as deduced. I'd have been here sooner, but the train was held up overnight because of slips on the track." He shook Charlie's hand gently, avoiding the bruises. "It must have been a nasty fight you were in, Mr Penrose Pyke. I hope it wasn't anything to do with Daisy and Oliver. Mrs Louisa Penrose didn't give me any details at our meeting on Monday, but the fact that she was asking if I had heard from Daisy lately had me worried. Daisy's letters had become irregular of late, but they suddenly stopped five weeks ago."

"Do you have a specific reason to be concerned about your sister-in-law, Mr Montgomery?"

"Daisy's husband has a history of mistreating her, but he is clever at pretending to be a loving husband, so he gets away with it. I mean to take her away with me, and I sincerely hope you won't try to stop me."

Charlie gestured ruefully at the crutches. "I'm not in a position to stop anyone, and I wouldn't if I could. How do you know about the mistreatment?"

"Daisy and my wife shared every detail of their lives until Barclay forced Daisy to move to Dunedin, where she knew nobody. My late wife was Daisy's sister, as I presume you know, but you may not be aware I have known both of them since we were children. Daisy is closer than a sister to me, so we continued to correspond when my wife died in March last year. Barclay tried to put a stop to it, but we managed to exchange letters with the help of her housekeeper, Mrs Freya Marcus. I received a letter from Mrs Marcus recently to tell me Barclay had fired her and locked Daisy in the house. I've been worried sick. In fact, I'd already been making arrangements to come to Dunedin before Mrs Penrose contacted me."

Charlie could feel the brandy going straight from his empty stomach to his head, which was already throbbing. But even if his brain had been in better condition, he doubted there would be an easy way to break the news. "We were hired to investigate the

189

kidnapping of Oliver Barclay, Mr Montgomery. He was taken late on Sunday night or early on Monday morning. A ransom note was left in his empty cradle."

"Ollie's been kidnapped? For ransom?" James Montgomery's shock was undoubtedly genuine. Several seconds passed before the words sank in. "Where's Daisy? I must talk to her immediately. She must be devastated."

"I regret to tell you that Daisy Barclay left the house last night during the storm, presumably to look for Ollie. Tragically, she was swept away in a swollen river. I know she was taken to hospital, but I cannot tell you her present condition for certain." Charlie quailed at the distress he was causing the other man, but he had to be honest. "I have to warn you that there have been unconfirmed accounts that Daisy Barclay did not survive the night. I understand Edward Barclay is currently making a statement to the police."

Montgomery's expression went through the usual sequence of emotions, starting at disbelief, moving to horror, flickering over anguish, before settling on pure unadulterated hatred. "I'll kill him if he has harmed Daisy."

Charlie felt for him, but he couldn't risk this man getting in the way of Oliver's rescue. "The police are conducting inquiries. Until that is completed, I urge you to restrain your anger against Mr Barclay."

"What about Ollie?"

"That's my job," Charlie said, "alongside the best detective in the police force."

After a dubious glance at Charlie's leg, James Montgomery nodded. "I will do whatever it takes to help Daisy and Ollie. I only regret I didn't act sooner to remove them from Barclay."

Charlie knew how he felt. He handed him a business card. "You could try the hospital, but the staff have been told not to talk to anyone. The reception clerk refused to say if Daisy had even been admitted. I suggest you ask for my wife, Grace Penrose Pyke, who is a medical student there and will have the information you need.

190

If she is not at the hospital, try our office on High Street. While you are there, I would be grateful if you would make a statement to whoever is there. My business partner, Alistair Stewart, his wife, Lily Stewart, or my wife. If none of them are there, go next door, where our housekeeper, Mrs Brown, will see to you. The statement should outline your knowledge of the relationship between Daisy and Edward Barclay, including any physical or other abuse you can testify to. Also, any information you might have on contacts the Barclays have in Dunedin, especially any person who might be willing to hide baby Oliver or anyone with a grudge against the family. I would take the statement myself, but I must excuse myself to follow up on crucial evidence."

Despite his distress and eagerness to rush to the hospital, James Montgomery had the decency to help Charlie into the waiting hansom cab, after promising to do as Charlie asked.

Prudence

Charlie squeezed his bruised body and crutches into the hansom cab and directed the cabbie to take him to Simeon Frobisher's cottage. The relentless tick of the clock and his overwhelming desire to have this nightmare over were all that kept him going.

The route took them across the Dundas Street bridge again, where the tangle of debris lining the muddy bank made Charlie appreciate just how miraculous his own survival had been. Having a thick skull came in handy. The volume of water had subsided within the space of a few hours to the point it was fast flowing, but no longer roaring. Passing over the bridge also reminded him to consider where Daisy had been heading last night. Simeon's house was one possibility, but Aggie and Freya both lived on the far side of the bridge too, along with the rest of the church community. Only Nathan Locke lived in the opposite direction.

Too many people, too little time. Despite Simeon Frobisher marshalling the congregation to knock on every door, the baby boy could still be in the vicinity, carefully hidden, if he wasn't already miles away. Nothing short of a full-scale search of every house would be needed to find him now, unless by a miracle he was with Simeon and Prudence.

Simeon's cottage backed onto a small stand of trees a short way up the Leith Valley from the city. It was a fine spot for a kidnapper, as a person could come and go through the trees without being seen. Charlie wished he had Blaze with him to sniff out any suspicious scents, but the dog would be at home, curled up on a comfortable blanket. Charlie sighed and handed over another generous tip to persuade the cabbie to wait for him.

Simeon answered the door at the second knock. "My goodness, Mr Penrose Pyke, you look dreadful. What on earth happened to you?"

"People with a criminal record don't always like being asked questions," Charlie said, which was true but irrelevant. The important point was that Simeon, and thus Prudence, did not know of his attempted rescue of Daisy Barclay. "I need to talk to Miss Winslow urgently."

"This is not a convenient time, because she is deeply distressed. I've already told you that Prudence knows nothing about Oliver's disappearance."

"I'm not here about Oliver, Mr Frobisher." Charlie ignored Simeon's reluctance and concentrated on navigating the steps and the hall with crutches that seemed to have a malevolent will of their own.

Prudence was in the sitting room, weeping and surrounded by baggage. Simeon put his arm around her protectively and passed her another handkerchief.

Nobody offered Charlie a seat, or even acknowledged his presence, but the half dose of painkiller had worn off, so he eased into an armchair with an internal groan. "Miss Winslow, I can see you'd rather not talk right now, but the matter is urgent. Why did you leave the Barclays' house this morning?"

"You were there last night, Mr Penrose Pyke. You know why. Edward said such terrible things. He punched his wife in the face. He's not the man I thought he was."

"Which is why you cannot trust him with your inheritance, Prudence," Simeon said. "I told you he was only after your money. Edward was constantly pestering Daisy for her inheritance, you know, and now he is turning his grasping ways on you."

"Enough, Simeon," Prudence said, between sniffles. "You were right, I admit it, but it's too late. I have already given Edward the two hundred pounds he needs to get Oliver back. And don't ask me to change my mind, because Oliver's life is at stake."

Charlie interrupted the brewing argument to get the interview back on track. "Did you hear Daisy leave the house in the middle of the night, Miss Winslow?"

"No, but I don't blame her after what happened. I thought your wife was supposed to be watching Daisy."

"My wife was drugged, Miss Winslow."

The colour drained from Prudence's face, except for her red-ringed eyes. "Edward drugged your wife? Oh, merciful heavens, I cannot believe I misjudged him so badly. When the policeman arrived to inform him of Daisy's death, I thought …"

What Prudence thought disappeared beneath the explosive force of Simeon's reaction. "Daisy is *dead*? Why didn't you tell me? Oh, that poor, sweet, innocent girl."

Prudence's long, hard stare cut a knife through his emotional outburst. Her reply, when it came, was a blunt statement of fact. "You're still in love with Daisy, aren't you? Honestly, Simeon, you call me a fool for believing Edward. I told you Daisy would never leave Edward for you."

Simeon avoided answering by rising from the sofa and pacing. He stopped in front of a wooden cross that had pride of place in the centre of the mantelpiece, his index finger tracing the shape distractedly. "I love you, Prudence, not Daisy. Never Daisy, although I liked her, and I won't apologise for feeling distressed by her sudden death. How did Mrs Barclay die?"

"I don't know," Prudence replied. "A policeman arrived during the night. Edward told me to go back to my room, but I overheard the policeman say Daisy's body had been found. Do you know what happened to her, Mr Penrose Pyke?"

"I know Mrs Barclay fell from a bridge into the river," Charlie said, sparing her the details of Edward's involvement for now, "and I have heard an unconfirmed rumour she died. However, I implore you to keep that confidential until it is verified, especially as the matter is subject to a police investigation." Charlie could see that Simeon and Prudence were about to fling more questions at him, which he would refuse to answer even if he could. Pain and patience did not mix; he waved a crutch to draw Prudence's attention back to him. "Miss Winslow, what were you going to tell me about your thoughts on the policeman's arrival last night?"

"When the policeman said Daisy's body had been found on the banks of the Leith, I thought ... I wondered if it was ... not an accident."

Simeon whirled to face her, his face contorted. "Prudence, I'm shocked you would say such a thing. Daisy Barclay would never, ever, contemplate suicide. She knows taking her life would be an unforgivable sin. Daisy is a godly woman with a child. A joyful lady, when away from her husband."

"You don't know everything about your precious Daisy, Simeon," Prudence said. "Edward begged me to move into the house six weeks ago to care for his wife because he feared she was not of sound mind. That's why he had to keep her locked in at night and watched during the day. He wanted me to make sure she didn't get taken advantage of by the type of men who exploit weak women. Edward even hinted he feared she would take her own life if left unsupervised, and now it seems he was right."

"It must have been an accident. Nothing will convince me Daisy attempted to take her own life." Simeon turned from Prudence to Charlie, his brow lowered over stormy eyes as a third possibility belatedly occurred to him. "Unless it was neither. Why would Edward have drugged your wife, if not to get to Daisy? I want the truth, Mr Penrose Pyke. Did Edward Barclay have a hand in Daisy's death?"

Charlie didn't like the sound of the raw anger underlying the choirmaster's question, and he had no wish to flame the flames of his fury. "Mr Frobisher, please refrain from jumping to conclusions. In fact, I believe Daisy drugged my wife so that she could leave the house. The ferocious storm last night meant visibility was poor, and the river was a torrent. Until the police investigation is complete, the most reasonable explanation is that

195

she slipped and fell into the floodwaters, especially given how distraught she was after the argument with her husband."

Simeon appeared far from convinced. Charlie tried again. "The police will be quick to intervene if anyone so much as whispers that Edward Barclay was implicated in his wife's fall. You could find yourself up on charges of obstructing justice." Charlie waited until he saw that Simeon understood. "Mr Frobisher, I would like to speak to Miss Winslow alone, please."

For several more seconds Simeon stood there, staring into the distance, then he headed to the door. "I should get back to the church, anyway. Prudence, I don't want to leave without assuring you once again that I don't have feelings for Daisy Barclay, only you. Stay here, my dear, and try to rest. You will always be safe with me."

"I know, Simeon. Thank you." Prudence said the words earnestly, but she must have been wondering, as Charlie was, whether Simeon was rushing out to confirm what happened to Daisy. Not that it would do him any good with the hospital staff's lips firmly sealed.

Charlie waited impatiently for the door to close behind the choirmaster, because he was eager to get an explanation for a point that had long vexed him: who had drugged Daisy on the night Ollie was taken and why? "Miss Winslow, why did you assume Edward Barclay drugged my wife?"

"Oh … ahh." Prudence locked her fingers into a ball and lapsed into silence.

"Come now, Miss Winslow. We know Daisy didn't wake up when Ollie was kidnapped because her cocoa was drugged. Was that why you assumed it was also Edward who drugged Grace last night?"

Her voice was a whisper as the tears trickled down her cheeks. "Edward always made Daisy a cup of cocoa in the evening to help her sleep. I thought it sweet of him to be so caring, until one night he admitted he sometimes put a drop or two of sleeping tonic in

196

her cup, but only because he was worried that lack of sleep would make her ill again. I didn't know before then, honestly."

"Which night was this?"

"Sunday."

"The night Oliver was kidnapped?"

Prudence nodded, but offered no explanation.

"Miss Winslow, I urge you to tell the whole truth. If not for Daisy, then for Oliver. What happened on Sunday night?" When Prudence didn't respond, Charlie lost what little was left of his patience. "Edward Barclay has a history of violence and abuse against his wife, Miss Winslow. He does not deserve your protection."

Prudence looked up at last. "I'm so ashamed I allowed myself to be fooled by him."

Her misery had Charlie regretting his outburst. "Good people are always the last to detect wilful deceit in others, Miss Winslow," he said gently. "Please, for Oliver's sake, what happened that night?"

"Edward and I went to the sitting room after Daisy retired. He said the strain of his wife's behaviour had become too much, and he confessed his growing feelings for me. Edward told me he wanted to divorce Daisy so we could be married." Prudence shook her head. "You'll think me naive to have believed him, because Daisy is so attractive, while I am not. But Edward wanted more children, which Daisy couldn't give him. He told me his wife had been unfaithful, and he wanted a good Christian wife. All I ever wanted was to make a home and have a child. I would have loved Oliver as my own."

"Edward would have had to prove Daisy was unfaithful to divorce her," Charlie said.

"Daisy only had to flutter her eyelashes and men like Simeon would run to do her bidding. That kind of power over men can turn a woman bad. I saw her in the park with a man, Mr Penrose Pyke.

They went to a secluded seat and talked together, with their heads close as if they were lovers."

"Can you describe him?"

"Tall, blond, handsome. He was attentive and caring towards her. Daisy was upset, and he consoled her. All I had to say was what I saw, then we could be a family – Edward, me and Oliver. We could leave Dunedin, go wherever we wanted. I've always had a yearning to visit the great opera houses of Europe, but I would have been happy anywhere. Edward had money invested, and I came from a wealthy family. It didn't seem impossible when he said it."

Prudence had seen what she wanted to see – evidence of Daisy's unfaithfulness rather than a tense meeting at which Daisy found out about her husband's appalling behaviour to Nathan Locke. Charlie didn't blame Prudence for her naivety. In his line of work, he saw many men like Edward Barclay, who could spin a lie as easily as breathing, whereas Prudence had lived a sheltered life caring for sick parents. She clearly didn't know Edward had lost his position at the bank and was as desperate for money as she was to be swept away to a better life. A life where dreams of the opera houses of Vienna and Paris might become a reality.

"What happened next, Miss Winslow?"

Her head dropped, hiding her eyes. "Edward tried to kiss me. I told him I wanted to be his wife but would not condone inappropriate behaviour right under his wife's nose. That's when he told me we would not be interrupted because he had added a little chloral hydrate to her cocoa to help Daisy get a good night's sleep." Tears dripped from the tip of her nose onto white-knuckled hands. "When I found out Oliver had been kidnapped that very night, I thought God was punishing us for our sins."

"Is that why you threw yourself into the search for Oliver?"

Prudence nodded. "I've been out all day, every day, looking for him."

And looking for salvation, Charlie thought. "You've been a hard woman to find, Miss Winslow. As the closest person to the Barclays, your evidence was crucial to our investigation. I even went to the railway station to look for you. You weren't there."

"I didn't stay at the station long because the person who was most likely to have seen the kidnapper leave with Oliver had just gone off duty. I went to find him, but he saw nothing. Not a single little blond boy was on the train that morning, so far as he recalled. I'm sorry. I suppose I ought to have realised you'd want to speak to me, but I had no relevant information to give you, Mr Penrose Pyke."

The planned divorce? The drugged cocoa? The fact that Daisy was being locked in her room like a prisoner while her husband lured another heiress into his web? Was Prudence really so naive she considered these facts irrelevant? Not likely. Prudence had been too embarrassed to admit her relationship with Edward Barclay and far too willing to turn a blind eye in exchange for a false promise.

Charlie tamped down his anger, because only a gentle touch would keep Prudence talking. "Miss Winslow, with the benefit of hindsight, do you think Edward took his own son?"

Her head shot upright again. "I know for a fact that he did not. That night, Edward and I talked for hours about our future together. I must have fallen asleep on his shoulder, because when I woke up it was morning and he was still on the sofa with me, asleep. Mr Penrose Pyke, I implore you to believe me when I say nothing happened between us other than conversation. Edward never left my side. He *cannot* have taken Oliver."

Prudence could be lying to cover for Edward, or indeed herself, but she seemed genuine in her denial. Charlie was inclined to believe her, if only because the distress shown by both Prudence and Edward at Oliver's disappearance appeared to be coming from deep within them. He was also ready to throttle her, because not knowing what happened that night had led him down a path where every clue had pointed to Edward Barclay, with Prudence as his likely accomplice. What if it was the wrong path?

Charlie took a deep breath before levering himself out of the chair with his crutches. "Thank you for your honesty, Miss Winslow." All he wanted to do was to go home and sink into bed, preferably with his wife beside him, and leave Detective Sergeant Kelly to sort out this abominable mess.

Prudence rose with him to open the door, obviously eager to see the back of him, but she couldn't resist a parting shot. "Mr Penrose Pyke, I hope you haven't been fooled by Daisy Barclay's fluttering eyelashes and engaging smile. She lured men in with her charm and lovely voice, as the Sirens lured men to their fate. If you're looking for suspects, I suggest you start there."

This was the second time Charlie had heard Daisy being compared to the mythical Sirens. Had he underestimated her? Was Prudence worried that Daisy had lured Simeon into helping her abduct Ollie?

Prudence must have regretted the implication of her words, because she hastened to add, "I don't mean Simeon, of course. She may well have used her feminine wiles on him, but Simeon would never stoop to committing a crime."

It occurred to Charlie, belatedly, that Prudence's desperation to find love with Edward could be partly a reaction to Simeon's besotted adoration of Daisy. After all, Freya had said Simeon wanted to marry Prudence, but her father had rejected his suit. How heartbreaking it would have been for Prudence to be free to marry Simeon at last, only to find his eyes had turned elsewhere. Perhaps what had begun as an attempt to regain Simeon's attention had ended with Prudence becoming tangled in Edward's web of promises and dreams. A tangled web indeed.

Prudence linked her fingers together in the classic prayer gesture, but, to Charlie, she looked less saintly than smug. Exceedingly smug, completely undoing the effect of her teary-eyed remorse. "You needn't worry about Oliver, Mr Penrose Pyke.

Once he is safe, you can rest easy that I will be there to look after him."

Charlie was at a loss for words. He took his leave with a tight knot in his stomach, fearing he had underestimated Prudence as well. What better way to gain attention than to be the heroine, spiriting baby Oliver away and "rescuing" him at the eleventh hour? His head hurt, his brain hurt, his whole body hurt, and he desperately needed a dark, quiet room to rest and think.

Fortunately, the cabbie was still waiting and eager to take him home in exchange for the diminishing contents of his pocketbook. Charlie would have swapped every last penny in it for a soft bed and a dose of painkiller, but it was not to be. At the corner of High Street, a wiry youth sprang out in front of them and waved the cab down.

Johnny Todd jumped up on the step of the cab and handed Charlie a note. "Left at the Barclays' house. You ain't gonna like what it says, Copper Charlie. Grubber says he's sorry, but it came while he was stuffing his face with pie."

"Not Grubber's fault, Johnny. I told him to take a meal break." Charlie realised the note must have been delivered in the short time between his visit to the Barclays' house and Grubber's return, which meant it couldn't have been left by Edward, Daisy or Prudence.

The last thing Charlie needed right now was more bad news, but he couldn't ignore the note. It was written in crude block capitals, bearing little resemblance to the first ransom note or to any of the handwriting samples they had gathered. It was also on a different paper stock and in a darker ink. Perhaps the kidnapper knew that handwriting and paper could be distinctive and was trying to baffle them with variety.

That was the least of Charlie's problems, because the note was a punch to the gut that left him unable to breathe. The ransom drop would now be tomorrow morning at eleven o'clock in the Dunedin Botanic Garden, a full day earlier than the previous deadline. The instructions were explicit: leave the ransom money in a canvas bag hidden within the bushes marked with a blue ribbon by the west corner of the south pond. No police, no private detectives, no tricks. The one thing the kidnapper did not specify was how and when Oliver Barclay would be returned; only that they would never see him again if the instructions weren't followed.

Charlie's head was ready to explode.

"One more thing, Mr Penrose Pyke."

Johnny's use of his real name jerked Charlie back to full attention. Whatever was coming next couldn't be good.

"Your wife's been looking for you. I don't think she's pleased you left the hospital. She told me to hunt you down and order you to go home, where she would be waiting for you." Johnny contorted his face into a mock grimace and jumped off the cab, slipping into the crowd like an eel through rushes.

Charlie told the cabbie to drive on. Grace on the warpath wasn't a cheery thought, but neither was the latest development in the case. He had a bad feeling about the second note, as if the magician orchestrating this show was deliberately distracting them, whilst Oliver was whisked away under their noses.

Resilience

Grace and Blaze sensed Charlie's arrival at the same moment. Grace because she was watching for him at the window, and Blaze because the border collie always seemed to know when Charlie was coming home.

According to Mrs Brown, Blaze had been pacing and whining all night, as if she instinctively knew Charlie was in danger. The dog had been frantic when Grace returned from the hospital this morning, and it had taken a lot of reassurance to get her settled again. Not surprising, because Blaze would have sensed how worried Grace was about leaving her husband in his condition. She had returned to the hospital as soon as she could, but he had already left, darned fool that he was.

But, right now, relief at his safe return outweighed any other emotion. As soon as Grace opened the gate, Blaze took off down the road in a blur of black and white. Grace's heart leapt to her mouth when their beloved dog threw herself at the side of a hansom cab until Charlie sent her back to the pavement. She was chasing her tail in circles like a puppy by the time Grace helped Charlie out of the carriage, but she settled into a more subdued ecstasy once Charlie had ruffled her fur and whispered sweet words in her ear.

Grace got her turn next, in the form of a lingering, if clumsy, embrace. There was no need to ask how he was feeling, because every battered, bruised, trembling inch of him suggested a man struggling to hold the grim reaper at arm's length.

She helped him up the path, wincing as he lurched forward. Charlie handled the crutches like a stick insect navigating a brisk breeze, not helped by Blaze weaving in and out of his legs. Being helpless was one of the few things her husband was terrible at.

"We have a visitor." Grace couldn't keep the excitement from her voice, knowing she was about to bowl him over with a surprise guest. He could certainly do with some good news.

Charlie groaned. "Is James Montgomery still here? I'd hoped he would have left by now. If I don't have an hour of uninterrupted peace to think, I won't be accountable for my temper. But before I go a step further on these blasted sticks, can you please confirm whether Daisy is dead? Before I left the hospital, I heard that Edward Barclay had attacked his wife, and you were seen taking a body to the mortuary."

"Come inside first, before you collapse. You look ghastly, but I'm sure I can cheer you up."

"Even you will be hard pressed to cheer me up today, Grace, because I have news too. We have run out of time. The ransom drop has been brought forward to eleven o'clock tomorrow morning."

"So soon?" No wonder her husband looked so grim.

"The kidnapper doesn't want to give us time to prepare, but we will be waiting."

James Montgomery met them at the steps with a broad smile, underscoring eyes shining with tears. He threw his arms around Charlie and embraced him gently. "You didn't say you suffered your injuries after diving into the river to rescue Daisy. I thank you, sir, from the bottom of my heart, for your bravery." James braced his shoulder under Charlie's arm and hoisted him up the steps.

Charlie allowed it, presumably because it was too exhausted to resist. He hobbled into the drawing room between his two helpers, letting out a yelp as a curly blonde head slowly lifted from the bundle of blankets on the sofa.

Daisy Barclay managed a feeble smile from a face that looked as if it had been through the ringer twice over. "Reports of my demise are premature, as you can see, Mr Penrose Pyke," she croaked. "Or Charlie, if I may, since I view you as my friend and heroic rescuer. I'm sorry to intrude upon your household, but Grace insisted I would be safer here."

When this short speech dissolved into a coughing fit, James rushed to her side, passing her a glass of water and propping an extra cushion behind her so she could sit up. Daisy winced, although her brother-in-law had been as gentle with her as he could.

Grace more or less pushed her dazed husband into a comfortable armchair and propped up his leg with a cushion on a table, before pouring him a shot of whisky with a morphine chaser. Not enough to knock him out, but enough to take the edge off the agony he was so clearly suffering. She'd have to examine his foot again, because she suspected one or more of the small bones might be broken. Having the ransom drop brought forward would at least bring this investigation to a quick conclusion, after which her husband would be on compulsory bed rest, even if Queen Victoria herself demanded his services. After all, Grace had access to drugs, handcuffs, and feminine wiles, and she wasn't afraid to use them.

Mrs Brown arrived on cue with a tea trolley laden with teapot, cups, milk, and a lavish spread of Charlie's favourite foods. "Nice to see you alive, Mr Penrose Pyke, though not for want of trying to kill yourself again, I hear. Eat up now, for I can see it's been hours since you last ate a decent meal. You need to rebuild your strength."

Charlie ignored everything but Daisy Barclay. A grin gradually spread across his face until the width of it pulled at his bruises and he winced. "A great pleasure to see you, Daisy. I cannot claim to have been heroic, as the water pulled me off my feet before I could reach you. To be honest, I cannot recall exactly what happened, except that I was tumbling through the torrent trying to grab anything I could and catch a breath."

"Don't you remember reaching me and holding my head up?" Daisy asked. "You even stopped the logs from hitting me and I distinctly recall you dragging me up that steep riverbank before I fainted. I would have drowned for sure without you."

Daisy had bruising and a nasty graze on what was visible of her under the blanket, which was testament to Charlie's success at shielding her from the worst of the knocks, but Grace could see she was every bit as exhausted as Charlie was from her ordeal. Daisy had suffered the worst of it last night as her body battled against shock and trauma, and a brief period without air thanks to her husband, before finally pulling back from the brink. Grace suspected Daisy had drawn from a well of hidden strength that had kept her alive for the sake of her missing son.

Charlie turned to Grace. "If Daisy is alive, whose body did you take to the mortuary?"

"Edward came to the hospital last night and tried to smother Daisy with a pillow," Grace said, "presumably to stop her from giving evidence against him. Fortunately, Declan was there to rescue her before any serious harm was done. However, we decided it would be better to remove Daisy from any further risk, so we covered her with a sheet and took her out of the hospital via the mortuary. More discreet that way. In the circumstances, we felt the fewer people who knew the better, given how quickly rumours spread. I didn't want to risk the kidnapper finding out what had happened and concluding his ransom demands wouldn't be met."

"You might have told me, Grace," Charlie grumbled. "Prudence Winslow overhead the policeman mentioning Daisy's body, and I wasn't in a position to deny her death."

Grace raised an incredulous eyebrow. "Correct me if I'm wrong, dearest husband, but you were told to stay where you were until I had spoken to you. By the time I got Daisy out of harm's way and ensured her condition was stable, you had disappeared, against explicit orders, medical advice, and common sense, stealing an elderly patient's crutches to make your escape."

Daisy made an odd gurgling sound that had Grace on her feet in an instant, until she realised Daisy was laughing. For a woman who had been through as much as Daisy had, she was remarkably cheerful. Charlie must have thought so too, because he gaped at her and shook his head, as if he might be hallucinating.

"Being alive and safe is an unexpected pleasure," Daisy said, "despite Edward's best efforts to silence me. And now I can be free of him forever, for no judge would refuse to grant me a divorce under the circumstances."

"I've seen men like him before," Grace said, "battering on the door of the women's refuge. Jealous and controlling, hiding behind a façade of godliness and charm, while harbouring a demon inside. It is not uncommon, believe me."

"He seemed so nice at first," Daisy said. "Edward convinced my father that he was an upstanding citizen with a bright future, and thus a much better match for me than the man I preferred. I was a weak-willed fool to give into my father's demands."

James Montgomery took Daisy's hand. "You made the sensible decision at the time, when the alternative was a struggling artist."

"Now a highly successful artist," Daisy retorted, "and the father of my delightful niece and nephews. My sister had more sense than me, you see. Once we have Ollie back, James has offered to take us back to live with his family. Ollie will grow up alongside his cousins in a loving home."

Charlie still appeared stunned by the turn of events, but not in the least contrite at Grace's scolding for his escape. He turned his intense green eyes on Daisy. "Rescuing Ollie is our only concern at this point. Everything else can be dealt with when that has been achieved. A new note was delivered this afternoon, informing us that the ransom drop has been brought forward to eleven o'clock tomorrow."

As deathly pale as Daisy's face had been, she went a shade paler. "Another ransom note?"

"You thought you knew who the kidnapper was, didn't you, Daisy?" Charlie said, "but this news has made you doubt."

"Yes. I mean no. I don't know."

"Please tell us who you suspect, Daisy. It's in your best interests to tell us anything that could help us find Oliver and get him back to you." Charlie waited in silence, but with his growing frustration obvious. Grace expected Daisy to give in and tell all, because people usually did when Charlie used that tone of voice.

Daisy sank a little lower into the blanket, stifling a yawn. "I'm sorry if I gave the wrong impression, but I saw no hidden meaning in the ransom note. Right now, I'm dreadfully tired and overwhelmed by all that has happened and I suspect you are too, Charlie." She paused to give him a chance to nod, which he didn't. "Honestly, Charlie, there is nothing to tell. You're right that I was startled at seeing the first ransom note, but that was only because the notepaper was so similar to the type used by Edward, as I told you. My reaction to the second note was simply because the change of date caught me by surprise."

Charlie was still looking at Daisy as if she had something to hide, but his eyelids were drooping from the effects of the morphine. "Now that the police have been brought in to investigate, I expect the kidnapper will be desperate to end this quickly."

Daisy's only response was a coughing fit from deep within congested lungs. James rubbed her back and handed her the glass of water. When Daisy had recovered, she cast them another doe-eyed plea. "Please, Charlie, will you come with us to the ransom drop and help bring my Ollie home to me? And you, Grace, for I know you have done as much as your husband to uncover the truth and you have been a friend to me when I needed one the most. I'll never forget how much you have done for me."

"We will be there," Charlie said, "but under no circumstances do I want you or James to show your faces outside the walls of this house until I say so. As soon as we have Ollie, we will bring him here to you."

"Could I not venture out wearing a hat and veil? Ollie is my son. He will need me."

"Dead women don't wear hats." Charlie glowered at Daisy with a fierceness powerful enough to scatter a gang of brigands. "And I don't need two more people to worry about when I am trying to catch a kidnapper." He raised a hand to stop her next plea. "That's my final word, Mrs Barclay."

Daisy flinched at his rebuke. "I understand. I cross my heart and promise not to be there tomorrow. To be honest, I'm not sure I am up to leaving the house for a few days, anyway."

"Charlie's right, Daisy," Grace added gently. "It will be easier if we can concentrate on our work without worrying about you. For now, you must go to bed and rest."

"We're forever in your debt," James said, as he picked Daisy up, blanket and all, with exaggerated care.

When they were alone again, Grace ran a practiced eye over her husband. "You need to rest too, Charlie. I can make the arrangements for tomorrow with the rest of our team and the police."

She could see Charlie was suffering, but she hadn't realised how bad it was until he agreed to her suggestion without a single grumble. Fortunately, James came back from putting Daisy to bed and lent his strength to helping Charlie up the stairs to the bedroom.

Grace settled her husband in bed, being careful not to snag his injured foot or put pressure on his wounds. When he was tucked up as snugly as a baby, she put a hand to his forehead, which glistened with sweat and radiated heat. "Perhaps I shouldn't leave you, my darling."

He brushed her hand away gently. "Just give me another dose of morphine, dearest wife, and put a plan in place to get Ollie back safely."

"You trust me?"

"Despite my grumbling, you have handled the crisis brilliantly. There's no one I trust more than you, Grace."

"Not even Alistair?"

"Not even Blaze. Now put me out of my misery."

Last Chance

Charlie awoke to a silent house. Three hours' sleep had restored him to a semblance of his usual self. Mentally, at least. Physically, he struggled to make it out of bed, because his pummelled muscles had stiffened while he slept and the pain in his foot was as bad as ever. Fortunately, he'd had the sense to keep his clothes on rather than face the impossibility of dressing on his own.

The next challenge was getting downstairs. James Montgomery had helped him up, but Charlie wasn't about to bleat for help. Using the banisters as a prop under his arm, he slid and hopped his way down, bumping the crutches behind him. Pathetic.

Mrs Brown came out of the kitchen at the noise and wordlessly took the crutches from him. "Two letters have been delivered for your wife, Mr Penrose Pyke. And Mr and Mrs Stewart called. I told them you were under doctor's orders to rest."

"Thank you, Mrs Brown." Charlie had never felt so grateful for her efficiency at fending off callers and not fussing over him. He took the crutches back at the bottom of the stairs and followed her to the kitchen, where the air was fragrant with the smell of home comforts. Mrs Brown was already cutting thick slabs of fresh bread by the time he took a seat at the table.

"Where is everyone?" he asked.

"Mrs Penrose Pyke is still out. Mr Montgomery is in the drawing room sketching. Mrs Barclay is sound asleep. I looked in on her a few minutes ago. She strikes me as one of those perpetually cheerful ladies who never lets on there is anything wrong until it all catches up with her and she collapses with exhaustion." Mrs Brown slid the plate of bread in front of him, along with a dish of pickles and cheese. "I made you a nice soft

211

potato and ham soup. I expect they didn't feed you properly at the hospital."

"Lumpy, glutinous porridge that would make you weep. I didn't bother eating, knowing you would feed me like a king." Charlie hadn't eaten the cold porridge he'd found beside his hospital bed, but only because his jaw had been too sore to eat and he had been too eager to escape.

He turned his attention to the letters. The first letter was from the woman they had met in the Botanic Garden on the first day, whose toddler had nearly fallen in the pond. She wrote to tell them not to worry about the man who had been watching the lady with the blond baby boy. The letter writer had asked around her friends and discovered that the lady was called Mrs Barclay and the man was only the choirmaster at the local church, who was acquainted with Mrs Barclay.

The day Blaze sniffed the woman's baby carriage seemed a lifetime ago. Unlike the woman, Charlie was not at all reassured to find out the choirmaster had been seen in the Botanic Garden, secretly observing Daisy and Oliver. The seemingly harmless Simeon Frobisher, who had failed to convince when he denied being in love with Daisy, was beginning to worry him.

The second letter was from Declan Kelly, who had looked up the files on the deaths of Aggie Gemmel's husband and son at Grace's request. Aggie's husband had died after being crushed by a dropped beam at a construction site a year and a half ago. The company had admitted fault and was paying Aggie a small pension. Her son had been born just over a year ago, which meant that Aggie had been with child when her husband died. The tragedy didn't stop there, because her infant son had died at the age of four months.

He mused on the new possibilities until the plates were empty. "Nothing like a hearty meal to heal all ills, Mrs Brown. Might we have tea in the drawing room?"

Charlie wanted to have a cosy chat with James Montgomery. Daisy had written to him, which meant James might know her thoughts about these people even though he had not met them. Talking to James rather than Daisy had another advantage – the man was an open book, whereas Daisy had, by necessity, learned to conceal her feelings. And James viewed Charlie as a heroic rescuer, while Daisy might harbour a lingering doubt that Charlie was still working on her husband's behalf.

James put down his sketchpad when Charlie entered, and helped him onto the sofa, with a soft cushion under his leg. "You are very kind," Charlie said.

"Caring for people comes from being a father to young children who miss their mother. Most people assume artists are self-centred people who care about nothing but their artistic creations, but that's more myth than reality."

Barclay had called his brother-in-law a ne'er-do-well artist, as if the man was halfway to being a rogue, which had coloured Charlie's image of James Montgomery before he met him. Now he could see Barclay was a poor judge of character. "May I see what you were sketching, James?"

James held out his sketchpad. "My children. I miss them dreadfully. They're staying with a friend for a few days."

The sketch, which displayed an artistry Charlie could only envy, showed children with bright smiles and curls like their Aunt Daisy. "You must miss your wife."

"Every hour of every day. It's going to be hard for the children to see Daisy again after so long, because she is so like her sister."

"Daisy will be excited to see them. I know she misses her sister very much. Women need close confidantes even more than we do, don't you think?" Charlie handed the sketchpad back. "James, I'd value your thoughts on various people Daisy met in Dunedin. Her letters to you and your wife might contain useful information Daisy herself has forgotten about. I've often found that an outside observer sees what those closest do not."

213

"I'll do whatever I can to help, Charlie. Ask anything."

"If you were not here, who do you think Daisy would turn to for help?"

James rubbed his chin with nimble fingers as he gave the question careful consideration. "She seemed close to her former housekeeper, Mrs Marcus. Freya, Daisy called her. They bonded over a common interest in painting, but I believe Daisy came to regard her as a trusted friend. Although, perhaps friend isn't quite the right word. Freya was more like a favourite older relative who allowed Daisy to be herself. A kind of comforting, protective grandmother figure. But I don't think Daisy would turn to Freya for help after Edward fired her, or even before. I got the impression that Daisy didn't want to impose too much on Freya, who was busy with her art and her own grandchildren. Daisy saw herself as a burden, although she was very grateful for the housekeeper's help and support."

"Did Daisy have women friends who shared a relationship more like the one she had with your wife?" Charlie asked.

"I suppose the closest bond she had was with a woman of about her own age who had lost a child. As I said, Daisy hates to be a burden. I believe she felt she was as much a support to this woman as the woman was to her. In an equal relationship, it is easier to ask favours, don't you think? I can't recall her name, but I know Daisy admired her for overcoming her grief and throwing herself into helping others. Volunteer work for charity, giving other young mothers advice, and such like."

"Agatha Gemmel? Also known as Aunt Aggie."

"That's her." James leaped up to open the door for Mrs Brown and her tea tray.

With a comforting cup of tea in one hand and a slice of Mrs Brown's ginger cake in the other, Charlie moved on to the trickier questions. "What about other men? Did Daisy have any male acquaintances in Dunedin?"

"Not if Edward could help it," James replied. "The only man I recall Daisy mentioning was a hapless choirmaster who bumbled his way into her affections. She felt sorry for him, because Edward was appalling rude to the man in front of the entire congregation over some trivial matter."

"The choirmaster admired her voice," Charlie explained, "and asked whether Daisy would consider private lessons. Mr Frobisher is not well versed in reading the feelings of his fellow man, or woman. He was mortified by Edward's anger, but the parish stood by him."

"Oh, I see. That explains it. Daisy went out of her way to be kind to him when Edward wasn't there, but she regretted it. The choirmaster began following her around like a puppy and leaving her little gifts. He'd 'happen' to be strolling in the park when she was there, for example. I remember laughing at her description of letting him down gently but firmly. Daisy has a wicked sense of humour when she is allowed to indulge it, but she is kind as well. Too kind. I hope the choirmaster took the hint. Daisy encouraged the man to seek solace with that dreadful woman friend of Edward's."

"Prudence Winslow?"

James nodded. "Daisy detested her, but she thought Miss Winslow was an excellent match for the choirmaster. Killing two birds with one stone, if you ask me. Getting rid of a man who was pestering her and a woman who was far too cosy with Edward. Just my impression, I hasten to add, since I have met none of these people. I might have it all wrong."

"On the contrary, James, you have been very perceptive. Did Daisy ever mention a man called Nathan Locke?"

James sipped his tea absently while he thought. "Was he the man who spilled a drink on her when they lived in Wellington? Daisy said Edward made a fearful fuss over it, I recall, but she has never mentioned the man in any of her letters from Dunedin."

Charlie took a risk and threw out a baited line. "I gather she only met Nathan Locke a few times."

"Daisy only talked about him to my wife once, if memory serves. From their giggles and teasing when they talked of him, I got the impression that he was a handsome fellow and amusing company, but I don't believe Daisy had any contact with him apart from the conversation at the Christmas party after the spilled drink incident. No more than half an hour chatting in a room full of people, and Edward flies into a rage. The man's deranged."

Half an hour of amusing conversation with a handsome, unattached man? A minute or two, Daisy had told Grace. No wonder Edward had his hackles raised.

"Did Daisy see him again in Wellington?"

"I doubt it after the fuss Edward made. Daisy and Edward went to Dunedin not too long after the incident, and she never mentioned Mr Locke again. I can see where you are going with this, Charlie, but there was never anything between Daisy and any other man after she married Edward. Daisy has a very strict moral code. She told her sister more than once that she had married Edward for better or worse, and she would stand by her marriage vow, 'until death do us part'. Tragically apt, since she came so close to dying by his hand."

"One last point, if you don't mind a personal question, James. Can you confirm Daisy sent most of her inheritance to your wife for her medical treatment?" Daisy had told Edward that was where her money had gone, but Charie wondered if she hadn't hidden it somewhere safe, planning to make her escape.

James gave him a pained smile. "Ellie's condition was incurable, yet Daisy sent us the money anyway. That's Daisy all over. She'd sacrifice anything for a loved one. I told her we didn't need the money, because I was selling my paintings for a good price by then, but she wouldn't hear of taking it back. I've kept the money aside for her, because I had the feeling that she would need it herself one day. You can be assured that Daisy is one presumed-dead woman who will be comfortably off into her dotage. Perhaps it was wrong of me not to return it. I certainly never meant to cause such a violent rift between husband and wife, but I didn't trust Edward, who believed it should be his money by right, as her husband. He was a man who clung to outdated values if they served his greed."

Charlie subsided into silence by way of a mouthful of ginger cake. James Montgomery's perceptions had been useful, but not conclusive. In fact, they had opened up new possibilities rather than the hoped for narrowing of suspects. A glance at the mantelpiece clock told him it was too late to make any further investigations today, even if he had been capable of it. In seventeen hours, at eleven o'clock tomorrow morning, all would be revealed. At least he hoped so. Charlie trusted Grace to make the necessary arrangements, but he loathed being out of the thick of the action.

James excused himself to check on Daisy, leaving Charlie to reflect on the information they had gathered. He must have dozed off, because he awoke to find Grace had brought Declan Kelly and the Southern Investigations team home with her. His business partner and mentor, Alistair Stewart, and his wife Lily Stewart, who was also Charlie's aunt. Grace's elderly great-aunt, Anne Drummond, and her new husband Kenneth Drummond, a retired barrister. And Johnny Todd, looking as disreputable as ever. Daisy and James had retreated to their rooms with a tray, true to their promise to stay in hiding.

Charlie watched on as the team agreed on their roles and strategy over the evening meal, leaving him feeling vaguely dissociated from reality. More than vaguely, if he was honest, since his thoughts drifted off at least twice, which meant he missed vital parts of the plan.

When the plates were cleared, Charlie roused himself to speak. "Am I to have a role?" All chatter ceased. He did not like the way they were smiling at him.

"My darling," Grace said, patting his arm, "how could we leave you out? I will explain your vital role tomorrow. Right now, I suggest we all have an early night."

If his wife meant this to be reassuring, she was very much mistaken, but he was too weary to argue. He allowed himself to be heaved up the stairs and put to bed like a child, before Grace disappeared again to see their guests out.

Charlie picked up the book Grace had by her side of the bed in an attempt to keep himself awake, knowing his wife's intention was to leave him to fall asleep before he had time to interrogate her. It was the book Daisy had given her. The eating regime it advocated seemed like a form of torture to him, but he was resolved to support Grace in whatever way she saw fit.

Their guests hadn't lingered, because Grace was back within minutes with a medicine bottle and a large spoon.

"Can't wait to knock me out again," Charlie grumbled.

"For your own good. Don't pretend you're not in pain, Charlie. Do you think I can't see your bruises and that hideously swollen foot and leg? You were mad to try to walk on it so soon."

"Can we talk first?" Charlie patted the empty space on the bed beside him. "Have a look at this letter." He fumbled on the bedside table for Declan's letter, knocking the book to the floor.

Grace eased in beside him and took the letter, scanning the contents at speed. "Poor Aggie, losing her baby son in such tragic circumstances. Sudden, unexplained infant deaths, with no prior illness, can leave a terrible emotional scar. Often, the parents find it hard to move on if they don't know the cause of death. The stigma can be unbearable."

"The grief I can understand," Charlie said, "but why the stigma? The report says there were no signs of injury or suffocation, and the coroner concluded he was a normal, healthy boy who died in his cot of natural but unknown causes."

"Charlie, my love, imagine you found your son dead in his cot one morning and nobody could tell you why. Imagine the guilt, wondering if you were to blame. And then the investigation, prodding and poking to see if you had caused or contributed to the death either deliberately or by negligence, fuelling more doubt and guilt. Doubly traumatic in this case, when Aggie was already suffering the grief of her husband's death. Finally, imagine knowing that people around you would be judging and whispering. A child dying of some obvious cause, like measles, would be far preferable to what these mothers suffer. Aggie, who is deeply religious, was probably wondering what she had done to provoke God's wrath."

Nausea swirled in the pit of Charlie's stomach at the very thought of it. His heart went out to Aggie for all that she had suffered. Now he understood the reason many of the local mothers were wary of her. He could imagine their gossip. *How could such a perfect wee boy die when he wasn't ill? What did that madwoman do to him?* They would not want their own children to be anywhere near such a woman, no matter what the coroner had decided, especially when she was so eager to hold their babies. On the other hand, he couldn't deny that the mothers who called her mad might have real cause for concern, since profound grief can manifest in unexpected and potentially dangerous ways.

"Daisy thought Aggie should be admired for her commitment to helping others as a way of overcoming her grief," Charlie said. "Aggie's support for Daisy was certainly welcome too, but I do wonder if Aggie became excessively attached to Ollie during a period of intense mourning, especially as her son's date of death was only a week before Oliver Barclay was born."

"I suspect you're right, Charlie. Aggie referred to Oliver's birth as a miracle. What if she saw Oliver as a miraculous gift from heaven to replace the son she had sacrificed?"

"If so, why didn't she take Oliver straight away? Why wait eight months? And why the ransom?"

"Madness takes time to sprout and grow, Charlie. Even if she isn't suffering from a form of mania, Aggie believes she has a

219

mission to help other children. Finding out Edward Barclay was an abuser might have been the final straw. Perhaps she saw herself as Ollie's saviour from a life with a cruel father. The ransom could be a misdirection to put us off the scent, but it's also possible she is running out of money now she doesn't have a husband to support her. A small pension is no substitute, especially as she has a large house to maintain."

Grace put the letter aside and tucked herself into the curve of his body. "Perhaps I am jumping at shadows, but that coroner's report is a timely reminder that Aggie's grief should not be underestimated as a potential motive. A belief in the righteousness of her actions would be stronger than legal considerations in her mind. You should see her house. Her dead son's room is set up as a shrine, as if she is constantly praying for forgiveness and seeking redemption."

"I agree, Grace. We'll have to keep a watch for Aggie tomorrow. On all of them, in fact. We have one point in our favour – no one but the kidnapper should know about the earlier date for the ransom drop."

Almost no one. Charlie was already regretting that he had told Daisy and James about the second note. Daisy was definitely hiding something. Charlie wondered if Prudence had been right to warn him about Daisy Barclay's character. And witness testimony now pointed to Simeon Frobisher being besotted with Daisy to the point of following her around and giving her gifts, even after Edward Barclay had warned him off so cruelly. How far would he go to help her?

"Honestly, Charlie, I'll be relieved when it's all over. All I care about now is getting Ollie back, alive and well." Grace slid out of bed to get the medicine bottle. She picked the book up off the floor. "Have you been reading the book Daisy gave me?"

"I want to support you in whatever way I can, Grace. I also want you to know that if I am fortunate enough to live a lifetime with

220

you, I will be the happiest man alive. Children don't matter to me as much as you think they do."

She bent down to kiss him, her eyes sparkling with tears. "This case has almost put me off having children. We have adorable godchildren, who come with the distinct advantage of being able to give the little devils back. All I want is for you to resist your compulsion to throw yourself into raging torrents and other potentially fatal situations, so that we can enjoy a long life together. Is that too much for a loving wife to ask?"

"I'll do my best." Charlie noticed the flapping cover of the book. "Sorry I dropped your book. I can seal the cover again."

Grace opened the book to tuck the loose paper inside. "There's an inscription hidden under the cover. *For my beautiful angel, with hopes for a brighter future.* No wonder Daisy covered the book to hide it from Edward."

"How do you know Edward didn't give her the book?" Charlie said, although he could see that it was not Edward's style.

"Edward scorned the book and its recommendations, because it wasn't written by a qualified doctor. Daisy found it in her knitting bag after a walk in the Botanic Garden and treated it as a gift from a fairy godmother. She thinks it probably came from Aggie, but Aggie denied giving her the book. Having seen the inscription, I'd have to say that 'my beautiful angel' sounds more like a lover than a friend."

"A book on remedies for infertility is hardly a typical choice of gift to a lover."

"Unless the lover wanted to give a gift that he knew she would value," Grace said. "Or unless he wanted a child too. I didn't like to say anything, but it is a little unusual to conceive after so many years of trying. By no means impossible, but uncommon enough to make me wonder if there was another secret to Daisy's sudden success within a few months of arriving in Dunedin." Grace advanced on him with the bottle and spoon. "Open wide."

"One of the odd truths about infertility," Grace continued, "is that it can be an incompatibility issue between husband and wife. There are cases of childless widows and widowers remarrying and having no difficulty conceiving."

Charlie took his medicine gratefully for once, knowing he would sleep better once the pain had dulled. He wasn't feeling as well as he pretended and he certainly didn't wish to hear any more about incompatible spouses. "It wouldn't do the lover any good. The law says the child belongs to the husband of the woman who bears the child, unless the husband denies he is the father."

"Which would leave the real father with little choice other than to take the law into his own hands if he wanted to have his child. Motives for kidnapping don't come stronger than that."

Charlie mumbled his agreement, but his thoughts were elsewhere. "Simeon Frobisher called Daisy his angel, in reference to her lovely voice. He also worshipped her, following her to the gardens and giving her little gifts."

"I simply cannot see Daisy and Simeon as lovers," Grace said. "Daisy may have been drawn to anyone who was kind to her, but I really cannot believe she would betray her marriage vows with anyone, least of all Simeon. And Simeon is not the type of man to have an affair with any woman, let alone a married woman. If he was involved in the kidnapping, it would more likely be because he believed it was a noble cause."

Charlie was not so sure about the purity of his motives. "Simeon has another motive, too, because he needs money to support a wife. He would have taken great delight at parting Edward Barclay from his money and leaving Edward's boot prints as a clue. Simeon's much smarter than he looks, and he's a meticulous planner. Revenge on Edward would have been sweet after Edward humiliated him."

"If Daisy did take a lover, which I don't think she did, then there is a more obvious candidate. A man with blond curls like Oliver."

Charlie knew exactly whom she meant – the Greek god who would attract admiring glances from women wherever he went. "Nathan Locke cannot have taken Ollie himself, but I suppose he could have paid someone else to do it, while he was giving himself an unshakable alibi in Port Chalmers. James said Daisy talked to Nathan for about half an hour at the Christmas party, rather than the couple of minutes she admitted to you. But Daisy never mentioned Nathan Locke in her letters from Dunedin."

Grace let out a puff of air. "Taking a lover is hardly the sort of thing one would discuss in a letter to one's brother-in-law. However, this is all pointless speculation. We have no proof, especially since Daisy also has blonde curls like her son. She'd have to have been a lunatic to risk her husband finding out, given his explosive reaction to the most minor of encounters with other men. If Daisy had been unfaithful to him, Edward would have killed her ..." Grace's sentence petered out as she realised the implication of her words.

"Daisy was brave enough to risk Edward's fury to help Nathan Locke get his job back at the bank," Charlie pointed out. "Would she do that for a man who meant nothing to her? We've been viewing Edward's jealousy as excessive only because Daisy told us so. But Edward was right about there being more to Simeon Frobisher's attentions than merely a choirmaster discovering an angelic voice. Perhaps Edward had been right to worry about Nathan Locke too."

"The white flower on the sundial did strike me as a gesture from a man who understood Daisy and her dire domestic situation."

Charlie felt a wave of drowsiness washing over him. "You're right about pointless speculation, my darling. Come to bed. We'll prise the truth out of Daisy in the morning."

Grace reached out to put the book on the side table, but something must have caught her attention because she froze, staring at the inscription, wide-eyed. She held it out to him. "Look at the handwriting."

The capital F in "For" had precisely the same elaborate curl as the F in "Friday" in the original ransom note. Whoever gave Daisy the little red book was the kidnapper, which narrowed the field of suspects, but not by nearly enough.

Blue Ribbon Debacle

Grace woke the next morning with a churning gut after a restless night of fearing the worst. If Daisy really did have a lover and he had taken Ollie, they would likely never see the baby boy again. Even if the kidnapper was solely after the ransom money, there was still the chance it could be snatched from under their noses without Ollie being returned. And then there was the possibility that word of Edward's attempted murder of his wife had reached the kidnapper, in which case he or she could take fright and view Ollie as a dangerous encumbrance.

Grace swung her legs out of bed, knowing that fretting over the many possibilities wouldn't help. Better to trust the plan she had put in place and hope she would not let her husband down after his touching faith in her abilities. How ironic that this dreadful case had drawn them closer together again, after a tough year of dashed hopes. The harsh reality of other people's troubles had a way of highlighting all that was wonderful in their own marriage.

Charlie was dead to the world, his face and torso a ghastly ash-white under the mass of livid purple bruises. He had tossed and sweated the night away until she had woken him for another dose of morphine. The sweating worried her, because Grace feared his lungs might have become infected from the filthy water, but he was sleeping calmly now. Perhaps it had been nothing more than the pain and effect of a hot summer night. She left him to sleep until the last possible minute, while she prepared for the momentous day ahead.

Mrs Brown was already in the kitchen. From the warm nook by the stove, the yeasty aroma of fresh bread set Grace's stomach rumbling, but she was determined to complete the full eight weeks of her new eating regime.

225

"I got some preserved trout from a friend whose husband is fond of fishing," Mrs Brown said, placing a fragrant dish of trout kedgeree in front of Grace. She had taken Grace's tentative request for a change of diet and turned it into an entirely new form of creative cookery, because there would be no dissatisfied bellies under her watch.

"Delicious. You are a miracle worker, Mrs Brown." Grace wanted to hug their housekeeper for her thoughtfulness, but Mrs Brown was old school – proud to serve and dedicated to her work, but keeping to strict boundaries of conduct.

Grace thought through the gaps in her plan while eating her breakfast, which was far superior to toast. By the time she drained her cup of lemon balm tea, she was confident that the kidnapper would have no hope of escape if he or she appeared at the ransom drop. She glanced up at the clock and choked on the last drops of tea. Was that the time already? She must have slept later than she realised. But she wasn't the only one. "No sign of our guests, Mrs Brown?"

"Quiet as mice, despite their early night. I expect they were both exhausted."

Too tired to wake up on such a critical day? Grace found that hard to believe at such a late hour. She went to Daisy's room and tapped softly on the door. No reply. Grace eased the door open. The bed was empty and neatly made. Daisy Barclay had vanished.

Grace raced along the corridor, knowing James Montgomery would be gone as well. There was nothing for it but to go ahead with the plan, because they had no time to waste searching for Daisy. Johnny would be here in an hour with the buggy to take Charlie to his assigned position, and she still had to get her husband up and dressed. Each person had to be in place well before the eleven o'clock deadline, so they wouldn't look like a team of hunters setting a trap for their prey.

She shook Charlie awake to break the bad news, but didn't give him time to dwell on it.

Grace kept up a chatter of information to distract him as she helped him wash and dress. "Alistair is already in place, watching from the hill with a telescope. Declan is arranging the ransom bag, using one of Johnny's more innocent-looking urchins to place it in position without attracting notice. The money is from Prudence, as you know, and Barclay will have a constable allocated to him, so he can't give us the slip. Lily will walk Blaze, and Anne –"

"I don't even get to have my dog?" Charlie grumbled.

Grace raised an eyebrow. Blaze had been a wedding present to them both.

"Our dog. Don't try to blind me with chatter, wife. I want to know what my role will be. I sincerely hope it will involve a horse so I can be mobile."

A horse? In his condition? Grace would have laughed if her husband hadn't looked so serious. "Charlie, dearest, you will be the supreme commander at the very centre of the operation." Grace had finished putting on his shirt and waistcoat and was now unwrapping her *pièce de résistance*.

"Don't think for a minute I'll agree to wear that," Charlie growled. His nose wrinkled as he sniffed the coat. "It smells like you dragged it off a week-old cadaver."

Grace forced his arms into an enormous baggy sack of a coat. It may have been respectable once, many decades ago, but the ensuing years had not been kind to the garment. From the ingrained smell and patched cuffs and elbows, Grace suspected it had been worn by the same man his entire life, having been too poor to buy a replacement and too lazy to clean it. She'd been left with little choice, as there had been nothing else big enough for Charlie in the church's charity box. The dear old lady who organised the charity box had been eager to hand it over for a good cause, or perhaps she was simply eager to get rid of it. Grace had also borrowed one of the bath chairs used to transport old folks, but Charlie didn't need to know that yet. She just hoped he didn't notice the hole in the bottom of the coat, which bore the teeth marks of a hungry rodent.

She tied a faded cravat around his neck and plopped a wide-brimmed hat on his head, which flopped over his face from the joint effect of long wear and humble origins. "There. You look just like that picture of Sherlock Holmes in *The Stand Magazine*."

"Grace, you and I both know that I look nothing like a detective. I look like an ancient geezer fallen on hard times who hasn't changed his clothes in half a century."

"I know," she said cheerily. "Perfect, isn't it? Nobody but your nearest and dearest will recognise you." Grace stepped back to survey her efforts. "Perhaps a pipe to complete the disguise?"

"No pipe, Grace. And no more of the supreme commander puffery. What do you intend for me to do?"

Grace leaned down to kiss him on the lips, avoiding the two-day-old bristles, which would be part of his disguise. "I am sorry about the costume, but it's critical that you and I aren't recognised at the ransom drop, because we can't risk the kidnapper taking fright. Disguising a six feet tall, broad-shouldered detective wielding crutches required some ingenuity."

Charlie looked at the threadbare cuffs, then back up at Grace, his eyes slitted with suspicion. "You wouldn't be planning on sticking me in the gardens as a scarecrow with my trousers stuffed with straw, would you?"

"Of course not," Grace said, but only because she hadn't thought of the scarecrow idea. "You will be an elderly man sitting in the sun reading a newspaper, whilst playing the vital role of our lookout. You will stay in one place, as necessitated by your injury, and you will keep your eyes on the ransom bag no matter what else happens. If you see anybody grabbing it, yell and we will come running. Don't give me that scowl, Charlie."

"I'll stop scowling if you stop grinning."

"Come on, let's get the old geezer down the stairs." Grace tried to hide her grin, but she truly hadn't visualised how amusing her husband would look in his disguise. In truth, she felt as if she was bursting with vitality for the first time in a long while. Was it simply the excitement of being in charge, with a better-than-average chance of being the one to catch the criminal, or was the new eating regime working already? It was too early to know, but Grace was determined to make the most of it while she could.

An hour later, Grace was in the Dunedin Botanic Garden, ambling from the main gate towards the south pond along one of the four paths leading from the entrance across the lower gardens. Another path intersected her route near the end of the pond, where her path split to allow access to both sides of the water. Thus, the ransom drop could be approached from every direction, with exits to the surrounding streets at all points of the compass. She had to hand it to the kidnapper. He or she had chosen the site of the ransom drop with care. The spot was open, yet bustling, with potential escape routes aplenty.

Grace stopped near the end of the pond and scanned the scene, which would appear to most observers to be an ordinary summer's day in the gardens. Artists painted the scene, readers ignored it, strollers admired it. On the sunny side of the lake, several families had spread picnic blankets on the grass between the pond and the main path through the gardens, allowing their children to roam free on the lawn or feed the ducks as they chose. A gentleman wearing cricket flannels was teaching his young son to bowl a cricket ball, cheered on by a lady with a baby carriage.

On the less crowded side of the pond, a group of lady cyclists knocked back glasses of elderflower cordial that probably contained gin, if their raucous laughter was anything to go by. An elderly lady and gentleman, each with a walking stick, strolled past them, making a show of averting their eyes from the unseemly frivolity. A Chinese lady hurried in a circuit around the pond, apparently trying to exhaust the boundless energy of her dog.

Except that it was no ordinary scene. The dog was Blaze and his minder, Lily Stewart, was having a hard job pulling the collie away from Grace and Charlie. The elderly couple were Anne and Kenneth Drummond, while the cricketers were the Kelly family.

Unfortunately, they were not the only familiar faces present. An artist of short stature stood a little further along the pond, where a clearing in the trees left the water visible. A pretty scene, but the artist seemed more interested in observing than painting, which didn't surprise Grace as she matched the description of Freya, the Barclays' former housekeeper. Aggie and the Guthrie family had laid out their picnic blanket not more than twenty yards from the bushes.

Grace could see no sign of Nathan Locke, Simeon Frobisher, or Prudence Winslow, or indeed Daisy and James. She knew that Edward Barclay was concealed somewhere nearby with his police guard, but she couldn't see them. They had allowed Edward to be present, despite his arrest, because there was no doubting his love for his son. Besides, they wanted to see his actions and reactions, which was why they had deliberately removed his handcuffs and given him an elderly guard. Declan and Grace were not convinced of his innocence in the kidnapping, and both were hoping Edward would use the opportunity to flee and lead them to Ollie, with the help of Blaze's nose.

Moira Kelly pushed her baby carriage up to Grace, leaning close as if to have a quiet chat with a friend. "See the middle bush? Alistair says the ransom spot was already marked with a blue ribbon when he arrived. The constable watching the area overnight saw nothing. The ransom bag is just visible if you bend down, but not likely to be seen by a casual passer-by."

Bending down wasn't possible in Grace's disguise, until Moira helped her onto a park bench on the less crowded side of the pond, before waving farewell. Grace reached down to extract a partly knitted baby jacket from her knitting bag, so she could see under the dense cluster of bushes. And there it was, a green canvas bag filled with Prudence Winslow's inheritance, tucked in a bush by the edge of the pond. The bag would have been all but invisible amongst the stems and leaves, except that a soft blue ribbon from a baby's bonnet was gently swaying in the breeze below it.

There was nobody else nearby, except for an old man in a wheeled chair near the short artist. Charlie looked every inch the weary old geezer, hunched down in the borrowed bath chair to disguise his height, with a crocheted blanket concealing his legs and a hat flopping over his face. Her husband looked as if he was asleep, but something in his posture told Grace he was deep in thought. He must have been feeding the ducks before she arrived because they were still clustered around him, quacking and pecking at his legs.

As if he sensed her presence, he glanced up. His fleeting smirk told her he hadn't missed the irony of her own disguise, before he lifted a newspaper to conceal his face. She heaved a sigh as she ran her hand over her enormous belly, which bulged under the ancient maternity gown Moira Kelly had lent her. Declan Kelly had suggested the disguise as a way to hide Grace's thin frame. Moira had stuffed an overly large cushion under the gown in her enthusiasm, but Grace had to concede it added to the deception and forced her to waddle like a woman about to give birth. All she had needed to complete the disguise was a ridiculously large hat to hide her face.

Grace hoped Charlie was keeping a close eye on the bag, because losing £200 to a devious kidnapper was the last thing they needed. She looked around again, spotting a few of Johnny's fleet-footed lads dawdling around the general area. Johnny Todd was slouched against a fence by the pond, smoking. She wasn't sure how old he was, because he looked about sixteen but acted twice that age. Grace would have to put a stop to that filthy smoking habit when this was over, but right now the lads blended in perfectly. It gave her peace of mind to know that none of their suspects could run faster than these young lads.

Lily walked by, flicking a glance at a bushy flax plant on the hillside, where her husband had been hidden since daybreak with

231

a telescope. Alistair Stewart had been briefed on the suspects and was watching for anyone or anything suspicious. Blaze was alert too, unlike the other dogs in the park that day, who were snoozing in the sun or chasing balls. It seemed they weren't the only ones to ignore the "no dogs" rule.

Blaze pulled at her leash every time the old man in the bath chair turned the page of the *Otago Daily Times* he was perusing. The old man let the paper drop now and then, as if the act of holding it upright was too much for his aged arms. Judging from the grim set to the old fellow's lips, which was all that could be seen of him under his broad-brimmed hat, he was not enjoying the lovely summer's day.

Grace adjusted the brim of the enormous straw hat she was wearing, so that it did not obscure her view entirely. Unlike her usual practical style of minimal headwear, the hat was weighed down with enough garish bows and artificial flowers and fruits to attract the interest of passing bees. Grace sat and fixed her gaze on the blue ribbon. She itched to be up and moving, but that was the job of others. Her role was the same as Charlie's – to keep watch on the green canvas bag in the bushes – but from a different angle.

There was nothing to do but wait. Grace knitted for a while with rather less attention than necessary. The irony of her "pregnancy" was not lost on her, but her main concern had been the seconds it would take her to shed the cushion-baby if it came down to a chase. Grace rubbed one foot across her other ankle, checking her concealed knife was secure in its sheath. She went back to knitting. After a quick count, she realised she had dropped at least three stitches in the last two rows. Knitting had never been her forte.

Patiently waiting was not her natural state either. Grace glanced at her pocket watch. Still fifteen minutes until eleven o'clock.

Moira Kelly stopped to chat to the mother of a fair-haired baby boy who looked about eight months old, but she moved on quickly. Grace couldn't see any other child who fitted Ollie's description, nor any suspicious baby carriages, boxes, or other means of hiding a baby. It might mean nothing, because there were acres of gardens in which to hide one small child while the kidnapper waited, but Blaze had not picked up the faintest trace of Ollie's scent either, which was worrying.

Mad Aggie unpacked a basket and handed out boiled eggs and sandwiches to the rescued Guthrie family. The parents and children looked freshly scrubbed, healthy, and happy. Aggie had clothed them in neatly pressed outfits in an outdated style, none of which quite fitted. At least one family had had their lives improved by this investigation, Grace thought, with satisfaction.

Was Aggie's presence here today coincidental? Possibly, since it was a glorious day to be outside. But highly improbable in Grace's opinion. How had she known that the ransom drop had been brought forward?

The Guthrie boy had scoffed his food and was now playing with a ball. The girl soon joined him, leaving Aggie holding the baby and the mother watching the toddler. Other children joined in the ball game until the lawn was a darting shoal of little bodies shrieking with laughter.

Grace switched her attention to the tiny artist and former housekeeper, Freya Marcus, who still hadn't picked up a paintbrush. Her head was perked to one side, looking intently at Charlie. Freya left her easel and strolled over to the old man in the bath chair with a tin in her hand. Grace told herself to look away, but she couldn't. Charlie took something from the tin and popped it in his mouth. If Freya had recognised Charlie, at least she had done so discreetly, under the guise of offering him a sweet morsel. After a brief conversation, Freya strolled back to the easel and picked up a paintbrush. Charlie made a note in his notebook and ripped it out, allowing it to flutter in the breeze.

Seven minutes to eleven o'clock. Anne and Kenneth Drummond strolled towards Grace at her signal. Grace tipped her head in Charlie's direction, hoping they would take the hint. Anne nudged Kenneth, who approached Charlie as one old man to another, exchanging a handshake and a few words, probably about the dreadful state of the world and how it wasn't like this in their day.

Meanwhile, Anne made light conversation with Grace about how delightful it must be for a young lady to be expecting the birth of her baby, and thus a life of ease watching the little sweetheart play in the park while she chatted to the other ladies about knitting and recipes. Grace parried her jest with a remark about how dreadful it was that some young ladies demanded the right to work like their husbands. Meanwhile, the fluttering paper disappeared into Kenneth's hand with a magician's skill. Perhaps he had learned the art of swapping discreet notes with the clients he defended in court back in his barrister days. Kenneth strolled back, stopping to admire a flower, before taking his wife's arm and dropping the note behind Grace's knitting.

Grace contemplated the square of soft lavender wool, which had started out as a jacket Lily had been knitting for Molly's daughter, before Grace ruined it with dropped stitches. She opened the note behind it: *Freya heard about of the change of ransom date from Aggie, who saw the note pinned to the Barclays' door when she went to deliver some baking to them. So much for our attempt at keeping it quiet. Freya is here because her dear friend Daisy, who is rumoured to be dead, would want her to be, for Oliver's sake. Perhaps she is hoping to be the one to rescue him? She'll have to join the queue.*

The note answered Grace's question about how Freya and Aggie came to be here today, whilst also suggesting that Freya didn't know Daisy was alive. Freya's concern for Oliver's wellbeing was both understandable and commendable, if that was indeed her motive for being here. Was Aggie here for the same reason?

Grace scanned the surrounding area again. It was the people she couldn't see who worried her the most. The kidnapper would probably remain hidden until the moment he or she ran up and snatched the bag. That is, if the kidnapper hadn't paid an unsuspecting accomplice. A few pennies to a lad would be enough to hire him to retrieve the bag and deposit it elsewhere. It is what Grace would do, and the reason they had so many people watching. If Grace had been the kidnapper, she would also create a distraction to divert any watchers' attention at the crucial moment, which was why she and Charlie would keep their eyes on the bag, no matter what.

Her watch ticked down towards eleven o'clock. Grace nearly leapt out of her skin when a brass band struck their first discordant notes from the direction of the band rotunda. The band certainly needed the practice. The oompah, oompah of the tuba drifted closer, painfully out of time with the clash of cymbals and the erratic thumping of a drum. All heads turned to a group of young musicians, who looked to be a high school marching band, as they paraded through the gardens. All heads except for those associated with the investigation team, whose eyes immediately swivelled to the blue-ribboned bush.

As the long hand of her watch clicked around to the hour, the band came to a ragged halt in front of the bush and split in two on the command of their harassed-looking leader, thereby blocking the views of both Grace and Charlie. At the same moment, a ball arched through the air, landing in the middle of the band. Grace couldn't see the children racing after it, but she heard the section of the band nearest Charlie erupt into discordant toots and thumps, as they become entangled with the children chasing the ball.

The ball emerged from the melee, flying towards the bushes, followed by the horde of children. The Guthrie boy Aggie had so recently welcomed into her home led the pack, whooping in delight. Grace glimpsed Aggie shoving the baby into his mother's arms and diving after the little lad.

Detective Sergeant Declan Kelly was hard on her heels, but he got taken down by the trombone player, who was trying to untangle himself from the French horn.

Grace jumped up and shed her cushion-baby, while the band frantically reorganised its jumbled ranks in front of her. By the time she had shoved her way through them, the blue ribbon dangled in an empty bush. She could hear the yells of the various members of their investigation team as they charged into the ruckus. Charlie gesticulated wildly, sending the diminutive artist towards the end of the pond, calling Ollie's name.

The band began playing again, almost, but not quite, in time to the whistled beat.

Declan emerged, gripping a startled Aggie, who was hunched over, clutching something to her body.

Johnny's lads had rounded up the children, while Alistair guarded the children's parents, who were frozen with the shock of the rapidly unfolding chaos, and Lily searched the nearby bushes with Blaze. All eyes were on Aggie, who uncurled her body and held out the ball.

Grace was the only person in a position to see the flash of movement bursting from the trees further down the pond, away from the crowd. To her horror, it was a person on a bicycle, riding at high speed towards the nearby side gate of the gardens, a green canvas bag balanced on the handlebars. Grace screamed at Charlie and pointed, but he didn't hear her over the hubbub.

She ran after the bicycle, but on foot it was hopeless. The person on the bicycle pumped the pedals as if his life depended on it and disappeared into the trees before she got a good look at him. Grace could hear a commotion behind her, but she concentrated on running as fast as she could after the rapidly disappearing inheritance of Miss Prudence Winslow.

A bicycle! Why hadn't she thought of it? Not even Johnny's lads could outrun a bicycle. The clever devil must have crept around the marshy edge of the pond to snatch the bag from the rear side. Charlie would never forgive her for not foreseeing the possibility.

A woman jumped in front of her, blocking her way. Grace pushed her aside, but the woman's arm grabbed hers.

"Grace, take my bicycle, if you can ride." It was Felicity Halbrook from the lady cyclists' club.

Grace jumped aboard, flinging an "I'll be back" over her shoulder as she pressed down on the pedals. The infernal machine wobbled alarmingly for the first ten yards until Grace's muscles remembered the correct way of balancing and steering without falling over. Up ahead, she glimpsed the other bicycle as it shot over a footbridge across the Water of Leith and disappeared from view again.

Her muscles were already screaming when she crossed the bridge and skidded to a halt in the street beyond, almost catapulting over the handlebars with an overzealous use of the braking mechanism. The street was empty, apart from a coal cart, whose driver was asleep in the seat as his weary horse plodded home.

Which way to go?

Grace was fairly sure the bag-snatcher was a man, which left Simeon Frobisher as the most obvious suspect. Or had they accepted Nathan Locke's alibi too hastily? James Montgomery was now a possibility too, if he had written the second note in order to scoop up the ransom money to secure Daisy's future. But Felicity had mentioned women wearing trousers for cycling, and Prudence Winslow had a similar profile to Simeon. Grace couldn't afford to make a mistake, with Ollie's life at risk.

Go left, toward Nathan? Right, towards Simeon and Prudence? Or some other unknown direction to James and Daisy? With the fleeing bicyclist getting ever further from her grasp, Grace had to make a choice.

She glanced behind her, but all she could hear was the sound of running feet, as yet too far away to help. Grace steadied the bicycle and turned right towards Simeon's house, because her glimpse of the bicycle rider put him at the top of her list. She'd only just got the pedals going in a steady rhythm when a ball of black and white fluff whizzed past her, leash bouncing and nostrils quivering with the scent of the chase.

Charlie, bless him, had had the good sense to spray the ransom money with eau de cologne. Blaze had been trained on the scent and was now racing ahead with a confidence that brought joy to Grace's heart. Blaze darted down one side street, up another, along the river path, weaving a winding route Grace could never have found on her own.

She was puffing now; her legs pumping around and around in an action her muscles were not used to. A child ran out from a house, causing Grace to veer and wobble alarmingly. The wheel caught the rounded edge of a cobble, throwing her off balance and into a pile of soiled straw waiting to be dug into a vegetable garden. Blaze was at her side in a flash, pushing her nose into Grace's hand and urging her up. Grace brushed straw off her skirt and contemplated leaving the evil machine where it lay, wheels spinning, but speed was more important than dignity right now. She remounted the bicycle and followed Blaze, who adjusted her pace for her less agile human companion.

Despite the twists and turns of the route, the general direction remained the same – towards the Leith Valley. Grace pulled up close to Simeon's cottage and hid the bicycle behind a hedge. Blaze came to her side at a gesture, accepting Grace's grateful hug as her due.

Grace eased her knife from the ankle sheath, all too aware that she was on her own and tackling a man who was dangerous enough to stoop to kidnapping a baby. For what? Because Daisy had refused Simeon's attentions? Because Edward had insulted him? To prove himself to Prudence Winslow? The oldest motive in the book – greed? Or had he done it at Daisy's request because he still worshipped her, which might explain Daisy's unexpected disappearance this morning.

Grace went around the back of the cottage first, noting the bicycle propped on the rear porch next to boots dripping with pond mud. She pulled the toy monkey from her waistband, where she had tucked it, hoping to return it to baby Ollie in triumph. Blaze sniffed Mama Monkey and circled the house, but she arrived back at Grace's side with an apologetic tilt to her expressive face.

There was nothing for it but to confront Simeon Frobisher. Grace checked the back door, finding it unlocked. Not a clever move, but he probably thought he had escaped unseen. She eased the door open, cringing as the hinges squeaked, and crept through the kitchen into the hall. The sound of a woman crying and a man comforting her drifted out of the far room. Grace plastered herself against the wall and held her breath.

"What were you thinking, Simeon? You might go to prison if you're caught." A woman's voice, rising in distress. Prudence, not Daisy.

"Don't worry, my dear," Simeon said. "I timed it to coincide with the weekly rehearsal of the High School Junior B brass band, which I have been attempting to wrench into some semblance of order with very limited success. I asked the music master at the school to take them today and explained they needed to practise their split-marching around the lake. Goodness knows they need the practice, but their utter lack of musical accomplishment did come in rather handy today."

Prudence's reply dropped an octave, but lost none of its tremor. "Are you sure nobody saw you, Simeon?"

"Absolutely sure. They thought it was that madwoman who is obsessed with babies. I thought you would be pleased I got your money back, my dear. You wouldn't have wanted Edward Barclay to have run off with your inheritance, would you?"

"No. Not anymore." A sniffle. "You were right all along. Edward Barclay was not a man to be trusted. Did you really mean it when you asked me to marry you?"

"With all my heart, Prudence. You cannot deny I would do anything for you, my love. Haven't I just proved it?"

"Oh, Simeon. I don't deserve you. After the horror of Daisy's death, I began to think Edward was capable of anything, even kidnapping his own child to get his hands on our inheritances. I can scarcely believe it was that madwoman after all, as I had thought at the start. What a relief that Oliver was rescued from that lunatic."

After a drawn-out pause, Prudence's voice pierced the silence again, almost high enough to risk shattering glass. "Oliver *was* rescued, wasn't he? Did you actually see him? Was he unharmed? I should be there with him. He'll need me."

"Oliver wasn't there," Simeon said. "Don't fret, my dear. The police will find him soon enough, or those private detectives will. I was sure they would be at the ransom drop today, but it was a man in cricket flannels who grabbed Mad Aggie. Prudence, we cannot say anything about retrieving the ransom money. The police would not understand that my rescue of your inheritance was driven by noble intentions."

Grace wanted to sink onto the floor and weep. She had seen the ball in Aggie's arms and the genuinely startled look on her face when Declan Kelly nabbed her. It was not the look of a cornered felon, but the bafflement of a foolish innocent who could not bear to stay away from the excitement of the ransom drop and the hope of seeing Oliver again. Simeon snatching the ransom bag may well have destroyed their last hope of finding the real kidnapper, who had presumably been watching from a well-hidden vantage point in growing fury.

She pulled herself together and entered the sitting room, allowing her anger to vent. "You are mistaken, Mr Frobisher. We had a dozen people there ready to grab the kidnapper. Between the antics of your brass band, Aggie's family, and your premature snatching of the ransom bag, the real kidnapper has slipped through the net, leaving Oliver's life in extreme peril. I suggest you both remain here and prepare yourselves for a visit from the constabulary. And don't bother trying to invent a story, because I overheard every word."

Grace stomped out of the room with Blaze at her heels, before Prudence and Simeon recovered from the shock. The last thing she heard as she left the house was Prudence wailing, "Oliver, my little Oliver," amidst a flood of tears.

As Grace banged open the back door, another thought occurred to her. Blaze gave a startled yelp at her sudden change of direction. At the sitting room doorway, Grace took a deep breath. "Mr Frobisher, a word alone, if you please."

Simeon followed her outside, his eyes darting in all directions as if he expected a police ambush.

"I want to be absolutely clear I understand correctly," Grace said. "Did you play any part in the kidnapping of Oliver Barclay?"

Simeon let out an anguished sob. "As God is my witness, I swear I had nothing to do with the kidnapping. I didn't mean for this to happen. It was only after I understood the depths of Edward Barclay's depravity that I came to believe he had taken Oliver in order to rid himself of Daisy and gain control of both her and Prudence's inheritances."

"Did you write the second ransom note?" Grace demanded, but Simeon did not reply. "Mr Frobisher. This is no time to conceal the truth. If you wrote the second ransom note, the real kidnapper might not know that you changed the date. We might still have a faint chance of catching the culprit and getting Oliver back at the original time, tomorrow at noon."

Simeon hung his head so as not to meet her furious glare. "I just wanted to get Prudence's money back to give her the future she deserves. Today's brass band practice seemed the perfect distraction."

Grace took that as a yes and sprinted for the bicycle.

What an utter, unmitigated disaster. Charlie would be furious.

A Helping Hand

Charlie watched on with helpless fury as the debacle unfolded.

The brass band marched off to inflict their cacophony on another part of the Botanic Garden, leaving Declan Kelly holding a football and a bewildered madwoman who insisted she had nothing to do with Oliver's abduction. The tension escalated when Freya returned to say she couldn't find Oliver anywhere, causing Aggie to collapse into hysterics.

Lily was nowhere to be seen, which meant she would be searching the vicinity with Blaze. Johnny's lads had rounded up the rest of the children, while Alistair and the constables detained the adults, but the ransom had disappeared and nobody had seen who took the canvas bag in the chaos.

All the while, Charlie sat on the sidelines in the wheeled monstrosity, wishing he had insisted on using crutches. He wouldn't have been quick enough to prevent the disaster, but at least he would be mobile now. Instead, he sat, fuming and thinking. The arrival of the chaotic brass band had thrown the carefully laid plan into disarray. He mistrusted such convenient coincidences, which suggested the kidnapper knew the band would be practicing in this spot. And one of the church ladies had told him Simeon Frobisher was known for his work as the choirmaster, but he also worked with the school bands.

He spotted Alistair Stewart and waved him over, sending him to stop and search the band, and ask them whether they had seen Simeon Frobisher or a green canvas bag.

Charlie cast off his disgusting coat and yelled to get Johnny Todd's attention. He sent Johnny and his lads scattering at a run to search the maze of paths through the gardens, although he knew he was too late. The agony of sitting and waiting was too much.

He put his hands to the wheels and found he could roll forward at a glacial speed in a more-or-less straight line.

Until a shadow fell across him. Charlie looked up into a face brimming with hellfire. Edward Barclay must have wrenched free of his elderly police guard, who was tottering in their direction, sporting a rapidly swelling eye.

"Where's my son?" Barclay yelled.

Looking into his client's furious eyes was the one of the hardest things Charlie had ever done, but Barclay deserved his honesty. Whatever his other crimes, he loved his son. "I'm so very sorry, Mr Barclay. We did our best."

"Your best?" Barclay shouted. "Your best was worse than useless. I've lost everything I love, thanks to your incompetence. You're fired, and don't expect me to pay your fee."

The rebuke was hard to take from a man who had tried to kill his wife at least twice, but it still stung deeply, because Charlie knew he had failed miserably. "We can still find Oliver," he said, hearing the tension in his own voice while watching his client's hands tightening into fists.

But the blow didn't come, despite the hatred contorting Edward Barclay's features, because the constable intervened by clamping handcuffs around Barclay's wrists, none too gently. "That's enough of your bile, Barclay. You've –"

Barclay shocked them both by bursting into rasping sobs on the policeman's shoulder. If Charlie had any lingering doubts over Edward's role in his son's kidnapping, it vanished at the sight of a man descending from fury into utter despair in the blink of an eye. The constable recovered his wits and led Barclay away, leaving Charlie alone again.

What Charlie needed now – aside from Ollie safe in his arms – was Grace by his side so he could put a new plan into action. He looked around. The spot she had been sitting was empty, the discarded cushion-baby flung on the ground, and she wasn't visible in the thinning crowd.

"Where's Grace?" he called, but nobody heard him. In rising panic, he bellowed at the top of his lungs. "Grace Penrose Pyke. Has anyone seen her?"

That got their attention. But all he saw was shaking heads.

A woman in cycling knickerbockers hurried towards him. Felicity Halbrook. "I lent Grace my bicycle. She was pursuing a man mounted on a bicycle with a bag on the handlebars."

A bicycle. How could he call himself a detective when he missed such an obvious means of absconding quickly with the ransom? "Was it a green canvas bag?"

"I think so. He rode past so quickly, I only caught a glimpse before I had to leap out of his way to avoid being run over." Felicity pointed a bony finger towards the side gate. "They went that way."

"Thank you, Miss Halbrook. Might I ask you to remain here until Grace returns?"

Felicity nodded. "I'm not leaving without my beloved safety bicycle. I wouldn't have lent it to anyone but Grace. You have an admirable wife."

"I know. Thank you for your presence of mind. You have saved us for a second time." Charlie stopped her as she walked away. "Wait, are you absolutely certain it was a man?"

"The person was wearing a man's trousers, but it is not unknown for women bicyclists to adopt such attire to allow them to cycle faster. One of our number won a bicycle race recently wearing trousers. You should have seen the horrified look on the race officials' faces when they discovered she was not a man."

"Did you notice anything else about the person on the bicycle?"

"He was rather ungainly, with flapping elbows and an awkward style, although the fellow was dashed quick on the pedals too. Slim, I'd say, but that was only a fleeting impression."

"That's most helpful, thank you." Charlie rolled the bath chair away to give himself a moment to think. Simeon Frobisher sprang to mind from the description. Indeed, it seemed as close to a certainty as he was likely to get, especially after the brass band incident.

However, Simeon's involvement was a blow to the direction Charlie's thoughts had been taking right up to the moment the band appeared and the green canvas bag vanished. While waiting by the pond for the ransom drop, Charlie had made good use of the quiet time to think. The last three days had been so chaotic he had hardly had a moment to focus on the evidence, especially since his little dip in the Leith, which had left his brain running at half speed until today. The pieces of the puzzle, which had seemed so contradictory, had fallen into a new pattern.

The importance of Daisy being drugged on the night of the kidnapping had struck him from the start, pointing squarely at either Prudence or Edward. Edward's boot prints outside the nursery window, the use of his notepaper for the ransom note, his craving for the inheritances of both women, and Prudence's willingness to do anything for Edward – the conclusion had seemed inescapable.

Until the moment Prudence admitted that Edward had drugged Daisy to give them time alone to discuss their future together. Prudence might have been lying about her and Edward having nothing to do with the kidnapping, but Charlie didn't think so. Add to that the evidence of the inscription in Daisy's little red book, which pointed towards someone who wanted to help Daisy, and therefore not Prudence and Edward.

Charlie knew he should have thought through the implications of those two points before now, but he'd been distracted by a deluge of new evidence pointing in other directions. It came down to this: if Edward and Prudence were not the kidnappers, then the real kidnapper did not know that Daisy had been drugged that night. Thus, the kidnapper must have expected Daisy to wake up during the forced entry to the nursery. The most likely conclusion was that the person was a friend, whose intention had probably been to help both Daisy and Ollie to escape from Edward.

If so, the person must have been shocked to find Daisy too drugged to move. The seal on the window was already broken, which meant the culprit could not simply walk away and come back another night. Did the person take the baby and use Edward's stationery to write a hastily conceived ransom note to cover the real reason for the break-in? A ransom note containing a clue only Daisy would recognise, so she could choose a suitable moment to make her escape and rejoin her son in safety. Unfortunately, Daisy had not seen the note until the night of the storm, forcing her precipitous departure from the house in the dark.

However, if that theory was correct, Oliver Barclay's disappearance had never been about the ransom, and thus the ransom drop should have been a distraction. Simeon Frobisher had just blown a gaping hole in his conclusion by taking the ransom money. Unless Simeon was the person who had been on Daisy's side all along.

Charlie knew where Simeon lived, but he doubted Simeon would keep Ollie at his home. Blaze could use her nose to track him to his lair. He looked around. Where was his beloved black and white detective? Lily had rejoined the team, but Blaze was not with her. The dog's absence brought him hope, because she would only have left the vicinity with Grace. A comforting thought, because he did not like to think of Grace alone with a desperate man.

He rolled himself over to the rest of the team, who were in discussion with Detective Sergeant Declan Kelly, whose cricket flannels were no longer white. Alistair returned and reported that none of the brass band had seen Simeon or the canvas bag.

"The ransom bag was taken by a man on a bicycle," Charlie said. "Simeon Frobisher, I believe. Grace followed him towards the side gate."

"Blaze ran away from me in that direction," Lily chimed in.

"We'll go after her," Alistair added. "Declan had the foresight to arrange transport by the main entrance. Don't worry Charlie. We'll get Grace back to you and ensure Frobisher is caught."

"Take a constable with you to arrest Frobisher," Declan said. "I'm going with Mrs Agatha Gemmel to search her house. And I'll send a constable to check the Barclays' house, in case the kidnapper has left the baby there. Send a message to the police station if there are any developments. And please, do it quickly, because DI Wallace is going to have me tarred and feathered if I return without the baby boy."

"We'll go home to see if Daisy has returned," Anne Drummond said.

Within a few minutes, Charlie was the only team member left in the Botanic Garden. Normal life had resumed around him, but he had never felt so alone. He turned to find Freya back by her easel, pale with shock and packing up her paints. He rolled over to her.

"I'm not sure what just happened," Freya said, "but there is no point in me staying if Ollie isn't here. I certainly won't be doing any more painting today."

Charlie wheeled the bath chair around to the front of the easel. "Your painting looks finished to me, Freya," he said, noting that she had signed it, which suggested she thought it was finished too. "It's wonderful."

The painting depicted people enjoying the delights of the flower gardens, not the pond, and the paint did not appear wet, which meant she hadn't touched it today. Charlie couldn't imagine what more Freya could do to improve the painting because every inch of the canvas glowed with the vibrant energy the artist brought to the world. The people were recognisable, even though they were not portrayed with traditional realism.

"Freya, would you do me a favour?"

"Of course, Charlie."

247

"I find myself stranded in this frustrating contraption, having been deserted by my wife and family. If I carry your equipment on my lap, would you be strong enough to push me to the main entrance, where my carriage awaits? I have important business to attend to."

"Certainly. I may look like a feeble old lady, but scrubbing floors and wielding paint brushes has given me hidden strength."

Charlie scribbled a note for Grace and asked Freya to give it to the woman in the cycling outfit. While he waited for her to return, he took the painting off the easel and laid both across his lap. Laughter bubbled inside him at the thought that his embarrassing disguise and pathetic helplessness had been vital in making the final breakthrough he needed to confirm his growing suspicions. Even his grumpy comment about being stuffed with straw and used as a scarecrow had helped him crack the case, although the crucial piece of the puzzle hadn't fallen into place until he saw the completed painting.

Freya returned and hung the paint box on the back of the bath chair. As promised, she had no trouble pushing the combined weight of man and art. "Don't look so downcast, Charlie. Realistically, what hope was there with such a short time to find the kidnapper? We must pray that Oliver will be left at the Barclays' house and all will be well."

"Now that Edward Barclay has fired me, Ollie's safe return is all that matters." Charlie glanced over his shoulder at her. "But you're wrong in thinking I don't know who the kidnapper is, Freya. I'm simply trying to decide what to do about it."

The bath chair veered slightly as Freya reacted to the news. "Does that mean you saw the person who took the ransom money, Charlie?"

"I didn't need to, because the ransom was nothing more than another infuriating distraction. I have to say, Freya, you are a devilishly clever person."

The squeak of the bath chair and the puff of Freya's breathing filled the silence before she spoke again. "I could say the same of you. The dedication shown by you and your wife has been impressive. I wanted to unburden my conscience to you when I met you in the gardens and you seemed so charming, but I couldn't quite trust myself to believe you would do right by Daisy, when the law would come down on Edward's side. A terrible mistake, as it turned out, almost costing two lives. I can only apologise most sincerely and thank you for saving Daisy after her vile husband tried to kill her."

Saving Daisy, Charlie noted, which meant Daisy had already contacted Freya to tell her she was still alive. He wasn't surprised, because he'd been sure Daisy knew who had her son. He had also noticed they hadn't stopped by the carriages waiting at the main entrance. "If you are kidnapping me too, Freya, I hope you will at least take me to where you hid Ollie."

"I won't risk an innocent person getting in trouble, Charlie. Anyway, Ollie isn't there anymore."

"You did say you had children and countless grandchildren locally, but I never had time to follow that lead. I take my hat off to you, Freya. It was like hiding a needle in a haystack." Charlie noted that Freya hadn't said where they were going, but he was happy to go along for the ride. "Arriving to find Daisy too drugged to escape must have been a terrible shock. To come up with the kidnapping plan on the spot showed great presence of mind, although might I also suggest you showed a reckless disregard for your future if you had been caught."

"It was a moment of madness, driven by desperation and panic rather than by presence of mind, but you are correct about the rest. I'm an old woman, Charlie. My future means less to me than the future of a woman I loved almost as a daughter. I truly feared for Daisy's life."

"Why, Freya?" Charlie wanted to be sure he understood her motivation before he decided what to do about her.

249

"When I was cleaning the study one day, I saw a letter from Barclay's solicitor. Edward was planning to divorce Daisy, or have her declared mentally incompetent, but I knew it would only be a matter of time before he realised that faking her death in an apparent accident would be easier. Even if I was wrong, I knew what he was planning and I couldn't bear to see mother and child separated. I kept an eye on the house after I was dismissed as their housekeeper, but Daisy was never left alone. Seeing Barclay sealing her in her room was the final straw. I knew I had to act. May I ask what gave me away?"

"Using Edward's old boots was a masterstroke of deception, but it also hinted at somebody who knew the house. When I found the boots, I noted a few bits of straw inside but gave it no further thought until this morning, when I realised that straw would be ideal to stuff the boots, allowing someone with much smaller feet to wear them. And then there was the way Oliver hadn't cried and his blanket had been neatly turned down, showing the kidnapper cared for him."

"I'll remember that next time I kidnap a baby," Freya said with a wry grin.

"However, I have to admit it wasn't until the ransom drop that my suspicions settled on you. Partly from finally having the time to review all the evidence and partly because our border collie was being unusually wilful about dragging her walker in our direction. When I saw your finished painting, I knew it was you that Blaze was after, not me."

Freya didn't speak again until she had navigated a series of potholes and a narrow alley between two streets. They were heading towards her cottage. She took a breather at the end of the alley. "All right, I give up. What was it about my painting that declared me a criminal?"

Charlie's gaze dropped to the painting on his lap, now signed with a single name, "Freya." "Such a small thing, a signature, yet so telling. The elaborate F in Freya matches the capital F of Friday in the first ransom note."

"A single letter was my downfall?" Freya expelled a half-laugh, half-groan. "I hope you realise that I never had any intention of taking the ransom money, unless Daisy needed it for her future survival away from Edward. And I didn't write the second ransom note."

"I know. Another unfortunate distraction to throw us off the scent."

"Not intentionally. Nothing turned out as planned. Daisy didn't realise the first note was from me, and they engaged your team to find Ollie. I panicked. It only got worse when I tried to reach Daisy but couldn't. When I heard the rumour Daisy was dead, I was beside myself with the fatal chain of events I was responsible for."

"Daisy didn't realise you had Ollie because she didn't see the original ransom note until the night of the storm. I presume she left the house to come and find you, having finally realised who had her son. May I ask what the clue in the note was?"

Freya smiled. "When I was in France studying art, I was particularly taken with the work of a painter called Claude Monet, who signed his work with an irregular flourish that often left the final 't' of his name looking like a misshapen Y. Daisy saw the two Monet paintings I brought to New Zealand. She adored them but misread his signature as 'Claude Money' the first time she saw it. It became a joke between us. 'Here's your Monet', she'd say, when paying my housekeeping wages."

The oddly shaped letters of the original ransom note had struck Charlie when he first read it. "Money for baby" it had read to everyone who saw it, but Daisy would have read "Monet" and known where to find Oliver. No wonder a look of relief had crossed her face when she finally saw the note. If only she had seen it sooner, a great deal of pain might have been avoided, including his own.

251

"Do you know what happened to the ransom money?" Freya asked.

"I suspect Simeon Frobisher took it, presumably to give the money back to Prudence Winslow. Barclay convinced her to hand over her inheritance for the sake of Oliver."

"That man! Barclay presents himself as a shining example of Christian morality, but he's as black as tar on the inside, and now it seems he is not even willing to spend his own money on saving his son. Daisy's better off without him, and so is Ollie. You do see that, don't you, Charlie, regardless of what the law says about a husband's rights over his child?"

"Edward was caught red-handed attempting to kill his wife, Freya. Ollie will no longer be a child by the time his father is released from prison."

The problem for Charlie was what to do about Freya. She could be charged with kidnapping and breaking and entering if her role in this nightmare came to light, despite Freya having acted in the best interests of Daisy and her son. As it stood, Charlie was the only one who knew who had taken Ollie. Grace would have a say too, naturally, but he already knew what her view would be – that justice and the law were not always the same. Charlie decided to wait until he saw Daisy's reaction to what Freya had done.

They had arrived at Freya's cottage. The tiny artist had more than enough strength to help him out of the bath chair and up the uneven stone steps to a gaily painted front door. She went ahead at that point to unlock the door.

As soon as Freya entered the cottage, Daisy pushed herself out of her chair and limped across the narrow space to her, flinging her arms around the old lady and kissing her cheek. "Freya, my dear, brave friend. We were worried when you were away for so long. Did –"

Daisy's question died on her lips as her gaze fell on Charlie, who had entered the cottage and shut the door behind him. Daisy moved between Freya and Charlie. "Freya saved me, Charlie, just as much as you did. If you have come to arrest her, I won't allow it, even if you have to arrest me instead."

James Montgomery, who was holding a blond-haired baby boy in his arms as if the infant was the most precious thing in the world, stood up to join Daisy. "*We* won't allow it."

Charlie couldn't keep his eyes off the baby, who held out his chubby little arms to Charlie and said, "Dada."

"Can I hold him?" Charlie asked. "I won't take him away from you. I just … it's been hellish not knowing …"

James exchanged a look with Daisy and handed the boy over. Ollie nestled into his arms and smiled the innocent smile of a dearly loved child. The warmth of his body, the fresh smell of soap, the softness of his hair against Charlie's cheek – all of it told him that Ollie had had the best of care. The relief of knowing the baby was safe sent tears down his cheeks.

Outside, the sound of horse's hooves moving at speed triggered a visceral reaction inside him. Charlie was about to hand the baby back and tell James to hide him, when the door opened and Grace barged in with Blaze at her side.

Grace's frantic eyes fell first on Charlie and then on Ollie, and then her fear drained away and a smile lit her face. Charlie handed Ollie to her, so that he wouldn't be the only one reduced to tears.

Ollie took one look at Grace and said, "Dada", while Blaze sniffed the baby and stiffened into her "target identified" pose.

"Why don't we all take a seat?" Freya said, the loose skin around her eyes wrinkling in delight.

James helped Charlie to shuffle to a sofa covered in a colourful patchwork quilt. Grace sat beside him, with Ollie still nestled in her arms, pulling on an escaped tendril of her dark hair. Grace brought out Mama Monkey and wiggled the stuffed toy in Ollie's sightline, making him giggle. He let go of her hair and reached for his beloved toy with a gurgle of joy.

Charlie was finding it increasingly hard to be cross at Freya for the chaos she had caused, especially as Ollie was now mimicking Grace by wiggling the monkey at them.

Freya took the stool by a spinning wheel, leaving an armchair for Daisy. James perched on the arm of her chair with his hand on her shoulder. She was still weak, pale, and bruised, but she radiated happiness.

"How did Charlie work out you had Ollie?" Daisy asked.

"A single capital F was my downfall," Freya said. "Daisy, darling, did you have to hire such a fiendishly clever detective? And now he has to arrest me. No, don't look like that, Daisy. What I did was a crime, although I'm proud of doing what I could to help you, even if it went so disastrously wrong. I only hope they allow prisoners to have paints and canvas."

Daisy shot a fierce glare at Charlie. "If you try to arrest Freya, I will swear I set the kidnapping up myself to escape my brute of a husband, and then forced Freya to look after my child."

Grace pushed back her tangle of hair and broke the silence following Daisy's outburst. "Charlie, could we not simply say Ollie was found on Freya's doorstep? It's not unreasonable to assume the kidnapper would take fright after hearing rumours of Daisy's demise and her husband's arrest for attempted murder."

All eyes turned to Charlie. "I owe Declan Kelly and Detective Inspector Wallace the truth, so they don't waste time searching for the culprit or lie awake at night fearing the kidnapper will strike again." He closed his eyes for a moment, before removing Ollie from Grace's arms and standing.

A simultaneous intake of breath rippled around the room. James and Daisy lurched to their feet to prevent him from taking Ollie away from them.

Charlie handed Ollie to Daisy. "However, there's no reason Ollie cannot stay with you. All I ask is that you write to Edward in prison now and then, so he knows Ollie is thriving in his new home."

Daisy buried her face in her son's blond curls, so like her own. "I suppose Edward deserves that much. Whatever else he is, Edward loved Ollie with all his heart. What will you do about Freya, Charlie?"

"As well as being the very best of policemen, Detective Sergeant Kelly is a devoted father and Detective Inspector Wallace is a doting grandfather. When the circumstances behind Freya's actions are explained, I strongly believe they will let the matter drop, especially as the kidnapping was never officially reported to the police and Edward Barclay has well and truly proved that Daisy was in mortal danger, as Freya believed when she attempted their rescue."

James stepped forward and pulled Charlie into an embrace that squeezed the breath out of him. "I can't thank you enough, Charlie. And Grace too. I wish there was something we could do to repay your kindness."

"Daisy gave me hope that I may yet have a child of my own," Grace replied, "and a book to show me the way. There is no more precious gift than that. Although Freya deserves credit for that too, as the little red book must once have belonged to her."

Freya dipped her head. "The book helped one of my own daughters. I couldn't be happier it has found the perfect home with you, Grace. After all, Freya is the Norse goddess of love and fertility."

"Perhaps you might write, Grace, and let us know if you are blessed as I was." Daisy held Grace to her for a long time, until Ollie's squirming separated them.

Freya sandwiched both of Charlie's outsized hands between her own tiny hands. Warmth tingled through his fingers as if he was being touched by the Norse goddess herself. "It's been a pleasure meeting you, Freya. We should leave you now. The police will be concerned that Grace and I are missing, and I am eager to share the wonderful news that Oliver is safe."

"I have the buggy outside," Grace said. "No more than a brief stop at the police station, though, Charlie. I've seen patients at death's door who looked in better shape than you."

A gross exaggeration, but Charlie had to concede his battered body was throbbing from top to toe.

"Wait, I have the perfect gift to express our gratitude to you." Freya darted into another room and returned with a painting in a similar style to her own. "This was painted by an exceptionally talented artist I met in France, but I think it is calling out to you."

"Freya, it's beautiful, but we can't take your gift." Charlie held it up in front of him but wasn't entirely sure what it was. The colour and brushwork were extraordinary – a seemingly random scatter of swirls and splodges of blue and red and yellow and gold. Freya took it and held it a few feet away until Charlie suddenly saw that the painting depicted a field of riotously coloured flowers.

"Flowers are a symbol of fertility too." Freya pressed the painting into his hands. "I know this gift will bring you good fortune as well as viewing pleasure. The artist will be famous around the globe one day, I am sure of it, so please consider it your fee for solving this case."

Freya was right. The painting did call to Charlie, even if it would always remind him of this extraordinary investigation and a tiny old lady who almost got the better of him with her fairy godmother's kindness, her cleverness, and her pixie grin.

"It's truly wonderful. Thank you, Freya. I will treasure it."

James helped Charlie out to the buggy and promised to return the bath chair to the church hall. Grace took the reins, and they headed away at a brisk trot, with Blaze balancing behind her, stretching her head into the breeze.

Charlie sat back and felt content in his certainty that this was the start of a bright new life for all concerned. Or perhaps he was delirious from a mix of pain and euphoria at finding the missing baby alive.

As for the painter being famous one day, Charlie didn't care if he never saw the signature "Claude Monet" again. He and Grace were closer than ever, and that was all the mattered.

Read on

In Book 9, **Shocking Deceptions**, Penrose and Pyke's hopes of a quieter life are dashed by a spate of baffling burglaries and a persuasive charlatan promoting a miracle cure.

NEW! Audiobooks of the *Penrose & Pyke Mysteries* are now available.

Visit my website for more details: https://RosePascoe.com

Thank You

Thank you for reading this story. If you enjoyed it, I would be very grateful if you would leave a rating or review to help other readers discover it.

Find out about other books and sign up for notifications of new releases at https://RosePascoe.com

Historical Notes

The story may be set in 1894, but the issues faced by the fictional characters are all too real in our modern era. Issues such as domestic violence and infertility must not be taken lightly in any context, but I hope that I have at least depicted the women in this story as being more than stereotypical "helpless victim" figures. As we all know, women have extraordinary reserves of resilience and compassion if they are nurtured with the right support.

The story depicts that most insidious and all too common form of domestic violence – a creeping, behind closed doors, corrosive abuse designed to diminish and control. How much worse it must have been in the Victorian era, when women's lives were dictated to a large extent by husbands, fathers, the church, and the law. Divorce was possible, but strictly limited and shameful. A husband could divorce his wife on the grounds of her adultery, but a husband's adultery was not of itself sufficient grounds for divorce. A wife also had to prove some other ground such as cruelty, desertion or bigamy. And, of course, the financial implications of divorce were even more serious for women in those days than they are now.

Early in the Victorian era, women had few property and contractual rights. In fact, a married woman did not exist as a legal person outside of the legal entity of her husband. This changed in New Zealand with the passing of the Married Women's Property Act in 1884. Needless to say, the attitudes of some men took a while to catch up with the law.

The right to own property was not the same as the ability to acquire it. While some families treated sons and daughters equally in terms of inheriting their parents' estate, it was common for sons to be given control of the assets, while daughters were expected to be supported by husbands, perhaps with a dowry to fall back on if they were fortunate. They might be given household chattels, such as dinner sets, or benefit from the interest on investments, but not have control of the capital.

Infertility, low fertility, and the challenges of managing our fertility are issues that affect all women. These days, advancements in medical sciences give us far more options for understanding and remedying fertility issues and choosing the number of children we have, as well as keeping the children we have healthy. Daisy and Grace would probably be tested for thyroid disorders and food intolerances, for example, while Aggie's baby would probably still be alive with our modern understanding of the causes of sudden infant deaths. The journey is never easy, all the more so for the judgement woman face, both uninformed and well-meaning, regardless of the reasons for a woman's lack of children or their parenting choices.

On a more positive note, the 1890s was also a time of significant change for women in New Zealand. Women were granted the right to vote in 1893, and flocked to the polling booths in astonishing numbers. Women transformed society in many ways, through their career choices (like Grace, the first woman doctors graduated in the 1890s) and their determination to take up new challenges, such as the new and exciting world of bicycling. The invention of the safety bicycle allowed women to ride in skirts, but that didn't stop some women from adopting "rational dress" to make cycling easier. Garments ranging from split skirts to knickerbockers and trousers shocked the conservative populace, resulting in outraged letters to the newspapers. Women did it anyway, because the bicycle brought them freedom.

Readers who know Dunedin, in the South Island of New Zealand, may not recognise some locations described in this book. Road layouts have changed and Lake Logan has since been drained to form Logan Park. The Dunedin Botanic Garden has also undergone a transformation, as described by Eric Dunlop in: *The Story of the Dunedin Botanic Garden* (published by the Friends of the Dunedin Botanic Garden in 2002). I have used maps and photographs from the era, thanks to the National Library and Hocken Library collections, but added fictional details where necessary to enhance the story.

Interested readers can visit my website to see images from the era (https://rosepascoe.com/). Look under the tab for this book and scroll down to the Inspiration section.

Acknowledgements

A huge thank you to my fabulous beta readers: Mary, Jenny, Kathy and Ross. Their continued enthusiasm is very much appreciated. Two writing friends have joined the beta reading group: Bronnie Thomas and Tracy Chollet. Check out their books on: www.tracychollet.com and www.bronniethomas.com.

About the Author

Rose Pascoe writes historical mysteries with a dash of romance, when she isn't plotting real-life adventures. She lives in beautiful New Zealand, land of beaches and mountains, where long walks provide the perfect conditions for dreaming up plots and fickle weather provides the incentive to sit down and write.

After a career in health, justice and social research, her passion is for stories set against a backdrop of social justice. Her heroines are ordinary women, who meet the challenges thrown at them with determination, ingenuity, courage, and humour.

Visit her at: https://RosePascoe.com

www.ingramcontent.com/pod-product-compliance
Lightning Source LLC
Chambersburg PA
CBHW011444170626
46816CB00008B/2509